Praise for

Significant Others

"Its good-natured knack for making you laugh out loud would be reason enough to recommend *Significant Others*; but aside from that, it is wise, compassionate, irreverent and painfully of the moment."
The Independent (London)

"A portrait of the devastating effects of the AIDS epidemic that achieves an intimacy that could scarcely be duplicated in any other format. While this hardly sounds like material for romantic comedy—miraculously, it is."
Publishers Weekly

"Maupin's ear for dialogue is as acute as his feeling for characterization, and the net result is as engaging a read as you are likely to encounter in many moons."
The Times (London)

"Armistead Maupin is a first-rate, world-class novelist, creating characters so vivid, complicated, tender, and true as to seem utterly timeless. . . . I'm willing to bet that fifty years from now Maupin's work will be read for its detailed descriptions of late-twentieth-century America, its rollicking humor and kind heart, its Chekovian compassion, its Wildean wit, its intricate . . . sometimes unbelievable but always utterly irresistible plotlines."
Stephen McCauley

"Like those of Dickens and Wilkie Collins, Armistead Maupin's novels have all appeared originally as serials. It is the strength of this approach, with its fantastic adventures and astonishingly contrived coincidences, that makes these novels charming and compelling. Everything is explained and everything tied up and nothing is lost by reading them individually. There is no need even to read them chronologically."
Literary Review

BY ARMISTEAD MAUPIN

Novels

Tales of the City
More Tales of the City
Further Tales of the City
Babycakes
Significant Others
Sure of You
Michael Tolliver Lives

Maybe the Moon
The Night Listener

Collections

28 Barbary Lane
Back to Barbary Lane

SIGNIFICANT OTHERS

OTHERS

Armistead Maupin

HARPER ● PERENNIAL

NEW YORK ● LONDON ● TORONTO ● SYDNEY

HARPER ● PERENNIAL

This work was published in somewhat different form in the *San Francisco Examiner*.

Grateful acknowledgment is made for permission to reprint lyrics from "The Teddy Bears' Picnic" by John W. Bratton and Jimmy Kennedy. Copyright © 1907, 1947 by Warner Bros. Inc. (renewed). All rights reserved. Used by permission.

HarperCollins books may be purchased for educational, business, or sales promotional use. For information please write: Special Markets Department, HarperCollins Publishers, 10 East 53rd Street, New York, NY 10022.

First Perennial Library edition published 1987. Reissued 1989.
First Harper Perennial edition published 1994. Reissued 2007.

Designed by Cassandra J. Pappas

LIBRARY OF CONGRESS CATALOG CARD NUMBER 86-46088

ISBN: 978-0-06-096408-5 (pbk.)
ISBN-10: 0-06-096408-1 (pbk.)

14 15 16 RRD 10 9 8 7

For Terry Anderson,
who took his time getting here

For Jane Stuart Maupin,
who has been there all along

NOTE TO THE READER

The Bohemian Grove is a real place whose rituals I have compressed, though not substantially altered, to suit the time frame of this tale.

Wimminwood is a fictitious entity based on the actual practices of women's music festivals in Michigan, California, Georgia and elsewhere.

I am indebted to my friends in both camps.

A.M.

Significant Others

Descent into Heaven

BRIAN'S INTERNAL CLOCK ALMOST ALWAYS WOKE HIM at four fifty-six, giving him four whole minutes to luxuriate in the naked human body next to him. Then the Braun alarm clock on the nightstand would activate his wife with its genteel Nazi tootling, and her morning marathon would begin.

Today, with three minutes to go, he slipped his arm around her waist and eased her closer until her back had once again settled against his chest. It was risky, this part, because sometimes she would jerk awake with a start, as if frightened by a stranger.

He pressed his face against her neck, then traced with his forefinger the shallow swirl of her navel. It was smooth and hard now, miraculously aerobicized into a tiny pink seashell. She stirred slightly, so he flattened his hand to keep from tickling her and made sure their breathing was still in sync.

At the two-minute mark, he eased his knee between her legs and tightened his grip around her waist. She groaned faintly, then cleared her throat, so he let his hand fall slack against her belly. She countered by squeezing his knee with her thighs, telling him not to worry, he wasn't smothering her, she needed this time as much as he did.

The French had it wrong about *le petit mort.* If you asked him, "the little death" was not so much the slump after sex as these few piquant moments of serious cuddling before the demands of Mary Ann's career sent her vaulting over his piss-hardened manhood in the direction of the toilet and the coffee machine.

Another Nazi, that coffee machine. Even now, as he fondled her navel again, it was grinding its beans in the kitchen. The sound of it caused her to shift slightly and clear her throat again. "Like that?" she asked.

"What?"

"My belly button."

"Mmm."

"Took seven hundred hours," she said. "I figured it out."

He chuckled at the tyranny of numbers that governed her existence. *Everything has a price,* she was telling him. It was her favorite theme these days.

She rolled over in his arms and poked her finger into his navel. "Hey," he muttered, uncertain whether the gesture was one of affection or reprimand. She wiggled her finger. "Watch out," he said. "You fall in there and we'll have to organize a search party."

He waited for a faint cry of protest, but none came. A half-assed "Come off it" would have sufficed, but all she did was remove her finger and prop herself up on one elbow. "Well," she said, "I guess I'm up."

He knew better than to argue with this pronouncement. He would only receive the standard recitation of her cryptofascist morning regimen. Aerobics at six. A bowl of bran at seven. A meeting with the producer at seven-thirty. Makeup session at eight. A meeting with staff and crew from nine to nine-fifteen, followed by promo shots for the next day's show and a session in the green room with this morning's guest celebrities. Life was a ballbuster for San Francisco's most famous talk-show hostess.

"So what's the topic today?" he asked.

"Fat models," she replied.

"Huh?"

"You know. Those porkos who model for the big-and-beautiful fashions."

"Oh."

"It's a huge racket." She laughed. "Pardon the pun." She bounded over him and swung her legs off the bed, yawning noisily. "The book's on the dresser if you wanna take a look at it."

As she headed for the bathroom, he brooded momentarily about the extra ten pounds around his waist, then got up and went to the dresser, returning to bed with the book. He switched on the bedside light and examined the cover. It was called *Larger than Life: Confessions of the World's Most Beautiful Fat Woman.* By Wren Douglas.

A glamorous star-filtered cover photograph seemed to confirm the claim. The woman was big, all right, but her face was the face of a goddess: full red lips, a perfect nose, enormous green eyes fairly brimming with kindness and invitation. Her raven hair framed it all perfectly, cascading across her shoulders toward a cleavage rivaling the San Andreas Fault.

"What is this?" Mary Ann was brandishing the roll of paper towels he had left in the bathroom the night before.

"We ran out of toilet paper," he said, shrugging. He could do without her rhetorical questions at five o'clock in the morning.

The alarm sounded.

"Fuck off," he barked, not to her but to the clock, which deactivated obediently at the sound of his voice.

Mary Ann groaned and lowered the roll of towels, banging it angrily against her leg. "I specifically told Nguyet to make sure we had enough to—"

"I'll tell her," he put in. "She understands me better." She also liked him better, but he wasn't about to say so. He'd shared a special rapport with the Vietnamese maid ever since he'd discovered she couldn't tell the difference between Raid and Pledge. His pact of silence about the incident seemed the very least he could do for a woman whose uncle had been killed in an American bombing run over the Mekong Delta.

"It's just a language problem," he added. "She's getting much better. Really."

Mary Ann sighed and returned to the bathroom.

He raised his voice so she could hear him. "Paper towels won't kill you. Think of it as a learning experience."

"Right," she muttered back.

"Maybe there's a show in it," he offered, trying to sound playful. "A dreaded new medical condition. Like . . . the heartbreak of Bounty butt."

She didn't laugh.

He thought for a moment, then said: "Viva vulva?"

"Go to sleep," she told him. "You're gonna wake up Shawna."

He knew what she was doing in there. She was reading *USA Today*, briefing herself for the show, learning a little about a lot to keep from seeming stupid on the air.

He picked up the book again and studied the face of the world's most beautiful fat woman. Then he switched off the light, burrowed under the comforter, and slipped almost instantly into sleep.

He dreamed about a woman who had tits the size of watermelons.

The next time he woke, his daughter was conducting a Rambo-style maneuver on his exposed left leg, propelling a green plastic tank up his thigh in an apparent effort to gain supremacy of the hillocks that lay beyond. Shawna invariably chose some sort of guerrilla theater over the simple expediency of saying, "Get up, Daddy."

He remained on his stomach and made a cartoon-monster noise into the pillow.

Shawna shrieked delightedly, dropping the tank between his legs. He rolled over and snatched her up with one arm, tumbling her onto the bed. "Is this my little Puppy? Yum-yum. Puppy Monster eats little puppies for breakfast!"

He wasn't sure how this Puppy business had begun, but he

and Mary Ann both made use of the nickname. In light of Mary Ann's distaste for the child's given name, maybe it was simply their way of avoiding the issue without being disrespectful to the dead.

Connie, after all, had named the little girl, and Connie had died giving birth to her. They couldn't just choose a new name the way people do when their pets change hands.

Was that what "Puppy" really meant? Something that wasn't theirs? Something they had picked out at the pound? Would the nickname hurt Shawna's feelings when she was old enough to consider its implications?

He seized his daughter's waist and held her aloft, airplane fashion.

The little girl spread her arms and squealed.

He rocked forward, causing her to soar for a moment, but his butt made a graceless landing on the toy tank.

"Goddamnit, Puppy. Mommy didn't buy that, did she?"

She managed to keep a poker face, still impersonating an airplane.

He lowered her to the bed and reached under him for the offending war machinery. "It's Jeremy's isn't it? You've been trading again."

The kid wasn't talking.

"I didn't buy it, and Mommy didn't buy it, and I know you don't take things that don't belong to you."

She shook her head, then said: "I'm hungry."

"Don't change the subject, young lady."

Shawna sat on the edge of the bed and let her head dangle in a loose semicircle. The little charlatan was condescending to cute as a last resort.

"What did you trade for it?" he asked.

Her answer was unintelligible.

"What?"

"My *Preemie*," she said.

She slid off the bed, hitting the expensive new carpet with a soft thud. "My Cabbage Patch Preemie." Her tone indicated that this was a matter of simple laissez-faire economics and none of his goddamn business.

He felt a vague responsibility to be angry, but he couldn't

help smiling at the inevitable scene in the condo across the hallway: Cap Sorenson, the ultimate Reaganite, returning home after a hard day of software and racketball, only to come upon Daddy's little soldier playing mommy to a premature Cabbage Patch doll.

Shawna tugged on his arm. "Dad-dee . . . c'mon!"

He checked the clock. Seven thirty-seven. "O.K., Puppy, go pick out a tape." This was his usual ploy to get her out of the room while he pulled on his bathrobe. It was no big deal to him, but Mary Ann thought it "inadvisable" that he walk around naked in front of Shawna. And Mary Ann should know; she was the one with the talk show.

"No," said Shawna.

"What do you mean, no?"

"No VCR. Go see Anna."

"We'll do that, Puppy, but not yet. Anna's asleep. Go on now . . . pick out a tape. Mommy brought you *Pete the Dragon* and *Popeye,* and I think there's—"

A whine welled up in the child. She pawed the carpet belligerently, cutting a silvery path through the powder-blue plush. He couldn't help wondering if parenting was an age-related skill like warfare—tolerable, even stimulating, at twenty, but inescapably futile at forty.

He looked his daughter in the eye and spoke her name—her given name—to signal his seriousness. "I want you to go pick out a tape before Daddy gets unbelievably mad at you. We'll go see Anna later on."

Shawna's lower lip plumped momentarily, but she obeyed him. When she was gone, he dragged himself to the bathroom and brushed his teeth. The floor was still wet from Mary Ann's frantic ablutions, so he mopped it with a damp towel and tossed the towel into the laundry hamper.

He hesitated before weighing himself, then decided that the ugly truth was a surefire antidote for his late-night jelly doughnut binges. The scales surprised him, however. He had lost four pounds in four days.

This made no sense to him, but he had never been one to argue with serendipity.

Shawna threw her usual tantrum over breakfast. This time her yogurt was the wrong color and there wasn't enough Perrier to make her cranberry juice "go fizzy." Would she ever tire of testing him?

After breakfast, according to custom, he let her pick out her clothes for the day. She chose a green cotton turtleneck with ladybugs on the arm and a pair of absurdly miniature 501's. He dressed her, then left her in the custody of Robin Williams and the VCR while he changed into his own version of her ensemble.

The clock said eight forty-six when he went to the window and peered down twenty-three stories into the leafy green canyon of Barbary Lane. From this height, Anna Madrigal's courtyard was nothing more than a terra-cotta postage stamp, but he could still discern a figure moving jauntily along the perimeter.

The landlady was making her morning sweep, brandishing a broom so vigorously that the ritual seemed more akin to exercise than to practical considerations of cleanliness. Later, she would cross the postage stamp diagonally and sit on the bench next to the azalea bed. For all her professed free-spiritedness, she was a creature of blatant predictability.

He lifted his gaze from the courtyard and surveyed their vista, a boundless sweep of city, bay and sky stretching from Mount Diablo to Angel Island and beyond.

There were no chimney pots or eucalyptus branches blocking their vision, no unsightly back stairwells or rocky rises framing some half-assed little chunk of water. What they had at The Summit was a goddamn *view*—as slick and unblemished as a photomural.

And just about as real.

Sometimes, when he stared at the horizon long enough, their teal-and-gray living room lost its identity altogether and became the boardroom of a corporate jet dipping its wings in homage to the Bank of America building.

Today, the sky was cloudless and the air was clear. No hint of the holocaust raging sixty miles south of the city. There, amid the brittle manzanita brush of the Santa Cruz Mountains, a jagged trail of fire seven miles wide had already blackened fifteen thousand acres and driven five thousand people from their homes.

But not here at The Summit. Nature wouldn't stand a chance at The Summit.

He sometimes wondered about that preposition. Should he tell people he lived *at* The Summit, *in* The Summit or *on* The Summit? Usually, when pressed, he admitted to 999 Green and left it at that.

If he was embarrassed, he had every right to be. He'd lived in the shadow of this concrete leviathan for nearly eight years, cursing it continually. Now, at his wife's insistence—and using his wife's money—he'd joined the enemy in a big way.

They had done it for Shawna. And for security. And because they needed a tax shelter. They had also done it because Mary Ann wanted a glossier setting for her "lifestyle" (God help her, she had actually used that word) than could ever be provided by the funky old bear of a building at 28 Barbary Lane.

Mrs. Madrigal had taken it well, but Brian knew she'd been hurt by their departure. At the very least, her sense of family had been violated. Even now, five months after their ascension, their old apartment on the lane remained empty and unrented, as if something had died there.

Maybe something had.

Life was different now; he knew that. The guy who had once waited tables at Perry's bore scant resemblance to this new and improved postmodern version of Brian Hawkins.

The new Brian drove a twenty-thousand-dollar Jeep. He owned three tuxedos and a mink-lined bomber jacket from Wilkes (which he wore only while driving the Jeep). Something of a fixture at Pier 23, he knew how to do lunch with the best of them.

When the new Brian went to parties, he usually ended up making man talk with the mayor's husband or Danielle Steel's husband—and once even with Geraldine Ferraro's husband.

8

O.K. He was a consort.

But even that took skill, didn't it?

And who was to say he didn't rank among the best?

When Shawna grew bored with television, he helped her into a windbreaker and briefed her for the trek to Barbary Lane. His basic requirements were two: Don't scream bloody murder on the elevator, and don't point at the doorman and yell "Mr. T!"

She did as she was told, miraculously enough, and they reached Green Street without a hitch. As they trooped along the crest of Russian Hill, his limbs felt curiously leaden; his temples pulsed a little, threatening a headache.

If this was the flu, he didn't need it. There were four major events in the next week alone.

Shawna insisted on being carried in his arms as they descended the steepest slope of Leavenworth, but she squirmed her way to the ground again as soon as they reached the rickety wooden stairs leading to Barbary Lane.

"Anna steps," she said, already recognizing the boundaries of another duchy. The lane, after all, belonged to Mrs. Madrigal. Even the grownups knew that.

There was a bulletin on the landing that confirmed the landlady's sovereignty: SAVE THE BARBARY STEPS—*Insensitive city officials have plans to replace our beloved wooden steps with hideous concrete ones. Now is the time to speak up. Contact Anna Madrigal, 28 Barbary Lane.*

Damn right, he thought. Give 'em hell, Anna.

Nevertheless, he took Shawna's hand as the beloved rotting planks creaked ominously beneath their tread. At the top, where the ground bristled with a stubble of dry fennel, he let her go and watched as she pranced between the garbage cans into the musky gloom of the eucalyptus trees. She looked like a child heading home.

9

By the time he'd arrived at the first clump of cottages, she was already playing havoc with Boris.

"Take it easy," he told her. "He's an old kitty. Don't pet him so hard."

She snatched her hand away from the tabby, cackling in her best mad-scientist fashion, then dashed up the lane again. The path at this point was paved with ballast stones, treacherous even for grownups.

"Slow down, Puppy. You're gonna hurt yourself again." He caught up with her and took her hand, leading the way toward the smoother, wider portion of the lane.

"You remember Anna's number?" he asked the kid.

Of course she didn't.

"It's twenty-eight," he said, feeling stupid as soon as he said it.

Why the hell should she have to learn *that?*

Because the house at the end of the lane was all he had to give a child.

It was all the lore he knew, his only storybook.

The door to the lych-gate was open.

The landlady stood in the courtyard, hunched over her largest sinsemilla plant. She was plucking its leaves with a tweezer, coaxing the potency into its blossoms. Her face suggested brain surgery in progress, but she was humming a merry little tune.

Shawna bolted into the courtyard, losing herself in the folds of Mrs. Madrigal's pale muslin skirt. The landlady gave a startled yelp, dropping the tweezers, then laughed along with the kid.

"It's the Feds," said Brian, grinning.

Mrs. Madrigal looked down at the creature clamped to her leg and stroked its hair affectionately.

"She's missed you," said Brian. "It's been two whole days."

The landlady's huge blue eyes swung in his direction momentarily. She offered him a dim smile before returning her attention to Shawna. "I've missed her too," she said to the kid.

It was asinine, but he felt a little jealous of Mrs. Madrigal's undivided devotion to Shawna. "I saw your notice," he said, searching for something to please her. "Are those crazy bastards really gonna tear down the steps?"

The landlady nodded soberly. "If we don't put up a fight."

She said *we,* he noticed; that was something. She still considered him part of the lane. "Well . . . if there's anything I can do . . ."

"There is, actually."

"Great."

"I thought perhaps if Mary Ann could say something on her show . . . you know, just a few words about preserving our heritage, that sort of thing." She fussed with a wisp of hair at her temple, waiting for his response.

"Yeah . . . well, sure . . . I could mention it to her. They have an awfully rigid format, though." He was backtracking now, remembering Mary Ann's aversion to what she called "hokey local items." Mrs. Madrigal's crusade would almost certainly fall into that category.

The landlady read him like a book. "I see," she murmured.

"I'll tell her, though. I'm sure she'll be upset about it."

Mrs. Madrigal studied him for a moment, almost wistfully, then began scanning the ground around her feet. "Now where did those damn things go? Shawna dear, look over there in that ivy and see if you can find Anna's tweezers."

He thought briefly of begging her forgiveness, then turned frivolous in his embarrassment. "Hey," he blurted, "you should grow your fingernails long."

Now on her hands and knees, Mrs. Madrigal looked up at him. "Why is that, dear?"

"You know, like those housewives in Humboldt County. Works much better than tweezers, they say."

She handled this clumsy inanity with her usual grace. "Ah, yes. I see what you mean." Falling silent again, she searched until she found the tweezers, then stood up and brushed her hands on her skirt. "I tried that once . . . growing my nails long." She caught her breath and shook her head. "I wasn't man enough for it."

He laughed, hugely relieved. In Mrs. Madrigal's repertoire, a proffered joke was the next best thing to forgiveness. When her eyes locked on his, they were full of their old familiar playfulness. He saw his entry and took it.

"I wonder," he said, "if I could ask a big favor of you."

She looked at him for a moment, then peered down at the child hanging on her skirt. "Tell you what, dear. Go into the house and look on the sofa. There's a nice new friend for you."

Shawna looked skeptical. "A Gobot?"

"You'll see. Be careful of the steps, now. The door is open."

As the child toddled away, Mrs. Madrigal beamed appreciatively. "She's just as smart as she can be."

"What did you get her?" he asked.

"Just a stuffed animal," came the mumbled reply.

It embarrassed him a little that the landlady spent money on Shawna. "You really shouldn't," he said.

She answered with a faint who-gives-a-damn smile, then said: "What sort of favor?"

"Well," he said, "my nephew is coming to town for a few days, and I wondered if . . . if he could stay at our old place."

She blinked at him.

"If it's a problem," he added hastily, "just say so, and I'll . . ."

"How old is he?"

"Uh . . . eighteen, I think. Maybe nineteen."

She nodded. "Well . . . there's no furniture, of course. There's a cot in the basement and maybe a chest of drawers." She tapped her forefinger against her lower lip. Her maternal juices were obviously functioning again. It cheered Brian to know that he could still do this for her.

"His name is Jed," he said. "He's in pre-law at Rice University. That's all I know, except that he's probably straight."

The landlady gave him a sly smile. "That's what he told you? He's probably straight?"

He laughed. "Well, he's currently in love with Bruce

12

Springsteen, so I just assumed he was."

"Now wait a minute."

"It's Michael's theory. Get him to explain it. He says every generation produces one male performer that straight boys are allowed to be queer for. It was Mick Jagger for a long time, and now it's Bruce Springsteen. So I figure the kid's straight."

"You and your featherbrained theories."

"It's not *my* theory. I just—" He cut himself off, realizing she'd addressed her remarks to Michael, who had sauntered into the courtyard from the house.

"What have I done now?" asked Michael.

Brian smiled at him. "I was just explaining your Springsteen theory."

"It's true," said Michael. "Straight boys will go all the way for him."

Mrs. Madrigal turned to Brian. "Is he including you in this sweeping generality?"

"Sure," Michael cut in. "He'd do it for The Boss in a second." He cast an impish glance in Brian's direction. "I mean, if he *asked* you, right?"

Brian actually got off on this. It was Michael's way of socking an arm in friendship. "You're a dipshit," he told him, socking back in his own fashion.

"I think it's great," said Michael. "Springsteen's done wonders for guys named Bruce. There used to be such a stigma attached." He paused for a moment, then added: "I'm late, y'all. I'd love to stick around and hash this out, but . . . Wren Douglas cannot be kept waiting."

It took Brian a moment to place the name. Then her face and chest flickered in his head like a soft-core video. "Oh, yeah. The fat model. You know her?"

"No, but I'm a major fan. Mary Ann got me a ticket for the show today."

Mrs. Madrigal looked confused. "She's . . . uh . . . heavy?"

"Yeah," said Brian, "but kind of hot."

"Kind of?" yelped Michael, with surprising indignation. "How about very?"

Brian gave the landlady a you-and-me glance. "And he should know, right?"

Michael headed for the lych-gate, stopping briefly to sniff a bud of Mrs. Madrigal's sinsemilla. He staged a little mock swoon for her benefit, then said: "Better be careful. They're busting people for this now."

"Well," said the landlady, remaining deadpan, "if Mrs. Reagan should drop by for tea, I trust you'll give me fair warning."

Mrs. Madrigal agreed to keep Shawna for a few hours, so Brian did some shopping at the Searchlight Market (Diet Pepsi, a box of Milky Ways and the new Colgate Pump) before returning to The Summit. Back on the twenty-third floor, he found Nguyet Windexing the kitchen window with what appeared to be the last of the paper towels.

And that reminded him: He had forgotten to buy toilet paper.

So what do you use when the paper towels are gone?

"Uh . . . Nguyet?"

The maid stopped Windexing and looked at him, a nervous smile on her face.

"This afternoon. When you go shopping. Buy toilet paper, O.K.?"

Her smile faded; he had lost her.

"Toilet paper . . . you know . . ." He considered miming it, then discarded the idea. Finally, he went to the bathroom and returned with the little cardboard tube.

Nguyet's face radiated understanding. "Ah," she said. "Shommin."

"Right," he replied. "Shommin. Buy Shommin this afternoon, O.K.?"

She nodded energetically and returned to her labors, watching out of the corner of her eye as he searched the pantry and came up with a box of Melitta No. 4 coffee filters.

Paper product in hand, he headed for the john, only to be stopped in his tracks by the monumental Wren Douglas, peering up at him from the bedside table. His cock stirred appreciatively, so he made a quick detour and took the book with him to the john.

Vanessa Williams would just have to wait.

Wren in the Flesh

RISING LATE IN HER SUITE AT THE FAIRMONT HOTEL, Wren Douglas ordered a hearty breakfast, then ambled into the bathroom to take stock of the cornucopia of miniature creams and shampoos that undoubtedly awaited her.

Hotel rooms were really the best part of a book tour. The bathroom bonuses you could stash away for future use. The king-sized beds with their sheets turned back and peppermint patties on the pillow. The thirsty, sweet-smelling towels and silent-flush toilets and TV sets hidden in armoires, ready to offer the transcontinental consolation of Mary Tyler Moore.

This was her sixteenth city in three weeks. Her fat rap had become a well-worn tape, almost too fragile to survive another playing. She was sick of the sound of her own voice and sicker still of the Ken-and-Barbie anchoroids who habitually asked her the same four questions.

Were you fat as a child? ("I was fat as a *fetus.*")

Do you think American women are being tyrannized by the current fitness craze? ("Not necessarily. Everyone should be as fit as possible, including fat people. The tyranny comes when we're told we should all look the same.")

What are your vital statistics? ("Two hundred and two pounds
... fifty-two, thirty-seven, fifty-seven ... five feet eight inches
tall.")

What do you think caused you to become an international sex symbol?
("Beats me, honey. Some guys just go for a girl with thighs
in two time zones.")

All that glibness had begun to catch in her throat like so
many dry cornflakes. She was biding her time now, counting
the cities—only Portland and Seattle to go—until the final
flight would spirit her back to Chicago, to her loft and her cat
and her hot Cuban lover with the permanent stiffie.

Not that she had hurt for attention on the tour. There'd
been that body-building cameraman in Miami, brick-
shithouse beautiful and full of surprises. And that cute kid in
Washington who'd taken her to dinner, entrusted her with his
virginity, and driven her to the airport the next morning,
whistling all the way. She'd done all right for herself, horizon-
tally speaking.

She mounted the scales in the bathroom, almost afraid to
look.

A hundred and ninety-two! Her worst fears confirmed!
Thanks to the rigors of the tour, she was losing weight like
crazy. If she didn't shape up and soon, the headline writers
would lose their two-hundred-pound sex symbol and she—
shudder, gasp—would be out on her ever-dwindling ass.

She savored this preposterous dilemma, then washed her
face with a violet-scented English soap.

Soon there would be blueberry pancakes to set things right
again.

Forty-five minutes later, she waited for her limousine on the
curb in front of the Fairmont. She was decked out in her
favorite touring ensemble: a low-necked turquoise sweater
dress cinched at the waist by a brown leather cummerbund.

The cummerbund and her boots—Victorian-style lace-up
numbers—gave her, she felt, the air of a good-natured
dominatrix. As her nerves grew increasingly ragged, she

needed all the authority she could muster when she faced her interrogators.

Her driver was a welcome surprise: young and dark, with pronounced Italianate influences and a set of lips she could chew on all night. As he whisked her down California Street toward her rendezvous with today's anchoroid, she asked him what he knew about the show.

"Not a whole helluva lot," he replied. "Just . . . it's called *Mary Ann in the Morning.*"

She let out a faint groan. She could picture the little fluff-ball already.

"My old lady watches it," said the driver. "It's real popular. She has on . . . you know, stars like yourself . . . Lee Iacocca, Shirley MacLaine, that kid o' Pat Boone's with the barf disease . . ."

"Right," she said.

"I saw you on Carson the other night."

"Oh . . . did you?" She hated it when they left you dangling. What the hell were you supposed to say?

"You were good."

"Thanks."

"We're the same age. I noticed that right off. You're twenty-eight and I'm twenty-eight."

"No shit."

He laughed and peered over his shoulder at her. "My ol' lady's big too, ya know?"

"Yeah?"

"Not as big as you, I mean. Not as big as I'd like her to be."

"I hear you," she said.

"I like 'em really big. Like you . . . if you don't mind my saying."

She found her little egg of Obsession, gave her tits a quick squirt, and lowered her voice an octave. "Not at all," she said.

"I didn't wanna sound like I was . . ."

"What's on our schedule this afternoon?"

"You mean . . . after this show?"

"Yeah."

He thought for a moment. "Just a personal appearance."

"Where?"

"You know . . . one of those Pretty and Plump shops on the peninsula."

She dropped the atomizer into her purse. "And then we're done until tomorrow?"

"Right."

"So . . . we've got time."

She noticed that he swerved the wheel a little, but he recovered instantly and curled those edible lips into a comprehending smile. "Sure," he said. "We got time."

Things went smoothly enough at the television station until the makeup man tried to camouflage her chins with darker makeup. "These babies," she told him sweetly, "are my bread and butter. What will people think if I'm obviously trying to hide them?"

"It won't be obvious, hon. You'll see. It's Light Egyptian, very subtle. Lena Horne uses it all over."

"Sweetie," she said patiently, "my chins and I are not of different races. If we were, I'd call them The Supremes or something, but we're not, O.K.?" He looked a little wounded, so she added: "Nice Swatch. Is it Keith Haring?"

He glanced down at his watch and answered with a lackluster "Yeah."

"Look," she said, trying another tactic. "You can go for broke when you do my eyes. How 'bout that? Turquoise, gold, whatever. There must be something you've always wanted to try."

As she'd expected, this did the trick. She had offered herself up as a palette, and the artist could not be contained. His eyes grew bright with obsession as he plunged into the depths of his kit. "I think there's an Aztec Gold in here . . . that on the lips, very lightly down the center."

"Super," she said.

"And a little pale purple powder just under the eyes."

"There you go."

Sometimes it seemed there wasn't a man on earth she couldn't handle.

* * *

An associate producer led her into the green room, which was peach and cream this time, with loads of hideous seventies Deco. On the walls were huge framed photographs of the fabled Mary Ann: Mary Ann with Raquel Welch, Mary Ann with Dr. Ruth, Mary Ann with Ed Koch, Mary Ann with Michael Landon.

"Make yourself at home," said the associate producer, backing toward the door. "There's coffee there . . . and sweet rolls and whatever. Mary Ann will drop by to say hello in a little while."

"Am I the only guest?" she asked.

He nodded. "Except for Ikey St. Jacques. We're taping him for 'Latchkey Kitchen.' "

"What's that?"

"One of our segments. Fifteen minutes at the end. Famous kids come on and . . . you know, teach latchkey kids how to cook for themselves while their parents are out working."

"Come on," said Wren.

"It's very popular." He sounded a little defensive. "We've had offers to syndicate it."

Wren tried to picture the tiny black star of *What It Is!* whipping up a quick-and-easy tuna casserole. "He's such a baby," she said. "He can't be a day over seven."

"Uh . . . look . . . I'm kind of rushed right now. I hope you don't mind if I leave you on your own for a while."

He was flustered about something, she could tell. "I'll be fine," she said. "Are you kidding? Alone with all this food?"

Laughing uncomfortably, the associate producer backed out the door and closed it. She puzzled over his behavior for a moment, then headed straight for the sweet rolls, remembering her dwindling weight. She had downed one and was repairing her lips with a napkin the next time the door opened.

"Awwriiiight, mama!"

It was Ikey St. Jacques, grinning like a jack-o'-lantern and cute as the devil in his tiny red-and-white workout suit. His hands were outstretched, Jolson-style, and one of them held a lighted cigar.

She tried to stay cool. "Uh . . . hi. You're Ikey . . . right?"

"I knew it," he said with a husky chuckle. "That fool lied to me."

"Who?"

"That candy-ass producer out there. He knows I like big mamas, so he lied to me, the sucker! I knew you was in here." He took a long drag on his cigar and looked her up and down. His head was no higher than her waist. "I saw you on Carson. I said to my agent, that is one foxy lady."

She wasn't buying this at all. "Look, junior . . ." She flailed toward the cigar. "Those things make me sick. The entrance was cute, but the bit is over."

He regarded her dolefully for a moment, then went to the table, reached up and stubbed out the cigar.

"Thank you," she said, extending her hand. "Now . . . I'm Wren Douglas."

He shook her hand. "Sorry 'bout that."

"Hey . . . no biggie."

"I come on strong sometimes. Don't know why."

She was beginning to feel like a bully. "Well, it was just that cigar. You ought not to smoke those, even for a joke. It'll—"

"Stunt my growth?" He laughed raucously. "I'm seventeen years old, lady!"

"Wait a minute. Says who?"

"Says me and my birth certificate. And my mama."

She drew back and studied him. "Nah. Sorry. No way. I'm not buyin' that."

"You think I'm lyin'?"

She shifted her weight to one hip and appraised him coolly. "Yeah. I think you're lyin'."

He glared at her defiantly and shoved his sweat pants down to his knees.

She took stock of the point he was making and responded as calmly as possible. "O.K. . . . Fine . . . we've established your maturity."

The kid wouldn't budge, arms still folded across his chest. "Say I'm seventeen!"

She glanced anxiously toward the door. "Pull your pants up, Ikey."

"Say I'm seventeen."

"Ikey, if somebody walks in here we could be arrested for . . . I don't know what. All right, big deal. You're seventeen. I'm sorry. I was wrong."

A half-lidded smile bloomed on the kid's face as he returned his sweat pants to their rightful position.

Wren clapped her hand to her chest and heaved a little whinny of relief. "God," she muttered to no one in particular.

Ikey moved to the table and picked up a sweet roll almost as big as his face.

"It seems to me," said Wren, now angered by his nonchalance, "you could find a subtler way to tell people."

The kid licked the edge of the pastry, then shrugged. "Saves talk."

"Don't give me that."

Another shrug.

"You *like* doing it."

He set the roll down and fixed her with the same sweet spaniel gaze he used on his television father. "Lady, if you spent your whole fucking life impersonating a seven-year-old, you'd rip your pants off every now and then, too."

She smiled, realizing his predicament for the first time. "Yeah, I probably would."

"I'm a fan of yours," he added. "I don't wanna fight with you."

She was embarrassed now. "Look . . . everything's cool, Ikey."

"Isaac."

"Isaac," she echoed.

"Can I light my cigar now?"

"No way." She softened this ultimatum with another smile. "I really can't handle 'em, Isaac."

He nodded. "Are you mad 'cause I called you foxy?"

"Not a bit. I appreciate that."

"Well, I appreciate what you're doing for . . . people who don't fit the mold."

In half a dozen words, he had explained the bond that

linked them; she was unexpectedly moved. "Hey . . . what the hell. I *like* doing it. I mean, most of the time. This is the end of a tour, so I'm a little antsy, I guess. You know how that can be." She wanted this to sound like a confidence shared with another professional.

He emitted a froggy chuckle. "Yeah."

"I watch your show all the time," she said.

This seemed to please him. "You do?"

"I think you're amazingly believable. Most TV kids are so cloying, you know . . . too cute for words. Plus, I like your scripts."

He gave her a businesslike nod. "They're gettin' better, I think." He hesitated a moment, then said: "Look, can I ask you something?"

"Shoot," she said.

"I don't want you to get pissed off again."

She smiled at him. "I've over that now. Don't worry." As a matter of fact, she felt completely comfortable around him. He'd done nothing but tell her the truth. "Go ahead," she said. "Ask away."

After another significant pause, he said: "Can I put my hand . . . in there?" He was pointing to her cleavage.

She pursed her lips and scrutinized his face. That spaniel look was doing its number again. "For how long?" she asked.

He shrugged. "Twenty seconds."

"Ten," she counteroffered.

"O.K."

"And no jiggling." She bent over to afford him easier access. "Make it quick. We've got a show to do."

Isaac's arm was engulfed to the elbow when the door to the green room swung open. The dumbfounded woman who stood there was the woman whose likeness adorned the walls. "Oh . . . excuse me. I . . . ."

"Hey," said Wren. "No problem." She removed Isaac's arm with a single movement and straightened up. "I lost an earring." She reached down and gave the kid's shoulder a pat. "Thanks just the same, Ikey. I'll look for it later."

The television hostess became a stalagmite, then cast her

stony gaze in Isaac's direction. "The director wants to see you on the kitchen set, Ikey."

The kid said "Yo" and strode toward the door. He gave Wren a high sign as he left.

"Well," said Wren, turning back to the anchoroid, "you must be Mary Ann."

The woman wouldn't melt. "You must be sick," she said.

"Now wait a minute."

"I've done shows on child molestation, but I never thought I would—"

"That child," said Wren, "is seventeen years old!"

"Well, I don't see what . . . Who told you that?"

"He did."

Thrown, the anchoroid thought for a moment, then said: "And I suppose that makes it all right."

"No," Wren replied evenly. "That makes it none of your business."

Member in Good Standing

THE SHOW HADN'T GONE AS MICHAEL HAD EXPECTED.
Instead of a freewheeling romp, there'd been stiffness and long silences and palpable tension in the
air. The trouble had begun, he suspected, when
Mary Ann introduced Wren Douglas to the studio
audience as "the woman who's shown America how to make
the most of a weight problem."

Whatever the cause, something had soured the interview
beyond repair, so he decided against requesting an introduc-
tion after the show. Mary Ann had already obliged him with
introductions to Huey Lewis, Scott Madsen and Tina Turner.
There was nothing to be gained by abusing the privilege.

Besides, it was eleven-fifteen, and he had a nursery to run.

The place had been his since 1984, when his partner, Ned
Lockwood, had moved back to L.A. The exhilaration of ownership had been a new experience for Michael, prompting
him to renovate and expand beyond his wildest imaginings.
He had built a new greenhouse for the succulents, then en-
larged the office, then changed the name from God's Green
Earth to Plant Parenthood.

The only problem with being sole proprietor, he had long

ago discovered, was that you couldn't call in sick to yourself. To make matters worse, his three employees at the nursery (two other gay men and a lesbian) knew subtle ways to trigger his guilt whenever he showed up late for work.

Actually, he relished his time at the nursery. The busyness of business helped him to forget how much he missed what had come to be known as "the unsafe exchange of bodily fluids."

If he remained idle too long, his euphoric past could creep up on him like a Frenchman pushing postcards, a portfolio of fading erotica fully capable of breaking his nostalgic heart.

It wasn't just an epidemic anymore; it was a famine, a starvation of the spirit, which sooner or later afflicted everyone. Some people capitulated to the terror, turning inward in their panic, avoiding the gaze of strangers on the street. Others adopted a sort of earnest gay fraternalism, enacting the rituals of safe-sex orgies with all the clinical precision of Young Pioneers dismantling their automatic weapons.

Lots of people found relief on the telephone, mutually Master-charging until Nirvana was achieved. Phone sex, Michael had observed, not only toned the imagination but provided men with an option that had heretofore been unavailable to them: *faking an orgasm.*

Michael himself had once faked an orgasm over the phone. Unable to come, yet mindful of his manners, he had growled out his ecstasy for at least half a minute, pounding on his headboard for added effect. His partner (someone in Teaneck, New Jersey) had been so audibly appreciative of the performance that Michael fell asleep afterwards feeling curiously satiated.

Most of the time, though, he ended up in bed with the latest issue of *Inches* or *Advocate Men,* his genitals cinched in the cord of his terry-cloth bathrobe.

He had learned several interesting things about pornography. Namely: (1) it wore out; (2) it reactivated itself if you looked at it upside down; and (3) you could recycle it if you put it away for several months.

Unlike most of his friends, he did not have sex regularly with a VCR. He had done that once or twice, but only at a JO buddy's house, and their timing had been so hopelessly out of sync that his only memory was of lunging through the sheets in search of the fast-forward button.

"What are you doing?" his buddy had asked when the video images accelerated and Al Parker and friends became the Keystone Cops.

Michael had replied: "I'm looking for that cowboy near the end."

And this was what bothered him about owning a VCR. If that cowboy was yours for the taking—yours at the flip of a switch—what was to stop you from abandoning human contact altogether?

He had taken the test in April, and it had come back positive. That is, he was carrying the virus or had already fought it off, one or the other. According to some doctors, this gave him (and a million others) a 10 to 25 percent chance of developing a full-blown case, but other doctors disagreed.

What did doctors know?

All *he* knew was that his health was fine. No night sweats or sluggishness. No unusual weight loss or mysterious purple blotches. He ate his vegetables and popped his vitamins and kept stress to a minimum. For a man who'd lost twelve friends and a lover in less than three years, he was doing all right.

Just the same, a mild case of the flu or the slightest furriness of the tongue was now capable of filling him with abject terror. The other paramount emotion, grief, became more and more unpredictable as the numbers grew. His tears could elude him completely at the bedside of a dying friend, only to surface weeks later during a late-night Marilyn Monroe movie on TV.

And people talked of nothing else. Who has it. Who thinks

27

he has it. Who's positive. Who couldn't *possibly* be negative. Who will never take the test. Who's almost ready to take the test.

To get away from the tragedy—and the talk—some of his friends had moved to places like Phoenix and Charlottesville, but Michael couldn't see the point of it. The worst of times in San Francisco was still better than the best of times anywhere else.

There was beauty here and conspicuous bravery and civilized straight people who were doing their best to help. It was also his home, when all was said and done. He loved this place with a deep and unreasoning passion; the choice was no longer his.

When he reached the nursery, a renegade Pinto was parked in his usual place out front. He spotted Polly among the arborvitae, clipping a can for a customer, and tapped the horn gently to get her attention. "Someone we know?" he hollered, pointing toward the offending car.

His young employee set her clippers down and wiped her brow with the back of her hand. "David's new squeeze," she yelled back. "I'll get him to move it."

He could see another parking space at the end of the block, so he decided not to make an issue of it. "That's O.K.," he told her. "Don't break up the lovebirds." It was lunchtime, after all, and David and his new beau were undoubtedly in the greenhouse making goo-goo eyes over Big Macs.

He parked and walked back to the nursery in the toasty sunshine. Polly was on the sidewalk now, hefting the arborvitae into the back of the customer's station wagon. "Sorry about that. Didn't know you'd be back so soon."

"No problem," he said.

Brushing the dirt off her hands, Polly followed him to the office. "How did it go? Did you bring me a lipstick print?"

"Shit," he murmured, remembering his promise.

"You didn't," she said calmly. "That's O.K."

"I didn't meet her," he explained. "She and Mary Ann had

rotten chemistry, so I decided not to risk it."

Polly shrugged.

"You're disappointed," he said. "I'm really sorry." So far she had cajoled lipstick prints from Linda Evans, Kathleen Turner and Diana Ross.

"Was she gorgeous?" Polly asked, leaning dreamily against the cash register.

"Yeah," he answered. "In a Fellini sort of way." He thought it wise to downplay the thrill of it all.

Polly sighed. "She's welcome in my movie any ol' day."

He amused himself by picturing the confrontation: the voluptuously rotund Wren Douglas putting the moves on pretty Polly Berendt, muscular yet petite in her faded green coveralls. "Well," he said, "she shows every sign of being hopelessly het."

"So?" said Polly. "I'm no separatist."

He laughed. The new lesbian adventurism was a source of endless amusement to him. If gay men could no longer snort and paw the ground in fits of purple passion, it seemed only fitting that gay women could. *Somebody* had to keep the spirit alive.

Polly slipped her hand around his waist and pressed her freckled face against his shoulder. "I want a wife, Michael. I want one bad."

"Yeah, yeah."

"Is it because I'm twenty-two? Is that what it is? Were you this way when you were twenty-two?"

"I was that way when I was thirty-two, but I got over it."

She tilted her face toward him. "My friend Kara went to a psychic last month, and she said that Kara's true love would show up within the month . . . and that she'd be driving a golden chariot."

"Right."

"I swear this is true. Kara met this girl called Weegie last month and they've been inseparable ever since."

"What about the golden chariot?"

"She was driving a Yellow Cab!"

He snorted.

"Kara called a cab from DV8 and Weegie drove up, and

that was it. Wedded bliss. Me . . . I look and look and end up with some former battered wife who takes me to see *The Women* at the Castro and hisses at all the sexist parts."

"Why are you telling me this?" he asked.

She hesitated, then said: "Cuz I wanna go to Wimminwood."

"Where?"

"A women's music festival up at the river."

He shrugged. "Go. You've got vacation coming. What's the problem?"

"Well . . . it's next week, when you're on vacation."

He saw her point; that left only David and Robbie to run the nursery.

"I really wanna go, Michael."

"Sure, but . . ."

"I've talked to Kevin," she added. "He says he'll be glad to stand in for me."

"Who's Kevin?"

She jerked her head toward the greenhouse. "David's new squeeze. He's had experience."

"He works at Tower Records, I thought."

"Yeah, but he's off next week . . . and he used to do gardening for an admiral when he was in the navy, and . . . C'mon, Michael, don't make me miss this opportunity."

He smiled at her. "Thousands of half-naked women going berserk in the redwoods."

"No!" she protested. "Some of them are *totally* naked."

He laughed. "You don't sound like somebody looking for a wife."

Actually, she reminded him of himself years ago, relishing the prospect of a weekend of lust at the National Gay Rodeo in Reno.

David's new boyfriend stayed at Plant Parenthood for the rest of the afternoon, making himself useful in the fertilizer shed. He was industrious, cheerful and seemingly honest. Michael saw no reason why he wouldn't serve as an adequate substitute for Polly.

At four twenty-five, Teddy Roughton called. "It's late notice," he said, "but there's a JO party at Joe's tonight. I thought you'd wanna know."

Michael felt faintly embarrassed. "Thanks, Teddy. I think I'll pass."

"Why?"

"I don't know. Those things make me feel . . . self-conscious or something."

Teddy clucked his tongue like a disapproving English matron. "Foolish, foolish boy . . ."

"I know, but . . ."

"He's got brilliant visuals, Michael. That chap from the Muscle System is coming."

Michael thought for a moment. "The one with . . . ?"

"That's riiight. And if that's not enough for you, Joe's rented *One in a Billion.*"

"Fine, but . . ."

"Think about it, at least. All right?" He might have been recruiting for a parish bake sale. "Eight o'clock. Joe's house. We'll see you if we see you."

The weather was unnaturally balmy at closing time, so Michael took down the top of his VW for the ride home. Tooling along Clement, he marveled at the warm silkiness of the air against his face. This was nothing less than a true summer evening, and the city smelled of steaks and hibiscus. His loins took note of the tropicality and began to lobby for their rights.

You remember that guy, they said, *that stud from the Muscle System with the beer-can dick and the pecs that won't quit. What would it hurt to sit in the same room with him? O.K., to sit there naked with him and two dozen naked guys and beat the old . . .* No, it was too embarrassing.

Think of it as the Explorers, his loins argued. *That camping trip in north Georgia, 1964. Guys around the campfire, weary from the hike. The sunburned necks, the smell of Off, Billy Branson's perfect smile flashing in the firelight, tantalizing beyond belief. The circle jerk that almost happened but didn't.*

Well, now it could happen.

When he arrived at 28 Barbary Lane, Mrs. Madrigal confronted him on the landing. "You'd better hurry," she said. "It starts in less than an hour."

He felt his jaw go slack. If she wasn't a closet clairvoyant, she sure as hell acted like one.

"I heard about it on the radio," she explained, as if that took care of things.

"You heard about what?" he asked.

"The welcome home," she said, "for those gay hostages."

The light dawned. Two of the thirty-nine American tourists held hostage by terrorists in Beirut had proved to be gay San Franciscans—lovers, no less. Upon their return to the States, they had faced the cameras as a couple, beaming proudly, moments before accepting the unconditional gratitude of Ronald and Nancy Reagan.

Michael had thrilled to the sight and had told Mrs. Madrigal as much.

"Where's the ceremony?" he asked.

"Eighteenth and Castro," she said. "They're blocking off the street."

He did some hasty calculation. The JO party was on Noe at Twenty-first, only four blocks up the hill from the rally. If he hurried, the evening might be made to accommodate both the erotic and the patriotic. "Thanks for the tip," he told his landlady.

She bent and picked up a plastic bucket full of cleaning gear. "Well, I thought you'd want to know, dear."

He pointed to the bucket. "Did Boris barf on the stairwell again?"

She chuckled. "Brian's nephew is staying with us for a few days."

"His nephew? Is he . . . grown?" Everything made him feel

older these days. At thirty-four, he still had trouble remembering that some of his contemporaries were the parents of teenagers.

"He's nineteen," said Mrs. Madrigal. "I'm fixing up Mary Ann and Brian's old place for him. Perhaps later you could give me a hand with that twin bed in the basement?"

"Sure," he answered. "Yeah . . . sure . . . be glad to."

His antsiness must have been obvious, for the landlady smiled at him. "I won't keep you," she said. "I know you've got a busy, busy evening."

That extra "busy" made him wonder again.

Back at his apartment, he took a quick shower and trimmed his mustache. Tonight especially, he was glad he hadn't shaved his mustache when everyone else had. It suited him, he felt, so to hell with the fashion victims who found him lacking in the new-wave department.

When it came time to dress, he dug to the bottom of his bottom drawer and found his oldest 501's. The denim was chamois smooth and parchment thin, and the very feel of it against his legs filled him with exquisite melancholy.

He left undone the middle button of his fly, just for old times' sake.

When he reached the Castro, he found a parking place on the steep part of Noe, then strode downhill in the direction of the music. On a platform in front of the Hibernia Bank, a gay chorale was already singing "America the Beautiful." Hundreds of people, some of them crying, had gathered in the street.

He wriggled through the crowd until he could catch a glimpse of the hostage/lovers. One was lean and blond and bearded. The other was also bearded, but he was darker and somewhat older, more of a daddy type. Michael could picture them together quite easily. He could see them on that hijacked plane, desperate when death seemed imminent, passing love notes under the murderous gaze of their captors.

Then the gay band broke into the national anthem, and the crowd began to sing. Michael noticed how many couples there were, how many broad backs settled against broad chests as tenor voices filled the warm night. The world was pairing off these days, no doubt about it.

The hostages took turns at the podium. They talked about home and family and the need for expressing love openly. Then they asked for a moment of silence for the sailor who'd been killed on their plane. When it was over, Michael wiped his eyes and checked his watch. He was already half an hour late for the JO party.

He strode briskly at first, then began to run up Castro as the band blared forth with "If My Friends Could See Me Now." At Nineteenth, he cut across Noe and completed his ascent to Joe's apartment. The house, as he'd remembered, was a potentially handsome Victorian that had been hideously eisenhowered with green asbestos shingles.

He caught his breath for a moment, then pressed the buzzer. Joe came to the door wearing nothing but cut-offs. "Oh . . . Michael. You're a little late, fella."

"It's over?"

"No. Just sort of . . . Round Two. C'mon in."

Michael entered the dark foyer and lowered his voice to a whisper. "Sorry," he said. "I was singing the national anthem and the time got away from me."

If his host appreciated the irony, he didn't remark on it. "Take your clothes off out here. Stack your stuff on the stairs." He slapped Michael's butt and slipped behind the bedspread separating the foyer from the parlor.

Michael stripped, piling his T-shirt, jeans and boots next to a dozen similar groupings on the stairs. He faced the hall mirror and checked himself briefly—for *what?* he wondered—before pulling aside the bedspread to greet his public.

The men were slouched on sofas and chairs arranged in a crude crescent in front of the TV set. On the screen, two men in business suits were sucking cock in an elevator. A few heads swiveled in Michael's direction, but most remained fixed on the movie, intent on the business at hand.

He scanned the room for available seating. Nothing was left but the middle section of a sofa on the far side of the room. Heading there, he passed in front of the TV set, and it occurred to him—perversely—that someone might shout "Down in front!" just to embarrass him.

No one did. He sat on the sofa, nodding gravely to his sofa mates, then glanced discreetly around the room at the other participants. This was Round Two, all right. As Teddy might have put it, there were very few members in good standing.

In a La-Z-Boy next to the window sat Teddy himself, cock in hand, smirking ruthlessly at the latecomer. Michael looked away from him, fearful of losing the moment altogether.

After a while, he got into it. There were some hot guys there—including that number from Muscle System—and the porn video suited his tastes perfectly. Once his self-consciousness had passed, he began to savor the sensation he had missed so dearly, the lost tribalism of years gone by. It wasn't the way it used to be, but it stirred a few memories just the same.

He was on the verge of coming when two men next to Teddy's La-Z-Boy rose and left the room. They were followed, moments later, by three others. Presently a small din was emanating from the foyer, where the dressing ceremonies had begun.

The guttural commands and primal grunts of the video were no match at all for the brunch being planned beyond the bedspread. "Don't do pasta salad," someone said quite audibly. "You did that last time and everybody hated it."

The fantasy collapsed like a house of dirty playing cards. As Teddy exited through a sliding door to the dining room, Michael caught his eye with a rueful smile. Teddy leaned over and whispered in his ear: "There's no such thing as being fashionably late for a JO party."

There were two other men left in the room. One of them,

the Muscle System hunk, was watching the screen with un-blinking single-mindedness; the other, in similar fashion, was watching Michael watch the hunk. It was getting too intimate, Michael decided, so he gave up the effort and left.

He dressed hurriedly, avoiding conversation, then remembered his manners and thanked the host. As he headed down Noe toward his car, he stopped long enough to admire the reddish remnants of a sunset behind Twin Peaks.

He could still hear the music down at Eighteenth and Castro.

A Handsome Offer

WREN DOUGLAS AND THE LIMOUSINE DRIVER HAD watched the sunset from her big bed at the Fairmont. The ripening nectarine sky had been a perfect backdrop for their postcoital cuddling, a pagan benediction of sorts.

"Does it do that often?" she asked.

"Sometimes," he replied. "When the weather's warm like this."

Idly, she massaged his temples with her fingertips, then worked her way up to his scalp. He gave a little faux-Stallone moan and repositioned his head against her chest, as if he were plumping pillows. His dark, curly hair was pungent with Tenax.

"This would make a fabulous ending," she said. "The credits should be rolling over that sunset. Here endeth the book tour."

"Two more cities," he mumbled.

She gave his cheek a reproving whack. "Don't remind me."

"Portland and Seattle, right?"

"Yeah."

"You don't wanna do it?"

"I wanna do nothing," she said. "I wanna lie around and be a total slug."

The bedside phone rang, mangling her reverie. "That's my publicist," she said. "I'll put money on it." With one hand still buried in the driver's curls, she grabbed the receiver and barked into it. "Yes, Nicholas my love, I'm still alive and I'm still on schedule."

There was no immediate response, no telltale bleat of laughter from the adenoidal Nicholas, so she realized her guess had been wrong. Eventually, the caller said: "I beg your pardon. I'm trying to reach Miss Douglas . . . Miss Wren Douglas?"

"You got her," she replied. "I thought you were somebody else."

"Oh," said the caller.

"What can I do for you?"

"Well . . . I have some business I'd like to discuss with you. My name is Roger Manigault. I'm chairman of the board of Pacific Excelsior."

Excelsior? What? The packing material? What could a fat girl do for an excelsior company? "Sorry," she said. "Never heard of it." Using her free forefinger, she traced the fleshy oval of the driver's lips, then popped the finger into his mouth. He sucked on it obligingly.

"We make aluminum honeycomb," explained the caller. "Among other things."

She didn't know what that was and she didn't care. "Oh . . . right. Why don't I give you my agent's number? You can tell her what you've got in mind. This really isn't the best time to discuss . . ."

"I'm in the lobby, Miss Douglas. I know this is irregular, but . . . time is of the essence. If I could have just ten minutes with you."

She looked down at the classic features of the fallen Pompeiian sprawled against her chest. "Look, Mr. . . . whatever. Maybe if you call tomorrow . . ."

"There's a handsome fee involved."

She hesitated a moment, remembering her lust for shoes,

envisioning how her Chicago loft would look with pink neon tubing around the windows. "Oh, yeah?" she said. "How handsome?"

The driver looked up at her and narrowed his eyes. She smirked and gave his earlobe a wiggle.

"Five thousand dollars," said the caller. "For three or four days of your time."

"Look, Mr. . . ."

"Ten thousand, then."

She muffled the receiver and spoke to the driver. "Find my Filofax, would you, doll? I think it's in the other room."

The driver looked puzzled.

"My appointment book," she explained. "It's in one of the drawers. Just check, O.K.?"

When he was out of the room, she uncovered the receiver and said: "Look, does this involve sex?"

The caller seemed prepared for that question. "No," he said quietly and almost immediately. "I can explain things better if you'll meet me downstairs. I'm in the Cirque Room."

"What's that?"

"The bar," he replied, "in the lobby."

"Fine. I'll see you there in fifteen minutes. What do you look like?"

"Um . . ." He faltered for a moment. "I'm wearing a gray pinstriped suit . . . and I have white hair and a white mustache."

"I'll find you." She hung up the phone.

The driver appeared in the doorway with her Filofax. "This what you mean?"

"That's it," she said.

He laid the Filofax on the bedside table and hopped under the covers with her. "So what's this shit about handsome?"

"A handsome *offer*," she replied, tweaking his cheek, "not a handsome man. Don't get that pretty Neapolitan nose out of joint."

"What kind of offer?"

"I don't know," she said, climbing out of bed, "but I'm about to find out."

After some indecision, she donned a pale blue sailor dress

with puffed sleeves and a dropped waist. It was cute and becoming (without being overtly sexy) and would do nicely for a business meeting.

As she tied the big floppy bow, the driver spoke to her languidly from the bed. "You comin' back?"

"You bet. Wanna stick around?"

He nodded. "How long?"

"Dunno. He's down in the bar. Hour or so, I guess." She patted the bow into place, then turned to face him. "Isn't your wife expecting you?"

He shook his head. "Tonight is PTA."

She slipped into her shoes and headed for the door, picking up her purse on the way. "Keep the bed warm. There's some champagne and Almond Roca in the fridge if you get hungry."

Down in the Cirque Room, she had no trouble spotting her mysterious caller. He sat ramrod straight in a corner banquette, so markedly military in his bearing that she half expected to find epaulets on his business suit. She guessed him to be about seventy.

He shot to his feet when he saw her approaching. This effort at gallantry—or at least *his* idea of gallantry—was far more endearing than she might have imagined. She smiled at him, then knelt by the glass he had knocked off the table, scooping up the scattered ice cubes.

"Please," he said, growing flustered, "don't do that."

She looked up at him. "Why the hell not?"

A waitress approached. "We have a little accident here?"

"I'm such a klutz," said Wren, glancing up at the waitress. "You'd think I could sit down without knocking the gentleman's drink over."

The waitress took the glass from her, then looked at the old man. "What was it, sir? I'll get you another."

"Scotch and water," he told her. "And whatever the lady's having."

Something kick-ass was in order, she decided, slipping into

the banquette. "I'll take the same," she said, then turned back to the man. "Your name makes no sense to me."

He didn't understand.

"Pacific Excelsior," she explained. "I thought excelsior was packing straw."

"Oh . . . no. In this instance it's a Latin word meaning 'ever upward.'"

She winked at him. "I knew that." She extended her hand and waited until he shook it. "Wren Douglas," she said. "And your name again is . . . ?"

"Boo . . . Roger Manigault."

"Boo-Roger. Interesting. Never heard that one before."

He smiled for the first time. "Some of my friends call me Booter. That's what I'm used to."

"Booter, huh? Why?"

"I played football," he replied. "Years ago. At Stanford."

"I like it. Can I call you that?"

"If you like."

She laid her hands on the table, palms down, and made a smoothing motion. "So . . . what's this about ten thousand dollars?"

He faltered, then said: "I have . . . well, a very comfortable lodge up in the redwoods. I'd like you to be my guest there for a few days."

She studied him for awhile, then gave him a rueful, worldly chuckle.

"I'm on the level," he said, reddening noticeably.

She shook her head slowly. "You lied to me, Booter. You've been a bad boy."

"I wanted you to meet me first. Before you said no."

"Get real," she said, just as the waitress returned with their drinks. She nursed hers for a while, saying nothing, regarding him out of the corner of her eye.

"I've never done anything like this," he said.

"That's a comfort," she replied dryly.

"Do you think I would . . . do this, if . . ."

"Where did you see me?" she asked.

He looked confused. "What do you mean?"

"What set this off?" She laughed. "I mean, ten thousand

41

dollars, Booter. That ain't whoremongering, that's . . . Christ, I don't know what it is."

"You're not a whore," he said glumly.

"Answer the question."

He looked down at his drink. "I saw your picture in *Newsweek*. I think you're an extraordinarily lovely woman."

She nodded slowly. "So you read my book and decided: What the hell—maybe I'll have a shot at it."

"No," he said.

"What?"

"I haven't read your book."

She drew back, affronted for the first time all evening.

"I stay busy," he explained apologetically. "There's time for a little Louis L'Amour but not much else."

"Are you married?" she asked.

"Yes."

"Are you really . . . you know . . . chairman of the board and all that?"

"You can check me out," he said. "I'm not a lunatic." He looked at her earnestly. "I'm sorry if I insulted you. I'm a rich man, but not a young one. I wanted to make it worth your while."

"Oh, please," she murmured, rolling her eyes.

He stood up to leave. "Let's forget I ever—"

"Sit down," she ordered, seizing his hand. It was large and fleshy, surprisingly strong.

He obeyed her.

"How old are you?" she asked.

"Seventy-one," he replied.

"I've had lovers that old," she said. "You'd know that if you'd read my book."

Generation Gap

BRIAN'S NEPHEW TURNED OUT TO BE A LANKY REDHEAD, as soberly and self-consciously devoted to the Wet Look as Brian had once been to the Dry. Jed was an average-looking kid, barely rescued from dorkiness by a rudimentary grasp of current teen fashion. (He affected hightop Reeboks of varying hues and let his shirttails hang out beneath his crew-neck sweaters.)

For some reason, Brian felt a little sorry for him.

"So," he said one night after dinner, "you're a sophomore next year, huh?"

Jed nodded, finishing off the last piece of pizza. They were seated at a card table Mrs. Madrigal had hauled up from the basement. Except for a bookshelf and a battered sofa, this was the only furniture in the candlelit room. Here and there, the landlady had compensated for the austerity by cramming jelly jars with yellow roses from her garden.

"I remember my sophomore year," Brian offered, trying to draw the kid out. "I screwed around the whole time. The ol' freshman terror had gone, and the girls started lookin' good."

No response. Zilch.

He tried again: "Guess things haven't changed all that much, huh?"

"I party some," answered Jed, measuring out his words, "but I have to keep my grades up if I want to be competitive in the job market."

Oh, right, thought Brian. Spoken like a true automaton of the state.

"Cissie and I have worked out a plan."

"Cissie's your girl?"

The kid nodded. "We wanna get married my first year in law school and start a family and all. But that takes money, so I figure I'd better graduate with at least a three point six or I won't get into Harvard Law School. The more prestigious firms never hire out of the . . . you know, minor law schools."

Brian repressed an urge to stick his finger down his throat.

"You gotta plan," added Jed. "Families cost money."

"Right."

"Of course, I don't need to tell *you* that. Look how long you and Mary Ann had to wait."

This observation was not so much malicious as naive, Brian decided. "We didn't have to wait," he said quietly. "It's what we both wanted. We were both in our thirties when we married."

"Wow," said Jed, as if he were digesting an entry from the *Guinness Book of World Records.*

Brian took the offensive, intent upon liberating the kid. "I enjoyed my time as a bachelor. It taught me a helluva lot about myself and the world. I think I'm a better husband because of it."

"Yeah," said Jed, "but wasn't life kind of . . . empty?"

"No. Hell, no." This wasn't entirely true, but he hated the kid's priggish tone. "I was an independent man. Sex helped make me that way."

Confronted with this hopelessly old-fashioned concept, Jed smiled indulgently.

"It's the truth," said Brian. "Didn't you feel more . . . in

44

charge of yourself the first time you got it on with a girl?"

The kid tugged at the cuff of his sweater. "There weren't any girls before Cissie."

"O.K., then . . . the first time you got it on with Cissie." Silence.

Brian studied his nephew's face, where the awful truth was blooming like acne. "Hell, I'm sorry . . . I didn't . . . I mean, lots of guys . . ."

Jed greeted his stammering with another faint smile, more smug than the last. "It's a matter of choice, Brian."

"Oh . . . well . . ."

"We don't believe in premarital sex. Neither one of us."

Premarital sex? He couldn't recall having heard that term since the early sixties, when it ceased to be a racy topic for high school debate teams. Who was this Cissie bitch, anyway? What gave her the right to pussywhip this innocent kid into a life of marital servitude?

"Jed . . . listen, man . . . maybe it's none of my business, but I think you're making a serious mistake. A little experimentation never hurt anybody. You owe that to yourself, kiddo. How can you be sure about Cissie if . . ."

"I'm sure, Brian. All right?"

Brian shook his head. "There's no way. You're too young. You haven't lived enough."

"I'm not interested in one-night stands," said Jed.

"You're scared," Brian countered, "and that's cool. Everybody's first time is . . ."

"Things are different now, Brian. It's not the way it was with your generation."

Or with your mother's, thought Brian. Sunny had had four lovers and an abortion before she got around to having Jed. How could life have changed so radically in twenty years? "Some things still apply," he told his nephew, hoping to God it was true.

Jed rose and dumped the pizza box into a Hefty bag in the corner. "I've had a long day, Brian." It was clearly a signal for the meddling uncle to leave.

"Yeah," said Brian. "Right." He stood up and went to the

door. "I'm up at The Summit if you need a tour guide or anything. Mrs. Madrigal says she'll be glad to answer any questions about the neighborhood."

"Forget that," said Jed. "She's too weird."

Brian didn't bother to reprimand him. Why waste his breath on this tight-assed little bastard?

Ten minutes later, back at The Summit, Mary Ann asked him how dinner had been.

"The pits," he replied.

"Well, I hope you were nice to him."

He gave her a peevish glance. "I was nice to him. He was the one who wasn't nice to me."

"What do you mean?"

"I dunno," he said. "Just rude and uptight." He saw no point in mentioning the virginity part. Mary Ann, no doubt, would find it "sweet."

"He's young," she said, stacking her dishes in the dishwasher.

Her phony generosity annoyed him. "You want me to invite him over?"

"No," she replied demurely. "Not if you think he's . . . difficult."

"Save your platitudes, then. The kid is an asshole."

She closed the dishwasher and looked at him. "What is your problem, Brian?"

A damn good question. He felt headachy still, and his gut had begun to seize up in a peculiar way. Was this weird fatigue a function of the flu? Or merely a function of being forty-two? Was that what made him so resentful of Jed's unspent youth?

"I'm sorry," he said finally. "My head hurts. I'm getting a bug, I think."

She frowned, then felt his forehead. "There's no fever."

He shrugged and turned away.

"I'll make us some hot chocolate," she said. "Go put your feet up."

"No, thanks."

"C'mon," she said. "Don't be so grumpy. It's sugar-free."

A soundless TV was their blazing hearth while she rubbed his feet. "Oh," she said after a long silence, "DeDe called this afternoon. She and D'or want us to come use the pool this Sunday."

He grunted noncommittally. He distrusted his wife's escalating chumminess with the Halcyon-Wilsons, not because they were dykes but because they were rich and social. Mary Ann was simply climbing in this instance, he felt almost certain.

"I thought it would be nice for Shawna," she added, giving his little toe a placatory tug. "I know you aren't crazy about them, but that pool is to die for."

"Whatever," he said.

"C'mon," she cooed. "Don't be like that."

"Fine. We'll go. I might be sick as a dog . . ."

"Oh, poor you." She pressed her thumbs into the arch of his foot. "You'll feel better by then, and—"

A ringing phone silenced her.

Brian reached for it. "Yeah?"

"It's Jed, Brian."

"Oh . . . yeah."

"I just wanted to thank you for bringing the pizza by. And the place and all. You're a real lifesaver."

"Well . . . sure. No sweat."

"You're a terrific uncle. I see why Mom likes you so much."

"Hey . . . no problem. We'll do it again, huh?"

"Sure," said the kid.

"Great. Then we'll—what?—check in with each other to-morrow?"

"You bet."

Brian hung up.

"Jed?" asked Mary Ann.

He nodded.

"He has manners," she said. "You have to admit."

"Yeah," he said absently, retrieving the towel he had thrown in so hastily. The kid, after all, was his own flesh and blood. He deserved a second chance.

Maybe all he really needed was a good piece of ass.

Ladies of the Evening

THE HALCYON-WILSONS DINED THAT NIGHT AT LE TROU, a tiny French restaurant on Guerrero Street.

"It means The Hole," said D'orothea.

DeDe, who was reapplying lipstick, looked up with exaggerated horror. "Ick. What does?"

"The name of the restaurant," said D'orothea. "Stop being misogynistic."

"Misogynous," said DeDe.

"What?"

"The word is 'misogynous,' while you're accusing me. But I fail to see how . . ."

"You were making a hole joke," said D'orothea. "You don't think that's demeaning?"

"Look, *you* brought it up. Besides, you make pussy jokes all the time."

D'orothea stabbed sullenly at her *bijane aux fraises.* "Pussy is friendly. Hole is not."

A woman at the next table looked at them and frowned.

"Tell the world," muttered DeDe. "Better yet, put it on a sampler. 'Pussy is friendly. Hole is not.'"

"All *right*," said D'or.

"You're just mad at me because I don't wanna go to Wimminwood."

"Well . . . I think that's indicative of your larger problem."

"My larger problem?"

"Your total resistance to anything you don't—"

"I told you," said DeDe. "I've already invited Mary Ann and Brian to brunch."

D'or scowled. "That's just an excuse. The fact is . . . you're threatened."

"Oh, right," said DeDe. "By what?"

"By women-only space."

DeDe snorted. "I was in the Junior League, wasn't I?"

D'or's eyes became obsidian. "Don't make fun of this. I won't have it. Wimminwood is very important to me."

"You've never even been there."

"I went to the one in Michigan. I know how it feels, O.K.? It's part of who I am, and it's . . . something special I want to share with you."

DeDe poked at her dessert. "That's what you told me when we left for Guyana."

Her lover gave her a long, incendiary look. "That was low."

Feeling the reprimand, DeDe looked away.

"You're becoming your mother," D'or added darkly. "Is that what you really want?"

"Talk about *low*," said DeDe.

D'or shrugged. "It's the truth."

"It *is* not. I'm nothing like her."

"Well, you're not a substance abuser." The very phrase was pure lesbianese, epitomizing everything DeDe hated about D'or's reemerging consciousness.

"C'mon, D'or. Can't you just call her a drunk and be done with it?"

This was a bit harsh, DeDe realized. Widowed nine years ago, her mother had struggled valiantly to keep the bottle at bay, never fully capitulating until her remarriage in 1984.

DeDe's stepfather had been their next-door neighbor in Hillsborough for as long as DeDe could remember. (That is, his tennis courts bordered on the apple orchard at Halcyon

Hill.) Her mother had married him nine months after the death of his first wife and moved into his rambling postwar ranch house.

That had left the mock-Tudor pile of Halcyon Hill for the sole tenancy of DeDe, D'orothea and the children. Absolutely nobody objected, since her mother and D'or were always at odds, and her mother's new husband had no intention of living under the same roof with his lesbian stepdaughter and her eight-year-old Eurasian twins.

By implicit mutual consent, they got tipsy on white wine spritzers at the Baybrick Inn.

When the floor show began, a sinewy stripper in full police drag made a beeline for their table, bumping and grinding all the way. DeDe giggled uncontrollably as the cop began gesturing lewdly with her nightstick.

"Did you set this up?" she asked her lover.

D'or's eyes were full of mischief. *"Moi?"*

"I'll get you for this. I swear."

"She's waiting. Give her something."

The stripper began to hump the back of DeDe's chair, egged on by the roar of a hundred women.

"Money, you mean?"

"Of course money!"

The cop doffed her helmet and held it out to DeDe, who fumbled frantically in her purse. The crowd was going wild. "D'or . . . how much?"

"The twenty."

"Isn't that a little too . . . ?"

"It's for AIDS. Give it to her."

She placed the bill in the helmet, to the sound of tumultuous applause. To show her gratitude, the cop leaned over and stuck her tongue in DeDe's ear.

* * *

"You looked utterly stricken," D'or told her later as they sped home to Hillsborough in their big Buick station wagon. "I wish I had a picture of it."

DeDe laughed along with her. "Thank God you don't."

When the city lights were gone and the highway became a dark ribbon through the hills, they both fell silent for the final stretch, with DeDe stealing occasional glances at the volatile, loving woman behind the wheel.

"D'or?" she said at last.

"Yeah?"

"Could we take the children?"

"Where?"

"Wimminwood."

D'or turned and smiled at her sleepily. "Sure."

"Well . . . maybe you're right, then. Maybe it would do us some good."

"Are you sure?"

"Yeah. I mean . . . I'm willing to give it a shot."

D'or reached over and squeezed her leg. "I figured that stripper would do the trick."

Their baby-sitter was a leggy freshman from Foothill Community College. When they got home, she was watching *Love Letters* on the VCR. Since they'd acquired the movie for the sole purpose of ogling the naked body of Jamie Lee Curtis, DeDe had the uneasy sensation their privacy had been violated.

The sitter, however, seemed totally oblivious of the smoldering eroticism on the screen. "This is so lame," she said without getting up.

D'or grinned wickedly at DeDe, who said: "Well, you two can settle up. I'll go look in on the children."

The kids were dead to the world, sprawled like rag dolls across their respective beds. Their almond-eyed faces seemed smoother and rounder than ever, gleaming like ivory in the bright summer moonlight.

A little healthy exercise in the woods would be good for

them, she told herself. There would be other children at Wimminwood, playmates with similar home environments. What better reinforcement could she find for them?

She adjusted Edgar's blanket, then leaned over and kissed him on the forehead. His eyes popped open instantly.

"You weren't asleep," she whispered.

"Did you have a good time?" he asked.

"Yes, darling." She sat on the edge of the bed and brushed the hair off his forehead. "How 'bout you?"

"That sitter is a retard," he said.

"Why?"

"She likes David Lee Roth."

"You didn't give her a hard time, did you?"

He shook his head.

"Go to sleep, then. In the morning I'll tell you about a great trip we're gonna take to the Russian River."

"D'or told me already," he said.

"She did? When?"

"Long time ago."

She wasn't surprised. It was typical of D'or to marshal the forces before mounting the attack.

"I can't go," Edgar added, "cuz I'm a boy."

"Who told you that?"

"D'or."

"Well, she must have been joking, darling."

"I don't think so."

"You misunderstood her, then. We're all going. We would never go anywhere without you." She pulled the blanket up under his chin. "Go to sleep now. Before we wake up Anna."

She descended the staircase to the foyer, her face burning with anger. She could hear the sitter's car spewing gravel in the driveway as she cornered D'or in the kitchen. "Did you tell Edgar he couldn't go to Wimminwood with us?"

D'or opened the refrigerator and took out a half-gallon carton of milk. "No. Of course not."

"He says you did."

"Well, I didn't, dammit. I told him just the opposite, in fact. I said we should all go this year, because he's not ten yet." D'or set a saucepan on the stove and poured milk into it.

"And?" prodded DeDe.

"And . . . little boys don't get to go when they're ten. It's the rule, DeDe. I wanted to be up front about it. Children can understand rules."

"This is what I hate, you know. This is exactly what I hate."

"Oh, c'mon."

"This doctrinaire bullshit, this . . . this . . ."

"You want some cocoa?"

"You hurt Edgar's feelings, D'or. A little boy doesn't understand what's so threatening about his penis."

"I'll talk to him—all right?"

"When?"

D'or opened the cabinet, removed a can of cocoa and handed it to DeDe. "Fix us some and bring it to the bedroom. I'll be there in a little while."

DeDe was still fuming when D'or finally joined her in bed. "Is he O.K.?" she asked.

"Just fine," said D'or.

"What did you tell him?"

"I told him they made that rule about little boys because ten-year-old boys were almost men, and men were all rapists at heart."

"D'or, goddamnit!"

"All right. Jesus . . . don't hit me."

"Then tell me what you told him."

"I told him I explained things all wrong."

"Is that all?"

"No. I told him it wouldn't be any fun without him along, and that I love him just as much as you do. Then Anna woke up and asked me what smegma was."

"*What?*"

"That Atkins kid called her smegma today."

DeDe groaned. "That little brat has the foulest—" The phone rang before she could finish the tirade. D'or reached for the receiver, mumbled hello, and passed it to DeDe. "It's your mother," she said, grinning. "Ask her what smegma is."

DeDe gave her a nasty look, then spoke into the receiver. "Hello, Mother."

"Don't use that tone with me."

"What tone? I just said hello."

"I can tell when you're being snide, darling."

"It's after midnight, Mother."

"Well, I would have called you earlier, but I got busy." "Busy" sounded more like "bishy."

"Go on, then," said DeDe.

"Were you asleep?"

"No, but we're in bed."

"Don't be vulgar, DeDe."

"Mother . . ."

"All right, I called to ask if you and D'orothea would come for lunch on Sunday. With the children, of course."

"That's sweet, Mother, but we've already made plans. I was giving a lunch myself, but I'm canceling it."

D'or smiled victoriously, then reached over and stroked DeDe's thigh.

Her mother wouldn't give up. "Oh, darling, please say yes. I'm gonna be all alone."

"Why?" asked DeDe. "Where's Booter going?"

"The Grove," said her mother bitterly.

"Oh. It's that time of year again."

"Do you realize," said her mother, "how many times I've been a Grove Widow? I counted it up. Thirty-two times. It isn't fair."

DeDe had heard this sob story all her life. Grove Widows, as they were popularly known, were the wives left behind by Bohemian Club members during their two-week encampment at the Bohemian Grove. The Grove was a sort of summer camp for graying aristocrats, an all-male enclave in the redwoods, whose secret fraternal rituals were almost a century old.

DeDe's father had been an ardent Bohemian, provoking her mother to bouts of acute depression during her annual ordeal of separation. Since her mother's new husband was also a Bohemian, the torment had continued unabated. "You should have married a commoner," DeDe told her.

"That isn't a bit funny."

"Well, what do you want me to say?"

"I want you to come to lunch."

"Mother . . . we're going away."

"Where?"

"Just . . . up north. We're packing the kids in the station wagon and taking off." Wimminwood, in fact, was only a mile or two downriver from the Grove, but to say as much would only heighten her mother's sense of familial desertion.

"I worry about her," she told D'or later. "I can't help it."

D'or pulled her sleep mask into position. "What's the matter this time?"

"Oh . . . Booter's taking off for the Grove."

"Christ," sighed D'or. "The crises of the rich."

"I know."

"This happens every year. Why didn't she plan something?"

"She did plan something. She invited us to lunch." DeDe reached over and turned off the light.

"And now you're feeling guilty as hell."

"No I'm not."

D'or paused. "Of course, we could always bring her along."

DeDe flipped on the light. *"What?"*

"Sure. Gettin' down with her sisters . . . tits to the wind. She'd like that."

DeDe turned off the light again.

D'or kept at it. "Turkey baster study groups, S and M workshops . . ."

"Shut *up*, D'or."

Her lover chuckled throatily and snuggled closer, hooking her leg around DeDe's. "It's gonna be great, hon. I can hardly wait."

DeDe said: "We don't have to go topless, do we?"

Another chuckle.

"Don't laugh. I think we should discuss it."

"O.K.," said D'or. "Discuss."

"Well . . . whatever we decide, I think we should be consistent."

"Meaning?"

"That we either both do it, or . . . you know . . . both don't do it."

"Maybe," said D'or, "if we both bared one breast . . ."

"Ha ha," said DeDe.

"Well, gimme a break."

DeDe paused. "I just think it would be disorienting for the children, that's all."

"What are you talking about? The kids've seen us naked plenty of times."

"I know, but . . . if one of us goes topless and the other one doesn't . . ."

"What you're saying is . . . you plan to keep your shirt on, and you want me to do the same."

"O.K.," said DeDe. "Yes."

"Why?"

DeDe hesitated. "We don't . . . well, we don't need to prove anything, that's all."

"Who's proving anything?" said D'or. "It feels good. What's the big deal? You went topless all over the place in Cabo last summer."

"That was different. It was secluded."

"This is secluded."

"Hundreds of people, D'or. That is not secluded."

"Well, they're all *women,* for God's sake."

"Exactly," said DeDe.

"What are you talking about?" asked D'or.

She was talking about jealousy, of course, but she couldn't bring herself to say it.

Something for Jed

THE DEFLORATION OF HIS NEPHEW BECAME BRIAN'S PET project. After reviewing half a dozen candidates for the job, he narrowed it down to Jennifer Rabinowitz and Geordie Davies, two Golden Oldies from his personal Top Forty. Jennifer, it turned out, was in Nebraska visiting her brother, so the honor fell by default to Geordie.

Geordie was thirty and lived alone in a garden apartment near the southern gate of the Presidio. They had met one night at Serramonte Mall while buying software for their Macintoshes. Feverish with lust, they had babbled clumsily about Macpaint and Macdraw before beating a hasty retreat to the parking lot. He'd followed her home in his Jeep.

Since that night—two, almost three years ago—he'd visited her cottage less than a dozen times. Neither her lover nor his wife had intruded on their lovemaking, which was refreshingly devoid of romance. Geordie was a true bachelor girl, who liked her life exactly the way it was.

The problem, of course, was how to set it up without scaring Jed off, but Geordie would probably have a few ideas of her own. When he called her cottage in midafternoon, he got her answering machine, which surprised him with its minimalist instruction to "leave your name and number at the tone." Usually her tapes featured barking dogs or old Shirelles tunes or her own unfunny impersonation of a Valley Girl.

His guess was that she was home auditioning callers, so he used his manliest tone of voice when he left his name and number. It didn't work, or she was out. You never knew for sure with Geordie.

By evening, he had decided to make his request in person. The scheme might not seem as cold-blooded if there was eye contact involved. "Do me a favor and fuck my nephew" wouldn't quite cut it on the telephone.

After dinner, he told Mary Ann he was going down to Barbary Lane to visit Jed.

She looked up from her homework, a book about scalp reduction, the subject of tomorrow's show. "Don't let her corner you," she said.

He didn't get it.

"Mrs. Madrigal," she explained. "She's obsessed with those steps. It's sweet, but it's a hopeless cause. Hasn't she told you about it?"

"Oh, yeah . . . she mentioned it."

"Personally," said Mary Ann, "I think she gets off on being colorful."

"I like the steps," he said ineffectually.

"Well, so do I, but they're lethal. And the city isn't about to build brand-new wooden ones." She returned to her book, closing the discussion.

He headed for the door. "I won't be late."

"Say hi to Jed," she said.

It took him twenty-five minutes to reach Geordie's cottage. He parked in the driveway of the house in front and made his way through the fragrant shrubbery to the rear garden. There was a light on in her living room.

He rang her bell, but there was no response. He had never before shown up unannounced, so it was entirely possible that her lover was visiting. She was probably madder than hell.

When she came to the door, however, her pale face seemed drained of all expression.

"I was going to call you," she said.

Escape to Alcatraz

O N HIS FIRST DAY OF VACATION, MICHAEL TOLLIVER took his mail to the Barbary steps and stretched out in the sunshine. According to the paper, there were fires still blazing to the south, and the warm spell showed no sign of imminent departure. His sluggish Southern metabolism had ground almost to a halt.

He plucked a stalk of dried *finocchio* and chewed it ruminatively, Huck Finn style. In the spring, this stuff was lacy and pale green, tasting strongly of licorice, a flavor he had never understood as a kid. It grew anywhere and everywhere, remaining lush and decorative in the face of constant efforts to exterminate it.

Finocchio, he had read somewhere, was also Italian slang for "faggot."

And that made sense somehow.

He set aside the less promising mail and tore into a flimsy blue envelope from England. These short but vivid bulletins from his old friend Mona had become enormously important to him.

Dearest Mouse,

The tourist season is upon us at Easley, and we're up to our ass in Texas millionaires. I'd say to hell with it, if we didn't need the money so badly. I am actually dating the postmistress from Chipping Campden, but I'm not so sure it's a good idea. She uses words like Sapphic when she means dyke. Also, I think she likes the idea of Lady Roughton more than she actually likes me, which is pretty goddamn disconcerting, since I don't *feel* titled. (Mr. Hargis, the gardener, insists on calling me Your Ladyship when there are tourists around, but I've got him trained to lay off that shit the rest of the time.)

Wilfred got a mohawk for his eighteenth birthday and has taken to lurking in the minstrels' gallery and terrorizing the tourists. He's grown at least three inches since you last saw him. The mohawk looks good, actually, but I haven't told him so, since I'm afraid of what he'll try next. He's signed up for fall classes at a trade school in Cheltenham, but he'll be able to commute from here.

They've finally heard of AIDS in Britain, but it mostly takes the form of fag-baiting headlines in the tabloids. According to Wilfred, their idea of safe sex is not going to bed with Americans. He misses you, by the way, and told me to tell you so. I miss you too, Babycakes.

MONA

P.S. Did you know there is still a Greek island called Lesbos? It's supposed to be wonderful. Why don't we meet there next spring?

P.P.S. If you see Teddy, tell him Mrs. Digby in the village wants to install an automatic garage door. I'm pretty sure this isn't allowed, but I want his support before I say no.

Smiling, Michael put down the letter. Mona's green-card marriage to Teddy Roughton was apparently the best thing she'd ever done for herself. By swapping countries with a disgruntled nobleman, she'd found a perfect setting for her particular brand of eccentricity.

And Teddy, obviously, was enjoying himself here.

*   *   *

Michael had yet to decide on the disposition of his vacation time. Some of it would be spent on reassuring domestic rituals: writing letters, painting the kitchen, helping Mrs. Madrigal with her garden. He had also promised to distribute fliers for her save-the-steps campaign, which had so far met with indifference in the neighborhood.

After lunch, he drove to Dolores Street for a Tupperware party hosted by Charlie Rubin. Charlie had come home after another scary stint at St. Sebastian's and was making up for lost time.

The Tupperware saleslady was a big-boned Armenian woman whose spiel had been written expressly for housewives. A creature of cheerful routine, she apparently saw no reason to alter the scheme of things now. When she proudly displayed the Velveeta cheese dispenser, the thirteen assembled men erupted in gales of laughter.

Mrs. Sarkisian smiled gamely, pretending to understand, but he could tell her feelings had been hurt. He felt so sorry for her that he bought a lettuce crisper immediately thereafter and later spent five minutes telling her in private how much it would change his life.

When the rest of the guests had straggled home with their booty, he joined Charlie on the deck. "Well, that was different," he said.

Charlie stared out at the neighboring gardens, a patchwork of laundry and sunflowers. "I always wondered what one was like," he said. "Didn't you?"

Michael nodded. "And now we know."

They were both quiet for a while. Then Charlie said: "I made a list when I was in the hospital, and that was on the list." He paused, then looked at Michael. "You haven't commented on my new lesion."

What was there to say? It was a dime-sized purple splotch on the tip of Charlie's nose.

Charlie cocked his head and struck a stately Condé Nast pose. "It doesn't suit me, does it? Should I get my money back?"

Managing a feeble laugh, Michael moved closer to him and

slid his hand into the back pocket of Charlie's Levi's. "It doesn't look so bad," he said.

"Please," said Charlie. "It makes me look like Pluto."

Michael smiled at him. "C'mon."

"Not even Pluto. He was friendly looking."

"You're friendly looking."

"Who were those guys who were always robbing Uncle Scrooge's money bin?"

"The Beagle Boys," said Michael.

"That's it," said Charlie. "I look like a Beagle Boy."

Michael reproved him with a gentle shake. "What else is on your list? Besides Tupperware."

Charlie thought for a moment. "A balloon ride, a fan letter to Betty White, finding you a husband . . ."

"Well"—Michael chuckled—"two out of three ain't bad."

"Don't be that way. There were some nice guys here today. Didn't you get any phone numbers?"

"No, I did not."

"Why not?"

"Because," said Michael, "I don't pick up men at Tupperware parties."

"You don't pick up men, period. You don't even date. When was your last date?"

"Stop nagging. It won't work. Let's go for a balloon ride."

Charlie inspected his nails. "Too late. Richard and I are going next week. You could join us."

"That's O.K.," said Michael.

"What about Alcatraz?" asked Charlie. "I've never been to Alcatraz."

"Neither have I," said Michael.

"It could be depressing, I guess."

"Yeah, maybe."

Charlie's fingers traced the grain of the railing. "I heard they gave the view cells to the worst offenders, because that was considered the greatest punishment. To see the city but not be able to go there."

Michael winced. "You think that's true?"

"Probably not," murmured Charlie.

"Let's check it out . . . take the tour."

"You sure you want to? It's awfully Middle American."

"And a Tupperware party isn't?"

Charlie smiled. "Did you absolutely hate it?"

"No. I thought Mrs. Sarkisian was very sweet."

"She was, wasn't she?"

A seagull swooped over the neighbor's laundry, then landed on the fence. "Everything is sweet," said Charlie. "It makes no sense to me at all."

Michael looked at him and thought of *finocchio,* popping up again and again through the cracks of the sidewalk.

Their tour boat was called the *Harbor Princess,* much to Charlie's amusement. The other passengers were a Felliniesque assortment of pantsuited tourist ladies and their husbands, plus a gaggle of Catholic schoolgirls in blue-and-gray plaid skirts.

There was also a singular beauty aboard—a strawberry blond with long, pale lashes and eyes the color of bleached denim. Charlie was sold on him.

"I'm telling you, Michael. He's cruising you like crazy."

Michael lifted his coffee cup and blew on the surface. "Don't make a scene, Charlie."

"Well, do something, damnit. Stop being coy."

"He's not even looking at me."

"Well, he *was,* for God's sake."

"Look at those gulls," said Michael. "It's amazing how long they can drift without flapping their wings."

Charlie heaved a plaintive sigh and peered out to sea. "What am I gonna do with you?"

A thin scrim of fog covered the island as they approached. The cellhouse was still intact, crouching grimly along the crest of the Rock, but many of the outbuildings were skeletal ruins, rubble overgrown with wildflowers.

Above a sign saying FEDERAL PENITENTIARY Michael could

barely make out the word INDIANS, painted crudely in red—obviously a relic of the Native American occupation in the late sixties.

They disembarked with the mob, flowing across the dock and past the ranger station into a building that felt curiously like a wine cellar, with clammy walls and low, arched ceilings. There, a ten-minute slide show assured them that inmates at Alcatraz had been the meanest of the mean, incorrigibles who deserved the isolation of the Rock.

Afterwards, they assembled at the rear entrance of the cellhouse to await further instructions. When their ranger arrived, he explained that due to the size of the crowd, visitors would be required to split up and choose among three lecture topics.

"The three topics," he explained soberly, "are Security Measures, Famous Inmates and Discipline."

Charlie leaned forward and whispered "Discipline" in Michael's ear.

Michael grinned at him.

As if reading their minds, the ranger added briskly: "Those of you who've chosen Discipline please follow Guy through the shower room to D Block."

"Oh, Guy," crooned Charlie.

By the time they had all assembled in the shower room, the demography of their tour group had become absurdly evident: Michael, Charlie, the strawberry blond, and at least two dozen girls from the Catholic school.

The ranger led the way into D Block, doing his best to herd the giggling children. "There were a lot of different names given to this area—solitary, segregation, special treatment unit, isolation. Prisoners here spent up to twenty-four hours a day inside their cells. They had their own shower facilities down there at the end of the cellblock, since they were forbidden to shower with the other inmates."

Michael and Charlie exchanged glances.

"Cells nine through fourteen were known by the inmates

66

as the 'dark cells' and were the most severe form of punishment on Alcatraz. The men stayed in total darkness inside these cells, which are steel-lined, and they were given mattresses only at night. They were fed twice a day on what was known as a 'reduced diet'—mashed vegetables in a cup.''

"Eeeyew," went the schoolgirls in unison.

"If you'd like to see what it was like to spend time in a 'dark cell,' pick a cell and I'll close the door behind you."

The children squealed with fun house terror, formed protective clumps, and crowded into the six chambers. Michael was headed for Cell 11 when Charlie grabbed his arm. "Use your head, dummy. Go for twelve."

He glanced toward Cell 12 and saw a splendiferous smile hovering above a sea of schoolgirls.

"Go on," said Charlie.

Michael hesitated, then entered the cell, watching the smile grow broader.

Seconds later, the ranger approached and closed the heavy door with a resounding clang. The tiny room was plunged into instant and total darkness, provoking another shriek from the girls.

Their mock ordeal lasted only a second or two; then the door swung open again, spilling light into the cell. The strawberry blond was no longer smiling, but he seemed a little closer than before. "Pretty creepy," he said.

"Isn't it?" said Michael.

"And we had company," said the man. "What can it be like when you're alone?"

Michael let the tide of children sweep him out of the cell. The man caught up with him and extended his hand. "I'm Thack," he said.

Michael shook his hand. "I'm Michael."

Charlie was watching them, arms folded across his chest, a triumphant gleam in his eye. "How was it?" he asked.

"Um . . . Charlie," Michael fumbled, "this is Thad."

"Thack," said the man, correcting him. "It was great. Didn't you try it?" He met Charlie's gaze without flinching, Michael noticed. A point in his favor.

Charlie shook his head. "I can't handle a crowded cocktail party."

Thack laughed, then turned back to Michael. "You guys from around here?"

"Yeah," Michael replied, avoiding his eyes. They were too easy to drown in.

"Isn't this kind of . . . touristy, for a local?"

Michael shrugged. "We'd never done it, so we thought it was time."

"Like New Yorkers and the Statue of Liberty."

"Right." Charlie nodded. "Is that where you're from?" He was hovering like a Jewish mother interviewing a candidate for son-in-law.

"Charleston," said Thack.

"West Virginia?"

"South Carolina."

"A Southerner!" exclaimed Charlie, far too gleefully. "Michael's a Southerner. You don't sound like one, though. Where's your drawl?"

Michael was squirming. "I think we'd better move it," he said. "There's another tour coming."

The three of them left the cellhouse through the main entrance and stood beneath the lighthouse, watching the fog erase the city. "I almost forgot," said Charlie suddenly. "I wanna take a picture of the shower room."

"You didn't bring your camera," said Michael.

"Didn't I? Damn." He gave Michael a glare that said *Shut up, stupid.* "Maybe they sell postcards or something."

"Right," said Michael.

Charlie turned to Thack. "Keep an eye on him, would you?"

As Charlie strode away, Thack asked: "Your guardian angel?"

"He thinks so," said Michael.

"Is that KS?" Thack touched the tip of his nose.

Michael hesitated, then said: "Yeah."

"I've never actually seen it."

Michael nodded. "That's it."

"Is he your lover?"

"No. A friend."

Thack turned back toward the city. "You live over there, huh?"

"Uh-huh. I can see this light from my bedroom."

"Must be nice."

"It is," said Michael. He snatched a pebble off the ground and flung it in the direction of the warden's house.

"This is my first time here," said Thack.

"How do you like it?"

"It's O.K.," said Thack. "The swimming isn't much."

"The ocean's a killer," said Michael, "but the river is nice. You should go up to the Russian River."

"I've heard of that. Where is it?"

"Up north. Not far."

Thack sat down on a low stone wall and yanked a weed from a crack.

"How long will you be here?" asked Michael.

Thack shrugged. "Another week. Give or take a few days."

"Where are you staying?"

"The San Franciscan. On Market Street."

"Well, if you need a tour guide . . . I mean . . . I'm on vacation myself right now."

"Oh . . . yeah. Well, sure."

"I'm in the phone book," said Michael. "Michael Tolliver. Spelled just like it sounds."

Thack nodded. "Great."

"Want me to write it down?"

"No," said Thack. "I'll remember it."

The return voyage to the city was marked by small talk and biographical data. Thack made a living renovating antebellum houses in Charleston. He was thirty-one years old, seldom ate red meat and never watched *Dynasty*. His full name was William Thackeray Sweeney, thanks to a mother in Chattanooga, who still taught high school English.

Charlie pressed Michael for details as soon as Thack had

left them at Pier 41. "I want to be matron of honor," he said. "That's all I ask."

"He won't call," said Michael.

"Why not?"

Michael shrugged. "He's a tourist. He wants instant gratification. He'll find somebody in a bar or order somebody out of the *Advocate.*"

"Don't be such a cynic," said Charlie. "It isn't becoming."

They took a cable car up Hyde Street, parting company at Union, where Michael disembarked and walked home to Barbary Lane. When he reached his apartment, Mrs. Madrigal came gliding up the stairs and called to him.

"Uh . . . Michael dear?"

"Yeah?"

"Brian was by. He asked if you'd give him a jingle."

"Did he say what it was about?"

The landlady shook her head.

"Probably his nephew," said Michael. "He's gay and Brian can't handle it."

She smiled demurely. "I don't think so."

"I hope not. I don't want him on our side."

She cast her eyes upward in the direction of Jed's apartment, then put a finger to her lips. "There are no sides, dear."

He tried to look contrite.

"He's young, that's all. I expect you and Brian can both be of help to him."

He seriously doubted this.

"Call Brian," said Mrs. Madrigal, heading down the stairs. "I think it's important."

The Boy Next Door

EAGER FOR ESCAPE, BOOTER MANIGAULT LEFT WORK
early and drove home to Hillsborough. He found
his wife drinking Mai Tais on the terrace, his maid
brooding in the kitchen. This was a tiresomely familiar scenario, since Emma was plagued by Frannie's drinking even more than he was.

"O.K.," he said, setting his briefcase on the kitchen table.
"What happened this time?"

The maid was poker stiff with indignation. "I told her she
was killin' herself, and she said none o' your business, nigger."

Emma had heard worse, of course. She had been with Frannie so long that she'd arrived as part of her dowry, along with
the crystal and the Persian rugs and the John Singer Sargent
of Frannie's grandmother.

The Sargent looked like holy hell in Booter's modern low-
beamed ranch house, but Emma and the other furnishings
had worked out fine. She was old and cantankerous, but her
loyalty was indisputable. In his eyes, that made her the last of
a breed.

"She didn't mean it," he told the maid quietly. "It's the whiskey talking."

Emma grunted, then rearranged her licorice-stick fingers on the tabletop. "Crazy ol' white woman, that's who was talkin'."

He left her and confronted his wife on the terrace. "Would you go make up with Emma, for God's sake!"

Frannie looked at him with red-rimmed basset eyes, then squared her jaw in a pathetic imitation of resolve. "I'd sooner fry in hell," she said.

"Did you call her a nigger, Frannie?"

She thrust out her lower lip.

"Did you?" he persisted.

"You use that word all the time."

"Not about people I know," he said. "Not to their faces."

"I've known her for forty years." She raised her bejeweled fingers to her head and repositioned her wig. "I can call her anything I want."

"She's a servant, Frannie. It isn't done."

"It's none of your business, Booter. Emma and I understand each other."

In a way, she was right about that. The two women bickered constantly, then drew blood, then made up. Emma and Frannie were more of a couple than he and Frannie would ever be.

"When are you leaving?" she asked.

"This afternoon," he replied.

"For how long?"

He hated this kind of third degree from a woman he still regarded as an old friend's widow. "Four or five days," he muttered.

She heaved a melodramatic sigh.

"Don't give me that. Edgar used to go for the full two weeks."

"It's not just the Grove," she said glumly. "You never take me anywhere."

She had said the same thing the year before when he'd gone to Europe without her for the fortieth anniversary of D-day. As a member of the American Battle Monuments

Commission, he'd been entitled to bring her along for the festivities, but he'd known better than to risk the embarrassment.

Emma, as usual, had held down the fort at home, while he trudged about the beaches of Normandy in a drip-dry blazer, only paces away from the President. Traveling alone had been his only option, given Frannie's drunken mood swings and her long-standing feud—dating back to gubernatorial days—with Nancy Reagan.

"We'll do something soon," he said.

She took a sip of her drink and stared forlornly at the distant hills.

"I'm making a speech," he said brightly, trying to pull her out of it.

"Where?"

"The Grove."

She grunted.

"It's a Lakeside Talk."

"Is that an honor or something?"

Damn right, he thought, annoyed by her deliberate indifference. Edgar, after all, had never been asked to make one.

"What's it about?" she asked.

"The SDI," he replied.

"The what?"

"Frannie . . . the Strategic Defense Initiative."

"Oh. Star Wars."

He winced. "We don't call it that."

"Well, I do. I don't care what that horrid old actor calls it."

He glowered at her, then turned away, catching sight of a diminutive figure as it dashed across the tennis court and up the lawn. It was little Edgar, Frannie's half-breed grandson, intruding once more on his peace and quiet.

"Damn it to hell," he muttered.

"Don't be mean to him," said Frannie.

"I'm not mean to him. When have I been mean to him?"

"Well, you aren't very nice. He's your grandson, for heaven's sake."

"Oh, no," said Booter. "He's *your* grandson, not mine."

"Well, you could at least show a little concern."

"Look. Just because DeDe had no more sense than to get knocked up by a chink grocery boy—"

"Booter!"

"At least that was normal," he added. "It's beats the hell out of this unnatural—"

"Edgar darling," Frannie called. "Come say hello to Gangie and Booter." She gave Booter a venomous look and polished off her drink just as the boy arrived breathless on the terrace. Booter couldn't help wondering what Edgar Halcyon would have made of this slant-eyed namesake.

"Mom sent me," said the boy.

"That's nice," said Frannie. "You want Gangie's cherry?" She held out her glass to the boy.

Little Edgar shook his head. "D'or won't let me."

"Don't be silly, darling. Just the cherry."

"It has red dye," said the boy. "It's poison."

Frannie looked confused, then faintly indignant, setting the glass down. Served her right, thought Booter. What did she expect from a couple of bulldaggers raising a child?

Little Edgar said: "Mom wants to know if you guys still have that two-person tent."

"I am not a guy," said Frannie, bristling.

The boy studied his grandmother for a moment, then turned to Booter. "It's the one Anna and me set up in the orchard last summer."

Booter nodded. "It's in the potting shed. On the shelf."

"Can we use it?"

"*May* we use it," said Frannie.

Booter ignored her. "C'mon, I'll help you get it down."

They walked together to the potting shed. "So," said Booter. "Your mother's going camping?"

"We're all going," said the boy.

"Well, you'll need more than one tent."

"I know," said Edgar. "We've got a pup tent for me and Anna."

Booter pictured this unwholesome arrangement and got a bitter taste in his mouth. "Where are you going?" he asked.

The boy gave him a guarded look, then shrugged. "Just camping."

When they reached the shed, he found the tent, telling Edgar: "I think those plastic rods are all present and accounted for. You'd better get your mother to check."

The boy hefted the bundle and said: "I can check."

"Good," said Booter. He reached behind a row of flowerpots and retrieved the plastic dinosaur he had found there two days earlier. "This is yours, I think."

The boy nodded, taking the toy. "Thanks," he said. "This one's my favorite."

"It is, huh? You know the name?"

"Protoceratops."

Booter steered the boy toward the door. "They were big fellas," he said.

"No," said Edgar. "This one wasn't."

"Well, maybe not that one . . ."

"They were only six feet long and three feet high. Their eggs were only six inches long."

"I see."

"I've got some of the big ones too. Wanna see 'em?"

"Not today, son."

"I could bring 'em over here. You wouldn't hafta come to our house."

"I'm busy, Edgar."

"Why?"

"Well, I'm going on a trip this afternoon. Just like you."

"Oh."

They walked across the lawn in silence. He was afraid Edgar might follow him back to the house, but the boy blazed his own trail when they reached the tennis court, squeezing through a hole in the privet before crossing the orchard to Halcyon Hill.

Call Waiting

CHARLIE DIDN'T BOTHER TO IDENTIFY HIMSELF. "WELL, has he called?"

"How could he," Michael answered, "when you keep calling to find out if he's called?"

"Bullshit. You've got Call Waiting."

"Well . . . he hasn't. O.K.?"

"He will. What are you gonna tell him?"

That was the burning question, all right. What *would* he say? *I like you, Thack. I'm attracted to you, and I think we could have something here. But I think I should tell you before we go any further that I'm antibody positive.*

Yeah, boy. That was the stuff of romance, all right. Who wouldn't be turned on by a line like that?

"I'll play it by ear," he told Charlie.

"What about the river?"

"What about it?"

"Why don't you take him there? You said he's never been."

"I can't afford it, Charlie."

"Ah, but I have a place."

"Since when?"

"Since my Shanti volunteer went to Boca Raton to inseminate a lesbian."

Michael laughed. "Great. Thanks for clearing *that* up."

"Well, it's a big compliment, actually. Who's asked for *your* semen lately?"

"Charlie, what the hell are you talking about?"

"O.K. Arturo—my Shanti buddy—has this great place in Cazadero. Only he can't use it now, since he's gonna be a sperm donor."

"Right."

"He took the test two weeks ago, and it came back negative, so the girls went into a huddle and sent him a plane ticket. Which leaves this great cabin completely empty. And I can't use it, since I'm going ballooning."

"Well, that's really nice, but . . ."

"Just remember it, that's all. When Thack calls."

"*If,* Charlie."

Michael's Call Waiting beeped.

"There," said Charlie. "Right on cue."

"Hang up," said Michael.

"No way. I want a report."

Michael sighed and tapped the button on his receiver. "Hello."

"Hi, it's Brian."

Against all reason, Michael's heart sank a little. "Oh, hi. Mrs. Madrigal said you came by."

"Yeah. I kinda wanted to talk."

"Oh . . . well, sure."

"Is this a good time?"

"Now? On the phone?"

"No. Could I come down?" Brian's solemn tone suggested urgency. Another fight with Mary Ann, no doubt.

"Uh . . . sure. Come on down." The phrase sounded faintly ridiculous, like an instruction to game show contestants, but he'd used it a lot since his friends had moved to The Summit.

"Thanks," said Brian.

Michael hit the button again. "It wasn't him," he told Charlie.

"Damn."

"I've gotta go now."

"Keep me posted," said Charlie.

Brian's smoky green eyes darted about the room, never lighting anywhere for long. His crow's feet seemed more plentiful than ever (McCartney's syndrome, Michael had once dubbed it), though they hardly detracted from his amazing chestnut curls and the twin-mounded rise of his sandpaper chin.

"How 'bout some coffee or something?" Michael asked.

Brian took a seat on the sofa. "No, thanks."

"I have decaffeinated . . . and Red Zinger."

"Michael . . . I'm in big trouble."

Michael pulled up his mission oak footstool and straddled it in front of Brian's chair. "What's the matter?"

Brian hesitated. "Remember Geordie Davies?"

Michael shook his head.

"The woman I met at the Serramonte Mall?"

"Oh, yeah."

"She's got AIDS."

"What?"

"She's got AIDS, man. I saw her yesterday. She's really sick."

Michael was dumbfounded. "How did she get it?"

"I dunno. Her lover's a junkie or something."

"Oh . . ."

"What the fuck am I gonna tell Mary Ann?"

Michael thought for a moment. "How often did you . . . see her?"

Brian shrugged. "Six or seven times. Eight, tops."

"I thought you told me . . ."

"O.K. I saw her more than once. It was no big deal. Neither one of us wanted a big deal." He chewed on a knuckle. "What am I gonna tell her?"

"Geordie?"

"Mary Ann, for Christ's sake!"

"Don't yell," said Michael calmly.

"We did anal stuff. Does that . . . you know . . . ?"

"You and Mary Ann?"

"No!" Brian's eyes blazed indignantly. "Me and Geordie."

"You mean . . . you fucked her?"

"No."

Michael drew back a little. "She fucked you?"

"Really funny, man! Really goddamn funny!"

"Well, I don't get it."

"She had these beads, O.K.?"

"Oh."

Brian paused, looking down at his feet. "They weren't very . . . big or anything."

Michael did his damnedest not to smile. "Brian . . . it's not that easy for a woman to give it to a man."

"It's not?"

"No. We'll get you tested. I know a guy at the clinic in the Castro. I'll make an appointment for you."

"You can't give them my name," said Brian.

"It's just a number. Don't worry."

"What sort of number?"

"Just a number you make up." He reached across and shook Brian's knee. "You've felt O.K., haven't you?"

"Yeah. Mostly. I felt kind of funky a few days ago, but it seemed like the flu."

"Then it probably was."

Brian nodded.

"You're gonna be all right."

"I've never been so damn scared. . . ."

"I know. I've been through this, remember?"

"Yeah, but . . . this is different."

"Why?"

"Michael, there are innocents involved here."

"What?"

"Mary Ann . . . Shawna, for Christ's sake."

"Innocents, huh? Not like me. Not like Jon. Not like the fags."

"I didn't mean that."

"Well, lay off that innocent shit. It's a virus. Everybody is innocent." He tried to collect himself. "I'll call the clinic."

"I'm sorry if I . . ."

"Forget it."

"I didn't know who else to talk to."

"You'll be all right," said Michael.

Brian looked him squarely in the eye. "I loved Jon too, you know."

"I know," said Michael.

These Friendly Trees

L IKE BOOTER, MOST BOHEMIANS ARRIVED AT THE GROVE by car from the city. The press in its endless fascination with money and power grossly exaggerated the number of Lear and Lockheed jets that landed at the Santa Rosa airport during the July encampment. Many of the members—well, some of them, anyway—were uncomplicated fellows with ordinary, workaday jobs in the city.

They came to the Grove for release from their lives, not to plan mergers, plot takeovers or wage war. So what if the A-bomb had been brainstormed there back in 1942? That, Booter knew for a fact, had been in mid-September, almost two months after the encampment had shut down.

The real function of the Grove was escape, pure and simple. It provided a secret haven where captains of industry and pillars of government could let down their guard and indulge in the luxury of first-name-only camaraderie.

Escape was certainly what Booter had in mind as he sped north on the freeway, away from Frannie and the city and the cruel vagaries of a career in aluminum honeycomb.

* * *

After an hour's drive, he left the freeway and headed west on the road to Guerneville, where sunlit vineyards and gnarly orchards alternated abruptly with tunnels of green gloom. When the river appeared, glinting cool and golden through the trees, so too did the ragtag resort cabins, the rusting trailers, the neon cocktail glasses beckoning luridly from the roadside.

He drove straight through Guerneville, doing his best to ignore the pimply teenagers and blatant homosexuals who prowled the tawdry main street. He had liked this town better in the fifties, before its resurgence, when it was still essentially a ruin from the thirties.

In Monte Rio he turned left, crossing the river on the old steel bridge. Another left took him along a winding road past junked cars and blackberry thickets and poison oak pushing to the very edge of the asphalt.

At the end of this road lay the big wooden gates to the Grove and the vine-entangled sign that invariably caused his heart to beat faster:

PRIVATE PROPERTY. MEMBERS AND GUESTS ONLY.
TRESPASSERS WILL BE PROSECUTED.

He drove through the gates and past the gray-frame commissary buildings, coming to a stop in front of the luggage dock and check-in station. Climbing out of the car, he adjusted his tie, brushed the wrinkles out of his suit, and inhaled the resinous incense of the great woodland cathedral that awaited him.

The familiar cast of characters was already assembled: the jubilant new arrivals, the blue-jeaned college boys who did the valet parking, the leathery rent-a-cops with their cowboy hats and huge bellies and belt buckles the size of license plates.

Sweating a little, he opened the trunk and hauled his two suitcases to the luggage dock marked "River Road." He was filled with inexplicable glee as he grabbed a stubby golf pencil and inscribed two old-fashioned steamer trunk labels with the words *Manigault* and *Hillbillies.* Why did this feel so much like coming home?

After relinquishing his BMW to a valet parker, he spotted Farley Stuart and Jimmy Chappell and sauntered up behind them. "Damn," he said, "we're in trouble now!"

Both men hooted jovially, clapping him on the back. Jimmy looked a little withered after his bypass operation, but his spirit seemed as spunky as ever. Farley, heading for the shuttle bus, turned and aimed a finger at Booter. "Come for fizzes tomorrow morning. Up at Aviary."

Aviary was the chorus camp. Farley was a valued baritone, an "associate" member whose talent alone had qualified him for a bunk in Bohemia. He wasn't an aristocrat by any stretch of the imagination, but he was a nice fellow just the same.

Booter pointed back at him and said: "You got a deal."

He knew already that he wouldn't go (he expected an invitation to fizzes up at Mandalay), but his burgeoning spirit of brotherhood made saying no a virtual impossibility.

He was amused, as always, when the guard at the check-in station punched him in, using a conventional industrial time clock. This, he'd been told, had largely to do with billing for food, as members were charged for any meals that occurred during their time at the Grove, regardless of whether or not they chose to eat.

The guard was one he liked, which comforted him, since this was the fellow who would know the most about his comings and goings.

When he was done, he found Jimmy and Farley holding the shuttle bus for him. He decided to walk, flagging them on—a joint decision, really, between a vain old man proud of his endurance and a wide-eyed boy ready to explore.

Somewhere up ahead, someone was playing a banjo.

The ceremonial gates, the ones meant to welcome rather than repulse, were a boy's own daydream, a rustic Tom Swiftian portal built of oversized Lincoln Logs. As Booter passed through them, a blue jay swept low over his shoulder, cackling furiously, and his welcome seemed complete.

He strode briskly, following the road into a forest so thoroughly primeval that some of it had been here when Genghis Khan began his march across Asia. Something indescribable always happened at this point, some soothing realignment of boundaries which contracted his world and made it manageable for the first time all year.

Sky and trees and river notwithstanding, the Grove was not the great outdoors at all; it was a room away from things, a cavernous temple of brotherhood, locked to the rest of humanity. There was order here, and a palpable absence of anarchy. No wonder it made him so happy.

He whistled as he passed the post office, the grocery store, the barbershop, the museum, the telegraph office, the phone bank, the hospital, the fire station. Other members, already anonymous in comfortable old clothes, moved past him in jocular clumps, brandishing whiskey in plastic glasses, calling his name from time to time.

At the height of the encampment, over two thousand men would be assembled at the Grove in one hundred twenty-six different camps. As Booter understood it, this made for a population density greater than that of Chinatown in San Francisco.

As he approached the Campfire Circle, he stopped to read the posters tacked to the trees—each a work of art, really— heralding gala nights and concerts, costume dramas and Lakeside Talks. His own address was somewhat drably listed as: *Roger Manigault: Aluminum Honeycomb and the Future of the Strategic Nuclear Defense Initiative.*

Another shuttle bus—this one labeled "The Old Guard"— bumped past him as he skirted the lake. Henry McKittrick was seated in the back, red-faced and solemn in his sweaty seersuckers. Booter gave him a thumbs-up sign, but Henry merely nodded, obviously still sore about the contract with Consolidated.

He headed down the River Road toward Hillbillies, immersing himself in the sights and sounds of the frontier community coming to life beneath the giant trees. The very name of the camps triggered half a lifetime of memories: Dog House, Toyland, Pig 'n' Whistle, Sons of Toil . . .

Someone was playing a piano—"These Foolish Things"— on the ridge to the left. To the right was a Dixieland band and a chorus practicing a classical number he didn't recognize. Their voices trailed heavenward, hovering like woodsmoke in the slanting afternoon light.

As night fell, he assembled with the others at the Owl Shrine for the Cremation of Care. The already drunken crowd fell silent as the lakeside organist began to play the dirge and the High Priest summoned his acolytes. Then the barge materialized, poled silently across the lake, bearing the palled figure of Care.

When the barge reached the shrine, two acolytes removed the pall, revealing the macabre effigy with its papier-mâché mask. The effigy was dutifully placed upon the pyre, but its incineration was halted, as always, by sinister, electronically enhanced laughter from the hillside.

All eyes turned toward the ridge as a puff of smoke and a flash of light revealed the presence of the ghostly white Tree of Care. From deep inside the tree thundered the voice of Care itself:

"Fools, fools, fools, when will ye learn that me ye cannot slay? Year after year ye burn me in this Grove, lifting your silly shouts of triumph to the pitying stars. But when ye turn your feet again to the marketplace, am I not waiting for you as of old? Fools, fools, to dream you conquer Care!"

The High Priest answered:

"Year after year, within this happy Grove, our fellowship has damned thee for a space, and thy malevolence that would pursue us has lost its power beneath these friendly trees. So shall we burn thee once again this night, and in the flames that eat thine effigy we'll read the sign that, once again, midsummer sets us free."

Then, after lighting their torches at the gas-jet altar fire, the acolytes descended upon the pyre and set Care aflame, piercing the night with shouts of ecstasy. The band broke into "Hot Time in the Old Town Tonight."

Booter smiled, feeling the old magic, then withdrew into the darkness as fireworks burst in the trees above the lake. When he reached the phone bank, he was relieved to see that no one else was there. He placed a local call.

"Yello," said Wren Douglas.

"It's me," he said. "Just making sure you're comfortable."

"Sittin' pretty," she said.

"Good. I'll be up there tonight."

"No problem," she replied.

Mary Ann's Good News

THE CLINIC WAS AN L-SHAPED CONCRETE-BLOCK BUILD-ing on Seventeenth Street between Noe and San-chez. Behind a row of ragged palms lay two distinct entrances: one for people taking the test, the other for people getting their results. Inside, while Mi-chael waited in the car, Brian was shown a videotape about T-cells and helper cells and the true meaning of HTLV-III. Then they drew his blood, and sent him on his way.

"Damn," he said to Michael, climbing into the VW. "You didn't tell me it took ten days."

"I thought you knew."

"Why would I know that?"

"Well, *I* took it, remember?"

"Oh . . ." Brian gazed absently out the window, weighing his options. He'd counted on coming home with a clean bill of health, a note from his doctor to soften the blow when he told Mary Ann about Geordie. But now . . .

"It's the lab procedure," said Michael. "Apparently it takes that long."

"Ten fucking days."

Michael smiled at him wanly, turning on the engine. "Ten non-fucking days."

"It won't work," said Brian.

"What do you mean?"

"Well, she'll know something's up." He gave Michael an admonitory look. "Don't make a pun out of that."

"You've never gone for ten days without doing it?"

"No."

"Well, I'm impressed."

Brian didn't laugh. Michael's flip tone was beginning to get on his nerves.

"What about rubbers?" asked Michael.

"We never use them," said Brian.

"Well, start. Tell her you think they're a safer form of birth control."

"Michael," he said, faintly annoyed. "I'm sterile, remember?"

"Oh, yeah. Sorry." Michael seemed to ponder this for a while before slipping into a reasonable facsimile of Dr. Ruth's Teutonic twitter. "Well . . . what about something in a nice decorative model . . . with whirligigs on the end?"

Brian laughed in spite of himself. "You bastard."

"Tell her," said Michael.

"No. Not yet."

"Sooner or later you're gonna have to. Sooner is always better than later."

"No it isn't. Why should she suffer for the next ten days?"

"Because you're suffering. And she's your wife."

Michael's logic annoyed him. "And I've been a great husband, haven't I?"

"Look, Brian . . . if you don't tell her now . . ."

"Forget it, all right? I have to do this my way."

"Fine," said Michael.

Twenty minutes later, Michael dropped him off in front of The Summit. The doorman fired off a friendly "Yo," but

88

Brian scarcely heard him as he made his wooden way to the elevator.

Could he fake it for ten days? Carry on his life as if nothing were wrong?

Making his ascent, he stood stock still and tried to read his body's signals. There was a heaviness in his limbs which may or may not have been there earlier. Some of the soreness seemed localized, a dim ember of pain lodged in a corner of his gut.

This could be anything, of course. Indigestion or a flare-up of his old gastritis. Hell, maybe it *was* the flu, after all. His headache seemed to have gone away.

The elevator opened at the twenty-third floor. He stepped out into the foyer to confront the insufferable Cap Sorenson, his face plastered with a shit-eating grin. "How's it hanging, Hawkins?"

"Pretty good," he said, adopting a similar hail-fellow tone. "Pretty good."

They changed places, Cap holding the door to get in the final word. "I closed that deal I told you about."

"Great."

"Forget great," said Cap. "We're talking megabucks this time."

Brian nodded. The elevator had its own way at last, obliterating Cap's idiot smirk.

He let himself into the apartment, moving to the window like someone walking underwater. The sun had swooped in low from the west, turning white buildings to gold: shimmering ingots against the blue. Far beneath him, the tangled foliage of Barbary Lane cast dusty purple shadows across the bricks of Mrs. Madrigal's courtyard.

Mary Ann emerged from the bathroom. "I wondered where you were."

What was she doing here? Hadn't she planned on working late tonight? "Oh," he said. "Michael and I drove out to the beach. Where's Nguyet? She was here when I . . ."

"I let her go home. I thought she could use an afternoon off."

"Oh."

89

She added: "I took off early myself. Just said to hell with it. Feels good." She rocked on her heels several times, a curious light in her eyes. "Guess what."

"What?"

"You're never gonna believe this."

He looked around, unsettled, distracted. "Where's Puppy?"

She frowned at him. "Will you let me tell this? She's riding her Tuff Trike at the Sorensons'."

He tried to look apologetic. "What's up?"

"Well . . . here's a hint." She paused, then sang: "Dah-dah-dah-dah-dah-*dah* . . . dah-dah-dah-dah-dah-*dah.*"

It made no sense to him whatsoever.

"C'mon," she prodded. "I know you know it. It's theme music."

He shrugged.

"Oh, Brian." She sang again: *"En-ter-tain-ment To-niiight . . . En-ter-tain-ment To-niiight."*

"Right," he said. "What about it?"

She beamed at him. "I'm gonna be on it, Brian."

"On the show?"

"Yes! They're doing a series about . . . you know, the best local talk shows. And they want me! Isn't that fabulous?"

He nodded, doing his best to echo her excitement. "That's really great."

"They wanna tape us here for part of it."

"Me, you mean?"

"Sure, you." She did a sort of Loretta Young twirl around the room. "You and me and Puppy and our drop-dead apartment high atop the city." She burst into triumphant giggles, flinging her arms around him.

He patted her shoulder and said again: "That's really great."

"I've been mentally decorating all day." She broke away from him and began to pace. "I think we need *lots* more flowers. Orchids, maybe . . . in those planters made out of twigs and moss."

He scarcely heard her.

She stopped pacing and scolded him with a little smile.

"Somebody looks out of it. What's the matter?"

"Nothing," he said.

"Are you still having those headaches?"

"No. I'm fine now."

"Good." She surveyed the room, obviously checking camera angles. "I want everyone back in Cleveland to be eating their crummy little hearts out. Oh . . . Jed stopped by this afternoon."

He grunted. He'd completely forgotten about the kid.

"Hey," she said gently. "I thought you were gonna give him a second chance."

"He's not worth it," he said.

"Well, he's leaving tomorrow afternoon. If you're gonna talk to him at all . . ."

"Look," he snapped. "I'll go see him—all right?"

She recoiled a little, shaking her hand as if she'd scorched it on a stove. "Somebody needs supper and a back rub," she said. "I'll fix us a drink."

The back rub meant what he thought it would mean. When he felt the pressure of her knees, the cool rivulet of cedar-wood lotion against his back, he knew she intended this as a prelude to sex.

"Guess what my show is about tomorrow?" She smoothed the lotion across his shoulder blades, then swept downward toward his ass.

"What?"

"Foreskin reconstruction. Is that gross or what?"

He laughed into the pillow.

"I have a book I'm supposed to read, but to hell with it."

He grunted.

"I'd rather play, wouldn't you?" She leaned down and kissed the left cheek of his ass.

He smiled at her and petted her head and looked at her as lovingly as he knew how. "I'm not up to it, babe. I'm sorry."

"That's O.K.," she said brightly, nuzzling his neck. "I like it up here too."

"Mmm. So do I."

"You're the best company, Brian."

"Thanks."

"We have the best time." She tightened her grip on him and sighed. "I can't believe it, really. All this and *Entertainment Tonight.*"

They lay there for a while, drifting off together. Then Mary Ann retreated to the armchair with her circumcision book, peering around it from time to time to catch his eye sympathetically.

He slept fitfully, waking all the way when she turned off the light and climbed into bed next to him.

"What time is it?" he asked.

"Almost midnight," she replied. "Go to sleep, baby."

It felt later for some reason. It should have been morning. He turned over several times, trying to find a position in which his muscles wouldn't ache.

"Are you all right?" she asked, snuggling against his back.

"Just . . . kinda warm."

"You're burning up."

"If you could just . . . move over a little."

She did so. "I'm gonna take your temperature."

"No. Forget it. I'm O.K."

"But if—"

"I want to sleep, Mary Ann!"

A wounded silence followed. Finally, she patted his butt and rolled over. "Feel better," she said.

He slept straight through until her alarm went off. She silenced it by saying "O.K.," then sat bolt upright in bed. "Brian, these sheets are soaking wet!"

He felt the covers. She was right.

She pressed his forehead, reading his temperature. "I think your fever's gone."

He felt much better, he realized. Maybe the worst was over.

She climbed over him and got out of bed. "You lucked out," she said. "It was one of those twenty-four-hour things."

"I guess so," he said.

She reached the bathroom and stopped, adding: "Change the sheets and get back into bed. You don't wanna push it."

"You're right, though. I feel fine."

"Never mind. Go to sleep. Nguyet can feed Puppy. I'll leave a note for her."

He drifted off in the damp sheets, sleeping for another three or four hours. When he woke, he heard Nguyet singing to Shawna in Vietnamese. Mary Ann's foreskin forum was blaring away full tilt on the set in the kitchen.

He eased the Princess out of its cradle and punched Michael's number. He answered with a breezy hello on the first ring.

"Let's go somewhere," he said, without identifying himself.

"Where?" asked Michael.

"Anywhere. I gotta get outa here, man."

"Are you watching her show?"

"The maid is watching it," said Brian.

"It's too fabulous. A new low. I love it."

"Michael . . ."

"You didn't tell her, did you?"

"No."

"You're going to, aren't you?"

"Yes. Soon. I gotta sort it all out first. Look, if we could just haul ass for a few days . . . go to Big Sur, the Mother Lode, whatever . . ."

"Just you and me?"

"Yeah."

"Brian . . ."

"I won't spend the whole time talking about it. I swear. I just need some company . . . some laughs."

"Ten days, Brian."

"Four, O.K.? Five. How's that?"

"Are you feeling O.K.?"

"Sure. Fine. Never better."

Michael paused, then asked: "How do you feel about the Russian River?"

"Great. What's up? You know a place?"

"I think so," said Michael. "A cabin in Cazadero. A friend said I could use it."

"Yeah? And you wouldn't mind . . . you know . . . ?"

"Putting up with a dork like you?"

Brian laughed. "We've talked about doing this."

"You're right."

"So let's do it."

"O.K.," said Michael. "You got a deal."

The Road to Wimminwood

THEY WERE HEADING NORTH AT LAST, D'OROTHEA AT the helm of the station wagon, DeDe in the navigator's seat. The children were in back, burrowed in a warren built of camping gear, arguing bitterly over ownership of the Nerds.

"Mom bought them for me," Edgar declared.

"She bought them for both of us," said Anna. "Didn't you, Mom?"

DeDe had heard enough of this. "Lay off me, you guys. I'm about to crack some heads back there."

"Ooooh," mugged Anna. "I'm really scared."

"I mean it, Anna."

"Well, Edgar ate all the Nerds, and you bought them for me."

"I bought them for both of you."

"Well, he ate all of them."

"You bought them Nerds?" asked D'or.

"I told her she could have some," said Edgar.

"You did not!" said Anna.

"What's a Nerd?" asked D'or.

DeDe knew what was coming next. "Never mind," she said.

"Let's see the box."

"D'or . . . don't read to me, please. I know they're disgusting."

" 'Sucrose, dextrose, malic acid and/or citric acid . . .' "

"All *right,* D'or."

" 'Artificial and natural flavors, yellow dye number five, and carnauba wax.' Yum-yum . . . carnauba wax . . . one of my personal faves."

DeDe let it go. There was no point in arguing with D'or when she was soapboxing about nutrition. DeDe addressed the children instead: "Can't you guys just cool it? We're almost there."

"How much further?" asked Anna, always the stickler for details.

"Not much."

"How much?"

"I don't know, Anna. Less than an hour."

"If we hate it, can we come home?"

"You won't hate it," D'or put in. "They've got a special duck pond just for kids."

"Big deal," said Anna.

"What's blue and creamy?" asked Edgar.

"Shut up," said Anna.

"And," D'or added, still on her sales pitch, "we get to sleep out under the stars, and eat our meals in the open air, and meet lots of—"

"What's blue and creamy?" repeated Edgar.

"Edgurr," whined Anna. "Shut your big trap."

"It's a riddle," said Edgar, leaning over the seat to confront D'or. "Give up?"

"Sit down," ordered DeDe. "You're gonna make D'or drive off the road."

"O.K.," said D'or, "what's blue and creamy?"

"Smurf sperm!" said Edgar, laughing triumphantly.

DeDe stared at him in horror. "Where did you hear that?"

The boy hesitated, then said: "Anna told me."

"I did not," said Anna.

"Yes you did."

"Liar!"

"All right, both of you! Let's keep it down back there!" This was D'or, raising her voice above the din. There was just enough menace in her tone to command the silence of the twins. DeDe both admired and resented D'or's flair for authority. Why couldn't mothers invoke such terror?

As they drove through Monte Rio, D'or turned to DeDe and said: "I guess ol' Booter's around here somewhere."

DeDe nodded. "Across that bridge and to the left."

"To the left, huh. Must be tough for the old fascist."

DeDe shot her a nasty look meaning *Not in front of the children.*

D'or persisted. "That's fair enough, I think. He laid a wreath on a Nazi grave."

"It was a reconciliation ceremony. You know that."

"Sure."

"And it was part of his official duties."

"Mmm."

"It was also a peacemaking gesture," said DeDe tartly. "Aren't you supposed to be in favor of that?"

D'or shrugged. "I don't notice him making peace with the Russians."

DeDe frowned at her lover, then turned and gazed out the window. She was hardly Booter's biggest defender, but she hated it when D'or used him to pick a fight. What was going on, anyway? Why was D'or looking for trouble?

"Mom?" said Edgar.

"Yes, darling?"

"How much longer?"

"Oh, two or three miles at the most. Do me a favor, will you?"

"What?"

"Don't tell that joke when we get there."

*   *   *

After Monte Rio, the landscape opened up to the blazing blue sky. The river wound lazily toward the Pacific, flanked by summer-humming thickets and shiny white thumbnails of sand. They crossed the bridge at Duncans Mills (groaning at the self-conscious Old Westernness of the storefronts), then turned left on the river road.

" 'Moscow Road,' " said D'or, reading the sign. "Now, here's a road worth turning left on."

DeDe smiled, feeling mellower now. She reached over and squeezed D'or's leg. "What an adventure," she said.

They followed the road into a small stand of willows, which obscured their view of the river. Next came an imposing hedge of evergreens and an equally imposing redwood fence. "The security looks good," said D'or.

It reminded DeDe vaguely of the approach to the Golden Door, her favorite fat farm of yesteryear, but she decided not to say so. She turned to the kids instead.

"So," she said, hoping her newfound enthusiam was contagious. "You guys are gonna have your very own tent."

The twins said "Yay!" in unison, their Nerd dispute all but forgotten.

"Look," chimed D'or. "Here we are."

A young black woman stood by the roadside, flagging them into the entrance. D'or slowed down, turned left, and spoke to the woman. "Registration?"

"All the way down," said the woman. "Park first and unload your gear. There's a shuttle to the land."

"The land of what?" asked DeDe.

The woman laughed and leaned into the car. "The land of Looney Tunes, if you ask me." She stuck out her hand to D'or. "I'm Teejay," she said. "Welcome to Wimminwood."

"Thanks. I'm D'orothea. These are DeDe, Edgar and Anna."

Teejay smiled and raised a pink palm in the window. "Hi, guys." Turning to D'or, she pointed at DeDe. "Tell her about the land," she said.

D'or gave her a high sign and drove on.

"Well," said DeDe. "Tell me about the land."

D'or smiled. "It's just a term for the encampment. It fosters a sense of community."

Maybe to you, thought DeDe.

D'or parked in a dusty clearing that was already chockablock with cars. Several dozen other arrivals were in the process of disembarking, hooting hellos, hoisting their bedrolls to their shoulders.

"We just leave the car here?" DeDe asked.

"You got it," said D'or. She turned to the kids. "O.K., gang, here's the deal. Everybody grab a handful of stuff. Mom and I will get the tents and the heavy things. You get the bedrolls and whatever's left."

The twins tackled this chore with uncharacteristic vigor. DeDe cast an optimistic glance in D'or's direction, then threw herself into the team effort.

Judging from the other new arrivals, their own paraphernalia was quite Spartan indeed. Some of these women were weighed down like pack animals, toting coolers and lawn chairs, Coleman lanterns, fishing gear and guitars. They converged, along with the Halcyon-Wilson household, on a central loading dock, then stood in line for registration.

"Pick a duty," said D'or, when their turn came.

"What?"

"What work duty do you wanna do?"

"Wait a minute," said DeDe. "Nobody mentioned any work duty."

"It's in the brochure, Deirdre. Don't be such a damn debutante."

DeDe would have put up a fight then and there, but the children were watching, and she didn't want to inaugurate their stay by setting a bad example. "What are the choices?" she asked icily.

D'or read from a list posted at the registration table. "Kitchen, Security, Garbage Patrol, and Health Care."

"Which one are you picking?"

"Garbage Patrol."

DeDe grimaced, but the choice made perfect sense for D'or. The woman loved to clean more than practically anything. "What's Security?" DeDe asked.

D'or shrugged. "Patrolling, mostly. Keeping an eye on things."

That sounded tame enough. Better than Kitchen, certainly, and a lot less icky than Health Care. "Put me down for that," said DeDe.

They were issued orange wristbands—plastic hospital bracelets, actually—which indicated they were festivalgoers rather than performers or technical people. This smacked of concentration camp to DeDe, and she couldn't help saying so.

"I know," said D'or, "but there's a reason for everything. All of this has evolved from past experience."

After registering, they walked back to their gear and waited with the other women for the shuttle. It arrived ten minutes later in the form of a flatbed truck—much to the delight of the children, who invariably applauded any form of transportation that promised to place their lives in jeopardy.

As they bounced along a rutted dirt road into the wilderness, DeDe shouted instructions above the engine noise. "Hold on to something heavy, Edgar. Anna, stop that. . . . Sit down this minute."

D'or threw back her head and laughed, a strange primal glint in her eyes.

Ten minutes later, the truck lurched to a stop in a clearing near the river. DeDe hopped down first, grateful for release, then gave the children a hand. Readjusting the belt around their double sleeping bag, D'or said: "Now we're on our own. Where you wanna camp?"

DeDe shrugged. "Someplace pretty."

D'or scanned the map she had picked up at registration before pointing downriver to a clump of trees. "The party-hearty girls are over there. The S and M group is half a mile behind us."

"Swell," said DeDe dryly. "What else?"

"Mom," chirped Anna. "Let's go down there. It's pretty next to the river."

DeDe draped her arm across her daughter's shoulders.

"Sounds good to me. What about you, Edgar?"

"I like the river," said her son.

DeDe turned to D'or. "How's it look on your map? Anything we should know about down there?"

Her lover caught the irony in her tone and reprimanded her with a frown. Then she said: "The Womb is up at the next cove, but that's fairly far away."

"The Womb," echoed DeDe, deadpanning. "I'm almost afraid to ask."

D'or lifted the bundled tent and began to stride toward the river. "If you're going to be snide about everything, I'd rather not hear it."

DeDe let it go. Turning back to the twins, she checked for dangling or abandoned gear, then said: "Now stick close, you guys. This is uncharted territory we're heading into."

"Oh, sure," said Anna, rolling her eyes.

DeDe helped Edgar rearrange the weight on his backpack, then hurried to catch up with D'or. "O.K.," she said. "Tell me about the Womb."

"Don't patronize me."

"I'm interested, O.K.?"

D'or hesitated, then said: "It's a place women can go when they need emotional support. This is a big festival . . . people can get hurt."

DeDe visualized a tent full of wailing women, all boring the Birkenstocks off the poor dyke who'd pulled Womb duty. But she now knew better than to say so. "It sounds very supportive," she told D'or.

When the time came to pitch their tents, they chose a stretch of riverfront property separated from the other campers by a stand of madrone trees. No one, not even D'or, had the slightest idea as to which plastic rods went where, but the process of finding out drew the family together in a way that warmed DeDe's heart.

Afterwards, flushed with their achievement, the four of them crammed into the larger tent and sat staring out at the light dancing on the water. They had been there only a matter of minutes when someone approached through the madrone trees.

The head that appeared through the tent flap had been shaved just short of bald. The remaining hair had been etched with a female symbol, with the circle part at the crown and the cross coming down to the forehead.

"Hello there," said the woman, smiling at them.

"Hi," they chorused.

She extended her hand to D'or. "I'm Rose Dvorak."

"I'm D'orothea Wilson. This is my lover, DeDe Halcyon . . . and our kids, Edgar and Anna."

The woman looked at Edgar for a moment longer than necessary, then addressed D'or. "I saw you come in. Just wanted to welcome you."

"Oh," said D'or. "Are you . . . uh . . . with the Wimminwood staff?"

Rose smiled in a way that was meant to convey both mystery and authority. "I'm pretty much all over."

Great, thought DeDe. Thanks for sharing that. "Do you know the way to the dining area?" she asked.

"Sure," said Rose. "If you come out, I can show you."

DeDe left the tent and followed Rose to the other side of the madrone trees. "Look," said Rose, when they were out of earshot. "That boy can't stay here."

"What do you mean?"

"Don't play dumb. This is women-only space."

"But he's not ten yet. He's only eight."

"Ten is the cutoff date for attendance. He still can't camp on women-only space. That's made perfectly clear in the regulations."

"Well, Jesus . . . what are we supposed to do with him? Float him on a raft in the river?"

The woman gave her a long, steely stare. "Have you read the regulations? Maybe that would help."

"Well, I've—"

"There's a separate compound for boys under ten. It's over next to the—"

"A compound?" said DeDe. "Give me a break. A *compound?*"

"It's called Brother Sun," said Rose.

"So . . . my daughter can stay with me, but my son has to be . . . deported?"

"I never used that word," said Rose.

DeDe was livid. This was Sophie's Choice without the choice. "Well, this is truly sick. This is really the dumbest thing I've ever . . ."

"They should have told you at the gate," said Rose. "I don't know why they didn't."

"Yeah. Must have been an oversight on the part of a *human being.*"

Rose's eyes narrowed noticeably. "I have an obligation to report the boy. My job is to ensure that this remains women-only space. If you're not willing to comply with the rules, you're free to leave at any time."

DeDe faltered, then turned, hearing D'or approach. "What's the matter?" D'or asked Rose.

"It's Edgar," said DeDe. "His wee-wee is a major threat."

D'or met the remark with a scowl and spoke to Rose. "He's not ten, you know."

"Ten has nothing to do with it," said DeDe.

This time D'or gave her a look which said: *Shut up and let me talk to the woman.*

"We have a separate camp for the boys," Rose explained, sounding far more placatory than she had with DeDe. "It's a courtesy we provide for women who can't leave their kids at home. If you'd like to see the facility . . ."

"But we came here as a family," said D'or. "Surely you can bend the rules enough to . . ."

Rose shook her head, a maddening smirk on her face. "You know where that would lead." She turned and swaggered away, yelling her final edict over her shoulder. "The person to see is Laurie at Brother Sun. I'll check with her later to see if he's situated."

"Let's go home," said DeDe.

"Now wait a minute."

"I won't stand for this, D'or. That woman will not tell me what to . . ."

"I know, I know." D'or slipped her arm around DeDe's waist. "She's a bitch. I'll grant you that."

DeDe felt a sudden urge to cry. At this rate, she'd be down at the Womb before she knew it. "D'or . . . why didn't you tell me about this compound business?"

"I didn't know, hon. Honest."

"Well, I think we should just leave. I couldn't possibly tell Edgar . . ."

"Hang on, now. We don't know what it's like. It could be very nice."

"Forget it."

"He'd be with other boys his own age. Haven't we talked about that? It would be like summer camp . . . only we'd be just a few hundred yards away. And we could visit him all the time."

"But he couldn't visit us. He'd feel excluded."

"How do you know, hon? He doesn't wanna go to the concerts. He told us so himself."

This was true enough, DeDe decided. Or were they just rationalizing their way out of a difficult situation? What if Edgar didn't understand? What if this marred him for life?

"Tell you what," said D'or. "Let's you and me go see this Laurie person at the boys' camp. If the place is the pits, we'll scrap the whole thing . . . pack our gear and find a good public campground somewhere in the area."

DeDe nodded tentatively. D'or was at her very best when building bridges over troubled waters.

Brother Sun turned out to be far nicer than DeDe had imagined. There were at least a dozen boys, and most of them were Edgar's age. Wasn't this what she had always wanted for her son? Edgar, after all, was the sole male in a household of women. For the time being, at least, an all-boy environment would probably do him a world of good.

Laurie, the boys' overseer, was fiftyish and warmhearted,

with an apparent devotion to her mission at Wimminwood. She referred to her charges as "the little hellions," but it was obvious that the boys liked her. The camp itself was a semicircle of redwood lean-tos, only yards away from a boys-only swimming hole.

In the end the decision was left up to Edgar. He took to the idea almost instantly, banishing any vestige of guilt DeDe might have felt. Only Anna put up a mild protest, faintly envious of this "special place for boys," but D'or assured her that there was plenty here for girls to do too.

Leaving Edgar at the compound, they set out across the land to get their bearings. They found women laughing around campfires and perched in trees along the river, women playing bridge and chopping wood and drinking beer with other women.

When they reached the central stage, a square dance was in progress. A hundred sun-flushed women, clad only in boots and bandannas, were do-si-doing to the music of a string band. Amused yet riveted by the sight, DeDe turned and caught her lover's eye.

"Well?" said D'or. "It's something, huh?"

DeDe nodded. It was something, all right.

Historical Interest

AT 28 BARBARY LANE, MICHAEL WAS PACKING HIS suitcase when the phone rang.

"Michael?" said the voice on the other end.

"Yeah."

"It's Thack Sweeney. The guy you met in solitary."

"Oh, hi." Didn't it figure? Didn't it just figure he would call now?

"I told you I'd call."

"Yeah, you did."

"Listen, what's your schedule like tomorrow?"

Shitfuckpiss, thought Michael. "Well, actually, I'm going to the river with a friend."

"Oh, yeah? Sounds like fun." If he was devastated, he didn't show it.

"What did you have in mind?" asked Michael.

"Oh . . . nothing much. Just hanging out."

Hanging out had never sounded so good. "This trip is kind of set," said Michael. "Otherwise . . ."

"I understand," said Thack.

Michael wavered, then asked: "What are you doing tonight?"

Thack laughed. "Lurking outside your door at the local mom-and-pop."

"Huh?"

"Well, not technically, but pretty close. The grocer says you're a block or two away. I was walking up Union Street and just decided to call. It's the wildest coincidence."

Michael wanted more than coincidence. "You're at the Searchlight?"

"That's the one."

"You . . . uh . . . want to come over?"

"Well . . . you must be packing."

"No. I mean, I'm finished. Come on over, if you want."

"How do I get there?"

"Uh . . . walk over the crest of Union, take a left on Leavenworth. Barbary Lane is on the left, halfway down the hill. There's a stairway you can see from the street."

"Got it," said Thack.

Michael hung up, sat down, smiled uncontrollably, stood up again and did a little jig around the room. Then he finished washing the dishes, gave the bathroom a quick onceover, and plucked the dead blossoms off his potted azalea.

When Thack arrived, ten minutes later, his cheeks had been pinched pink by the fog. "Boy," he said, coming into the apartment. "You didn't warn me about those steps."

"Oh, no," said Michael. "Did one break?"

Thack nodded. "I bailed out just in time."

"Where was it?"

"Up near the top . . . just before you reach the part with the killer stones. Get many lawsuits?"

Michael smiled at him. "The lane dwellers are used to it."

Thack looked around him, like a dog sniffing out his bedding, then went directly to the window and peered out to the bay. "The lane dwellers, huh? Sounds almost anthropological."

"Well, it is . . . kinda."

"Like an Amazonian tribe or something. Well, there it is, all right."

"What?"

"The Alcatraz lighthouse. You said you could see it from here."

"Oh . . . yeah. That's it. Look, if you don't mind making yourself at home, I should go fix that step."

"Now?"

"It's kind of . . . an agreement we all have. There are planks in the basement already cut to fit. It shouldn't take that long."

"This I gotta see," said Thack.

"If you'd rather wait here . . ."

"No. Go on, lead the way."

So Michael went to the basement, with Thack on his heels. He took a plank from a stack of ten (marked *SOS—Save Our Steps* by Mrs. Madrigal) and found a hammer and the appropriate nails.

"The steps are in jeopardy," he explained, as they crossed the courtyard into the pungent darkness of the lane.

"As are the steppers," said Thack.

"If the city gets another complaint, they'll tear them down, no questions asked. They've already got plans to replace them with reinforced concrete."

"Can't have that," said Thack, a little too deadpan about it.

Michael looked at him, then continued: "We're buying time right now, trying to get public support." He gave up the pitch, wary of Thack's irreverence.

When they reached the steps, the broken one was immediately apparent, white as a dinosaur bone under the Barbary Lane streetlight. Michael pulled the fragments free and removed the rusty nails with his hammer.

Thack squatted next to him. "The support beam is almost as rotten."

"I know."

"Hardly seems worth it."

Michael looked up at him. "I thought you said you were a preservationist."

Thack shrugged. "Antebellum stuff. These steps don't have any historical interest."

Michael lifted the plank into place. "Maybe not to you."

Thack watched him hammer for a while, then said: "Gimme that."

"What?"

"Do it right, if you're gonna do it. Gimme the hammer."

Michael blinked indignantly.

"You hammer funny," said Thack.

Michael considered several retorts, then handed him the hammer. "I'm a nurseryman, all right?"

Thack made the nail disappear in three deft strokes. In spite of his mild humiliation, Michael actually enjoyed the moment, his eyes fixed on the set of Thack's jaw, the corded white flesh of his neck. When he had finished, Thack sat on the mended step and patted the spot next to him. "Try it out," he said.

Michael took a seat. "I guess this seems kinda dumb to you."

"What?"

"Caring so much about these steps."

"I dunno," said Thack.

"I've been here almost ten years, so this place is kind of in my blood."

"Yeah. I'm that way about Charleston. I'd have a hard time leaving it."

"Well," said Michael, "then you understand."

Thack drummed his fingers against the railing.

"How long will you stay?" asked Michael.

"Oh . . . four or five more days."

Michael nodded, mad at himself for capitulating to Brian's panic. It was high time he started catering to his own needs again. "You know," he began, "if you'd like to join us at the river . . ."

"Thanks," said Thack. "I wouldn't horn in on your date."

"Oh," said Michael. "He's just an old friend."

"Oh."

"He's straight," Michael added. "I'm sure he wouldn't mind. I mean, I was the one who asked him. It's no big deal." He felt a little traitorous saying this, but Brian would just have to deal with it.

"Well," said Thack. "It does sound like fun."

"You bet."

"Three buddies in the boondocks."

"Right," said Michael a little uneasily. What sort of compromise was he accepting? "You'll like Brian, I think. He's a great guy."

They stayed there on the steps, bantering jovially under a lemon-drop moon. Half an hour later, having established a late-morning rendezvous, Thack bid Michael a hearty farewell and set off to catch the cable car at Union and Hyde.

Elated but a little confused, Michael called Brian and broke the news to him. He took it well, all things considered.

"No problem, man. It's your cabin."

"Well, it's our trip, though. I didn't wanna . . . you know . . . impose my . . ." He didn't finish, since it would have been an outright lie. He had done what he'd wanted to do. Why pretend to be considerate now?

"It's O.K.," said Brian. "I just wanna get away. You didn't tell him about . . . Geordie and all?"

"No," said Michael. "Nothing."

"Good. That's strictly between us, Michael."

"I know," said Michael.

Settling In

WREN'S NEST, AS SHE HAD COME TO THINK OF IT, was an oversized redwood bungalow with porches on three sides and a huge central fireplace built of smooth stones. It was perched on the ridge above Monte Rio, the last house on the road. From her porches she could look down on a squadron of turkey vultures, circling endlessly above the sleepy river.

There was a washer and a dryer, a black-and-white TV set, an assortment of comfy old chairs and couches. The refrigerator had been extravagantly stocked with wines and exotic deli food. The linen closet would have been ample for a family of six.

After several days in this cleansing environment, her end-of-tour tension had all but disappeared. She had lost track of time again, and the sensation was pure bliss. Life was a random pastiche of reading, eating, sleeping, sunning, wandering, and eating some more.

Sometimes, she would drive down to the Cazadero General Store in the white Plymouth Horizon Booter had rented for her use. She would loiter there with a dripping Dove bar, marveling at the time-warpy blend of tourist kitsch, organic grains and tie-dyed T-shirts. Most of all she adored the bulletin board, with its folksy index cards about belly-dance classes and "fixer-uppers" and solar panels for sale.

Her only other foray into the outside world had been to see *Some Like It Hot* at the movie house in Monte Rio. The Rio Theater was an entertainment in itself, a riverside Quonset hut with a Deco facade, noble in its failure to be grand. After the show, a chubby teenager had recognized the world's most beautiful fat woman and requested an autograph.

Comforted to learn that her fame was still intact, Wren had written "Think Big" on the kid's popcorn box.

Her agent had been pissed, of course. Not to mention her PR man, to whom fell the sorry task of canceling her Portland and Seattle engagements. Neither one of them believed her cock-and-bull story about this impromptu getaway, and her now-delayed return to Chicago had alternately wounded and enraged her lover, Rolando.

She didn't give a damn, really. She was more content now than she'd been in ages, and she was being paid handsomely for it. Her bed time with Booter had totaled less than two hours so far, and his requirements had been reasonable and few.

Besides, she liked the old buzzard.

"Where is it?" she asked him when he arrived for his third visit. It was late afternoon and they were standing on the porch.

"Where's what?"

"You know. This mystical scout camp of yours. Point it out to me."

He gestured vaguely off to the left. "You can't really see it from here. It's a sort of bowl. You can only see it from Bohemian property. That's the beauty of it."

She gave him a teasing look. "When you're plotting world domination."

He smiled thinly and shook his head.

"Don't you swim in the river?" she asked.

"Sure. That part down there with the platform. We call it the swimming pool."

She followed his finger to a gray pier, a row of tented changing rooms. "Those teeny little people . . . they're Bohemians?"

He nodded.

"They don't look very Bohemian from here."

He chuckled. "And even less so close up."

She laughed. "And there are no girls allowed?"

"Not during the encampment."

"I bet I could get in." This made him flinch a little, so she added: "Not that I would, of course."

"The gate guards are pretty smart," he said.

"I'd swim the river," she said. "I'd wait until it got dark and I'd swim the river naked, with my clothes in a plastic bag. Then I'd—"

"I hope you're not serious."

She shook her head, smiling. "I like making you nervous, Boo-Roger."

His relief was evident. "I don't know you that well," he said. "I don't know when you're joking."

"I was right, though, wasn't I?"

"About what?"

"Getting in. That beach is your weak flank."

He shrugged. "You'd still be a woman. You couldn't do much about that. You'd be spotted the first time you showed your face."

She smiled as cryptically as possible.

"How about a drink?" said Booter.

"You're on," said Wren.

She left him there in the dwindling light and went to the kitchen, returning minutes later with a couple of Scotch and waters.

"Thank you," said Booter.

She clinked her glass against his. "I'm a helluva gal."

He smiled faintly, then turned his gaze back to the river. "So it's . . . back to Chicago after this?"

"Yep."

"You like it there?"

"I adore it," she said.

"What about San Francisco?"

"What about it?"

"Did you like it?"

She shrugged. "It was O.K."

"Just O.K.?"

She laughed. "Good God!"

"What?"

"You're all alike here."

"How so?" he asked.

"You demand adoration for the place. You're not happy until *everybody* swears undying love for every nook and cranny of every precious damn—"

"Whoa, missy."

"Well, it's true. Can't you just worship it on your own? Do I have to sign an affidavit?"

He chuckled. "We're that bad, are we?"

"You bet your ass you are."

He swirled the ice in his glass, then took a gulp and set the glass down on the porch railing. "You have a . . . uh . . . beau back in Chicago?"

"Sure," she replied.

"Nice fellow?"

She smiled at him. "Don't know any other kind."

He nodded. "Good." The light in his eyes seemed almost paternal.

"He's Cuban," she added, just to catch his response. It showed in the set of his mouth, a brief involuntary twitch of the mustache. "Thought so," she said, smiling slightly.

"What?"

"You're a bigot."

His jaw became rigid.

"It's O.K.," she said, wiggling his fleshy old earlobe. "It's your generation, that's all. Tell me what your wife is like."

He was thrown off balance for a moment.

"Do you *like* her?" she asked.

"She's a fine lady," he said finally. "She drinks a little too much, but she's . . . very nice."

"I'm glad."

"That she drinks?"

She made a goofy face at him. "That you like her. That she likes you."

"Oh, we're friends," he said. "Most of the time."

"Amazing. After . . . how many years of marriage?"

He smiled. "Almost two."

She laughed. "C'mon."

"We were next-door neighbors for thirty years," he explained. "We were married to other people, but . . . they died. So it made sense."

"Were you in love when you were still married to the other people?"

"We aren't in love now," he said.

She nodded. "But she's still your significant other."

He gave her a blank look.

"Your spouse and/or lover and/or best buddy."

"Somewhere in there," he said.

They laughed in unison, creating a momentary intimacy which seemed to unsettle him as much as it did her. "Actually," he said, shaking his drink, "I was closer to her husband."

"Oh?" She arched an eyebrow at him.

"Nothing like that," he said.

She aped his expression, looking stern and jowly. "No, of course not."

"He was in my camp," said Booter, "down at the Grove."

Wren gazed down at the distant swimming platform, conjuring up the happy couple, genial and spider-browed, stretched out platonically on the gray wood.

"He was a good man," Booter added.

Wren nodded.

"He died about ten years ago. He brought a mistress here himself. He told me so."

"I'm not your mistress," said Wren.

"No," said Booter. "I meant . . ."

"That her first husband fucked around too."

"Yes," he said meekly.

"Does she know?"

He shook his head.

"Did your first wife know?"

"No." He looked decidedly uncomfortable. "This hasn't been a regular thing."

"Uh-huh."

"It's just that . . . when I saw you—"

"I know," she said, cutting him off, "and I'm the kinda gal who takes that as a compliment."

He gave her a hapless look.

"Lighten up," she said. "We understand each other."

Up a Creek

HONEY-BLOND MEADOWS FLEW PAST THEM IN A BLUR as the VW left the freeway and headed west toward the river. Michael and Brian were in the front seat; Thack was in the back. This unromantic arrangement had been Thack's doing, since he had climbed in first, but Michael had chosen not to take it personally.

"Well," said Brian, out of the blue. "Mary Ann wasn't exactly thrilled."

"About what?" asked Michael, playing it safe. As agreed, he'd said nothing to Thack about Geordie.

"This trip," said Brian. "I didn't give her much notice."

"Oh."

"I'm gonna miss *Entertainment Tonight.*"

Michael didn't get it. "Can't you tape it?"

"No, I mean . . . I'm gonna miss being on it."

Thack leaned forward. "You were gonna be on *Entertainment Tonight?*"

"You didn't tell me that," said Michael, even more impressed than Thack.

Brian shrugged. "She was gonna be on it. I was just gonna

be there. Part of her goddamn persona."

"Hey," said Michael. "Ease up."

"That's what she said. *Persona* is exactly the word she used."

"Well . . ."

"Your wife is in show business?" asked Thack.

"She's got her own talk show," Michael explained.

"That's great," said Thack, turning to Brian. "What sort?"

"The regular sort," said Brian. His tone was colorless, bordering on hostile.

"She's good," said Michael, trying to keep it light. "She got some major dish out of Bette Midler. . . ."

"What about here?" Thack pointed to the side of the road.

"What?" asked Michael.

"We're off the freeway. Let's put the top down."

"Oh . . . right. Good idea." Michael swung off the road into the dusty parking lot of a fruit stand.

"I could use something cold," said Thack. "How 'bout you guys?"

"Sure," said Michael. "Apple juice or something."

"Yeah." Brian nodded. "Fine."

"I'll get 'em," said Thack. "You get the top." He slid out from behind Michael's seat and strode toward the fruit stand.

Michael turned and looked at Brian. "You O.K.?"

"Yeah."

"This was a rotten idea, huh?"

"No."

"Well, you don't seem to be having a good time."

"Would you be?" Brian wouldn't look at him. "This was gonna be our time, man. I mean, this guy is perfectly nice, don't get me wrong. . . ."

"I'm really sorry," said Michael.

"Don't be. I can handle it."

It didn't look that way to Michael. "I thought this would work out great. He likes you, Brian . . . I mean, he seems to. And you seem to like him."

"C'mon. He likes you a helluva lot more than he likes me." He threw up his hand in a gesture of resignation. "That's cool. I'm a fag hag. I can handle it."

Michael laughed. "Stop it."

Brian offered him a game smile. "I just don't wanna be in the way."

"C'mon."

"Well, you guys are an item."

"Says who?" asked Michael, nursing the faint hope that Thack had told Brian as much when he, Michael, had run back to the house for his sunglasses.

"Well . . . I just assumed."

"We don't *all* go to bed with each other, Brian."

Brian shrugged. "This one looks like he might."

"How can you tell?"

Another shrug. "I can tell with you guys."

"Oh, yeah?" It amused him that Brian considered himself an expert on fags—prided himself on it, in fact. "Wrong again, Kemo Sabe."

"We'll see."

"This is strictly brotherly."

"O.K."

"Maybe even sisterly, for all I know." There hadn't, after all, been so much as a peck on the cheek the night before.

Thack returned with the juice. "Nice job," he said, handing them the bottles.

"Of what?" asked Michael.

"Taking the top down."

Michael grimaced. "Oh, fuck." He set down his juice and reached for the chrome clamps at the top of the windshield. "We started talking and . . ." Standing up, he pushed back the accordion roof until it fell into place of its own weight.

"Sunshine," said Thack, vaulting into the back seat.

"Hey," Brian said to him, "why don't you let me get back there?"

"I'm fine," came the reply.

"You sure? It's kinda cramped, isn't it?"

"No. Really. It's great. I can stretch out and look up at the redwoods."

"It's not much further," said Michael, disassociating himself from Brian's effort to remedy things.

* * *

When they reached Guerneville, Michael announced: "Here
it is, boys—our humble tribute to Fire Island."

Thack, who'd been recumbent in the back seat, sat up with
telling suddenness and scanned the men along the main drag.
Seeing this in the mirror, Michael felt some distant cousin of
jealousy, nasty but manageable, like a paper cut on the finger.

"I came up here once," said Brian, "to the jazz festival."

Michael turned and smiled at him. Sterile or not, this man
was breeder through and through. "Best of Breeder," he had
called him once. Surely there were gay men somewhere who
revered jazz, but Michael didn't know any.

"Do they get good people?" asked Thack.

"Brubeck," said Brian. "I saw Brubeck here."

"No shit," said Thack.

Brian said: "Tell Michael how good he is. Michael hates
him."

"I don't *hate* him," said Michael.

"He hates him," said Brian.

"I like tunes," said Michael. "Call me crazy, but that's the
way I am."

Thack kept his eyes on the sidewalk. "This is a nice town."

"It's too much like Castro Street," said Michael, mouthing
the stock criticism. It wasn't really true, but he resented the
place for consuming so much of Thack's attention. "I'm glad
we're gonna be out a ways."

"Where is Casanova?" asked Thack.

"Cazadero," said Michael. "We follow this road along the
river until we get a few miles past Monte Rio. Then we hang
a right and follow Austin Creek for a few more miles. We're
at the mercy of Charlie's map."

"We'll find it," said Thack.

What they found was a smallish, newly built structure in the
redwoods along Austin Creek. Its siding was plywood, the

front door was aluminum, and the main room was paneled with the sort of pregrooved faux walnut used in rumpus rooms the world over.

Michael's heart sank. The yawning stone fireplace he'd envisioned had been usurped by a hooded atrocity built of shiny orange metal. There was a comfortable sofa (herringbone corduroy, obviously late seventies) and a decent bathroom, but the place was nowhere near the stuff of fantasy.

And nowhere near big enough.

"Where's the bedroom?" asked Brian.

"Let's see," said Michael, his depression mounting.

"You're lookin' at it," said Thack. "That sofa converts, I think, and there are two studio couches."

Brian gave Michael an accusatory glance. "Did you ask Charlie whether . . ."

"Yeah," said Michael, "of course. He said he was sure it had at least three rooms."

"Uh-huh," said Thack. "This room, the kitchen and the bathroom."

"Shit," said Michael.

Brian looked around. "We can put a studio couch in the kitchen."

"Oh, sure," said Michael.

"This'll be fine," said Thack. "There's plenty of room for all of us." He peered out the aluminum-frame window. "There's a great view of the creek."

Michael looked over Brian's shoulder. "Yeah. It's really . . . close." Even closer were a rusting pink trailer and another prefab cabin, slightly more soulless than theirs. "I fucked up, guys. I'm sorry."

"Hey," said Brian.

Thack just shrugged it off. "We've got a fire," he said brightly. "A place to swim. Big trees. Good company. I'm happy."

They unloaded the car in silence. Then Brian stretched out on the sofa while Michael and Thack made an exploratory trek to the edge of the creek. When they returned, their roommate was fast asleep and snoring.

"Hey," whispered Thack. "Let's take some beers to the creek."

"What beers?" asked Michael, increasingly disturbed by Thack's chatty-fratty demeanor.

"Check the fridge," said Thack.

Michael did; there were two six-packs of Oly inside. A minor consolation, but a welcome one.

Back at the creek, Thack said: "Hunkering."

"What?"

"That's what this is called in the South."

"They still call it that, huh?"

"Oh, yeah." Thack kicked off his loafers and rolled up the cuffs of his khakis. "I know lots of gay boys who are hunkering fools."

Michael followed Thack's example, doffing his Adidas, finding a flat place on a sunny rock, sliding his pale feet into water which was surprisingly warm.

Thack handed him a cold Oly. "It isn't officially hunkering until the beer is in the hand."

"Right," said Michael.

From neighboring rocks, they lifted their bottles in unison. "To the woods," said Thack.

"To the woods," said Michael.

The beer and blazing sunshine lulled them like a finger on the belly of a lizard. After a long silence, Thack said: "How did you two meet?"

"Me and Brian?"

"Yeah."

"Well . . . he used to live in my building. Him and his wife both. I've known them since they were Swinging Singles."

Thack smiled. "What's she like?"

Michael thought for a moment. "Perky. Sweet. Ambitious. Too serious about the eighties."

"Oh."

"It doesn't bother me. She was just as serious about the seventies."

"Are you friends with her?"

"Oh, sure," said Michael. "Not as much as I used to be, but . . . well, I see her off and on." He trailed his fingers in the water.

Thack skinned off his T-shirt. His chest was white-skinned and pink-nippled, distractingly defined. Michael caught the briefest whiff of his sweat as the T-shirt went over his head.

"Something's bothering Brian," said Thack.

"Why?"

"Well . . . I think I must rub him the wrong way."

"No, you don't. He likes you. He told me so."

"He did?"

"Yes."

Thack took a sip of his Oly. "I like him too, actually. I wish there were more straight guys like him."

"He's fighting with Mary Ann," said Michael, telling a medium-sized white lie. "He gets a little weird when they fight." That was certainly true enough. "He's a great guy most of the time. Funny, generous . . ."

"Hot," said Thack.

Michael felt the sting of that paper cut again. "Yeah, I guess so."

"You guess so?"

"Well, I've known him such a long time. We're more like brothers or something. I know he's good-looking, but I really don't think of him that way."

He was jealous, he realized suddenly. He was actually jealous of Brian.

Campfire Tales

DRIFTING BACK INTO CONSCIOUSNESS, BRIAN STIRRED on the sofa. The corduroy gave off a faint aroma of mildew, which tingled in his nostrils. He could hear a noisy bird behind the house and Michael's laughter down by the creek.

He wasn't sure whether he'd been there for thirty minutes or three hours. The headache that had nagged him on the road had subsided somewhat, but the spot in his gut was still burning. He was hot all over, in fact, and his mouth tasted foul.

His tongue made its usual rounds, searching for raw spots that hadn't been there earlier. Finding nothing, he propped himself up on his elbows and gazed out toward the creek. Michael and Thack were still sunning on the rocks.

Brian found his shaving kit and dragged himself into the bathroom. He splashed water on his face, then brushed his teeth, then examined his face in the mirror. His grinding fatigue had made itself known in charcoal smudges under his eyes.

He left the house and walked down to the creek. The guys

didn't see him approaching, so he hollered: "How 'bout some grub, men?"

"We gotta go shopping," Michael answered.

"That's what I meant. I'll do it. Tell me what you want." Thack sat up. "Great."

"Take the car," said Michael.

"Nah," said Brian. "I need the exercise. Whatcha want?"

"Hot dogs," Thack replied, "and baked beans and nachos . . . and stuff for a salad."

"And Diet Pepsi," Michael added. "You know where the store is?"

"Yeah," said Brian.

"We'll get a fire going," said Thack. "We thought we should cook out."

"Good," said Brian.

He left them and headed toward the Cazadero road. It was late afternoon now. Dusty shards of sunlight pierced the redwoods along the creek. As he walked, a family of quail scurried to avoid him. A blue-bellied lizard flickered like a gas flame, then dove into a mossy woodpile, extinguishing itself.

With a mission in mind, he felt better already, picking up his pace as he passed the little green-and-white frame church that marked the edge of the village. By the time he'd reached the Cazadero General Store, he was calmer than he'd been in days.

After assembling the food they needed (plus a Sara Lee lemon cake for dessert), he waited in a short line at the cash register. The woman in front of him—huge breasts, huge hips, startling green eyes—turned and smiled warmly.

"Dinner?"

He looked down at the contents of his red plastic shopping basket. "Yeah. We're gonna cook out."

Her emerald eyes widened. "We?"

"My buddies and me."

"Ah." Without actually smiling, her full mouth registered amusement at some private joke. Something about her seemed familiar, but he was positive they'd never met. He would have remembered for sure.

He looked around the store. "This place is handy. It's got a little bit of everything."

"Yes," she replied. "Doesn't it?"

There was flirtation in her tone, but he pretended not to notice. What was left of his libido had been beaten into cowering submission. He had never gone for such a long time without being horny.

The woman paid for her purchases and left. As the clerk tallied his bill, Brian peered out the doorway in time to see her cop another glance in his direction.

Grinning, she fluttered her long pink fingernails at him, then climbed into a white sedan and drove away.

Thack had found firewood under a plastic sheet behind the house, but there wasn't enough for a big fire, so Michael foraged for flotsam along the creek.

When he returned to the cabin, Thack was hunched over his fire, blowing on a stack of crisscrossed twigs. The sky was still indigo, but here beneath the trees, darkness had come early. The light of the fire cast a coppery glow on Thack's pale features.

Michael laid the wood down. "Your faggots, milord."

"Aye, and fine faggots they are." He smiled. "This isn't illegal, is it?"

"What?"

"Building a fire."

Michael shrugged. "Someone's obviously done it here before."

"Right," said Thack, feeding a dry branch to the flames. "Good enough for me." He looked up at Michael and smiled again—fire builder to wood gatherer—and Michael smiled back. It was a moment of prehistoric domesticity. Words would probably have ruined it.

* * *

A nearly full moon looked down on them as Michael finished off his salad. "We should've done baked potatoes," he said. "You know . . . in mud."

Brian said: "When did you ever bake a potato in mud?"

"When I was a scout."

"You were a scout?" asked Thack, sounding a little too amazed.

"I was an Eagle," he replied. "Thank you very much."

"So was I," said Thack.

"Really?"

Thack nodded.

"I never made it past Tenderfoot," said Brian. "I hated it."

"Why?" asked Michael.

"Well, it was fascist, for one thing. We had a belt line at my troop. You know, where we all took off our belts and whipped this other guy's butt while he ran past us."

"That's not fascist," Thack said dryly. "That's all-American."

Michael threw another log on the fire. "I hated it too. I did it, but I hated it. My father had been an Eagle, so damned if I wasn't gonna be one too."

"I liked camping trips," said Brian. "I liked that part."

Thack nodded. "Same here."

"I went to Philmont," said Michael. "You know . . . that Explorer camp in New Mexico?"

Both Thack and Brian shook their heads.

"Well . . . anyway, it was a big deal. Guys went there from all over. It was a big deal for me, anyway. I found out about love."

"Oh, God," groaned Brian.

Thack chuckled.

"I was fourteen," Michael said, "and my Explorer troop went on this two-week trip to Philmont. We went by bus, and we stayed at army bases along the way. . . ."

"What did I tell ya?" said Brian. "Fascist."

Thack laughed, then turned back to Michael, waiting for him to continue.

"They fed us army food, and we bunked in barracks buildings, and went to movies at base theaters, and . . . God, I'll never forget those soldiers as long as I live. Most of them were just four or five years older than I was, but . . . *vive la différence.*"

Thack said: *"Vive la similarité."*

Brian laughed.

"It was total fantasy," Michael continued. "I wouldn't have had the slightest idea what to do. But . . . it got my engines going. I was hornier than a two-peckered goat by the time I got to Philmont."

"Isn't he quaint?" said Brian, turning to Thack.

"One night," said Michael, ignoring them, "we were camped in this canyon, and there was this hellacious hailstorm, which knocked down our tents and got everything wet, so we were more or less adopted by this group of older scouts—"

"Wait a minute," said Thack, grinning. "Didn't I read this in *First Hand?*"

"First what?" said Brian.

Michael ignored them. "So . . . we went over to the other camp, and dried off in front of the fire, and this older scout shared his poncho with me. He put his arm across my shoulders, and I sort of . . . leaned against him." He stared into the firelight, remembering this.

"And?" said Brian.

"And . . . I just leaned against him. It was the most comfortable, wonderful, amazing thing. . . ."

"That's it?" said Thack, joining in the torment.

Brian looked at Thack. "Pretty scorching stuff."

Michael scowled at them both. "You had to be there." He picked up a stick and used it to rearrange the embers. "That's all anybody wants, isn't it? That feeling of being safe with somebody." Hideously embarrassed, he looked at Brian, then at Thack, and dropped the stick into the fire.

Later, back at the house, the three of them went about their separate rituals of ablution, passing each other like salesmen in a boardinghouse, toothbrushes in hand, unnaturally formal. Brian went to bed first, falling asleep almost instantly on one of the studio couches. Thack stripped to his underwear and took the other couch, leaving Michael with the convertible sofa, which he didn't bother to convert.

He slept fitfully, awaking just before dawn. Thack was still asleep under his blanket, breathing heavily. Brian stood across the room in his boxer shorts, awkward and disoriented as a wounded bear.

"You O.K.?" Michael whispered.

Brian held up a corner of his sheet. "Look at this," he said. It was drenched with sweat.

"There's fresh linen in that cedar chest," said Michael. "I'll just get—"

"What the fuck's happening, man?"

Michael took a sheet from the chest and flung it over the studio couch. "Lie down," he said.

"Look, Michael . . ."

"Go on. Lie down."

Brian lay on his stomach. Michael blotted his back with the wet sheet, then kneaded the knotty muscles above his shoulder blades. There was a moment of deceptive quiet before Brian began to sob into the cushions.

"Hush," whispered Michael. "It's O.K. . . . It's O.K."

DeDe's Duty

DAY BROKE AT WIMMINWOOD. DEDE WAS THE FIRST IN her family to stir, rubbing her eyes until they focused on the smooth green ribbon of river, the shimmering willows along the shore. She slipped free from the comfy entanglement of D'or's arms and eased herself out of the sleeping bag.

She sat there naked for a while, hugging her knees, listening to the wrens in the madrone trees. As much as she treasured D'or and the kids, she couldn't help savoring a moment when the world was all hers.

Things had gone beautifully, so far. Edgar had acclimated instantly to Brother Sun, displaying a knack for communal living which had dazzled even Laurie, his overseer. When his NCQ (Non-Competitive Quotient) was measured, he had beaten the socks off all the other kids in the compound.

DeDe, D'orothea and Anna had sampled most of the wonders of Wimminwood. They had played New Games, learned to face-paint, and splashed in the river like overheated ponies. The night before, with a thousand other women, they had sprawled on their backs under the stars while Hunter Davis sang to them:

You're the perfect match / for the imperfect me / coming on when I hold back / holding back when I come on / and darling I love you.

Hearing those lyrics, DeDe had turned and gazed at the miraculous planes of her lover's face, the bottomless black eyes tilted toward the moon.

Then, almost instinctively, she had reached for her daughter's hand, so small and silky-cool in the evening air.

She was happy, she realized. She had everything she wanted. D'or had been right about Wimminwood.

They ate breakfast, as usual, in the open-air vegetarian "chow hall." Food servers clad only in aprons and boots, all four cheeks ruddy from the grills, plopped mounds of steaming oatmeal onto their plates, ordering stragglers to "move it, please, *move it.*"

They found a place at a picnic table with three other people. "Listen," said D'or, digging into her oatmeal, "Anna and me thought we'd go visit Edgar, then maybe check out the Crafts Tent."

DeDe looked at her daughter. "Shopping again, huh?"

"D'or said it's O.K."

"We have a limited need for stoneware, you know."

Anna made her grumpy face.

"The same goes for tattoos, temporary or otherwise."

The little girl shot D'or an accusatory glance. "Did you tell her?"

D'or acted as negotiator with DeDe. "Maybe just a little one, huh? Femme. Something in Laura Ashley."

DeDe laughed in spite of herself. "Well, you're the culprit if it doesn't wash off."

"Yay!" crowed Anna. The child was a chronic shopaholic, DeDe realized. Like her grandmother. Like DeDe herself back in her post-debutante, pre-People's Temple days. Was it something in the genes?

"Aren't you coming with us?" asked D'or.

"No," said DeDe. "My work duty is this afternoon, so I'm gonna goof off for a while."

"Go to a workshop," said D'or.

"I might," said DeDe.

"There's one just made for you in Area Five."

"What?"

D'or's lip curled mischievously. "Check it out. Ten o'clock. Area Five."

Alone again, DeDe stood at the bulletin board and considered her options:

9:00–10:00   CRYSTAL WORKSHOP: Cleaning and caring for quartz crystals. How to use different crystals for healing, dreaming and meditation. Mariposa Weintraub, facilitator. Area 8.

9:00–10:00   BODY AND FACIAL HAIR: In slides, stories and song. Bonnie Moran, facilitator. Area 3.

9:30–11:00   YOUR DIET COLA IS OPPRESSING ME: How the patriarchy kills fat wimmin through dieting and harassment. Sandra Takeshita, facilitator. Area 4.

10:00–11:00 DOWRY DYKES SUPPORT GROUP: A chance for wimmin with money to share with each other their feelings about the personal and political issues connected with inherited wealth. Leticia Reynolds, facilitator. Area 5.

Dowry Dyke, huh? So *that's* what she was. Finally, she had an identity.

She was still smiling at D'or's little joke when a woman next to her made a snorting noise. "What do you do if you're not hairy, fat or rich?" She herself was young, lean and tomboyish.

DeDe smiled at her sympathetically. "Something with crystals, I guess."

"Yeah." The tomboy scuffed the ground with the toe of her loafers.

"Have you been to one yet?" DeDe asked.

"What? A workshop?"

"Yeah."

"Well, I went to the pottery one yesterday."

"How was it?" asked DeDe.

"Disgustingly PC. It's called 'The Herstory of Pots.'"

"Forget it," said DeDe.

"Our facilitator kept talking about the Hispanic influence on pottery, and finally I said, Don't you mean 'Herspanic'? and she looked at me like I'd just pissed in the punchbowl."

DeDe laughed.

"I told her, Pardon me but I gotta go . . . I'm late for my hersterectomy."

DeDe giggled. "Did you really?"

"No." She ducked her head in the most beguiling way. "I thought of that later."

"Esprit de l'escalier," said DeDe.

"What?"

"It's just an expression. For thinking of things later."

"Oh."

They looked at each other sheepishly, both at a loss for words.

"Have you been to many of the concerts?" the young woman asked at last.

"Hunter Davis," said DeDe. "Kate Clinton."

"Wasn't Kate Clinton a riot? Your little girl is gorgeous, by the way."

DeDe was confused.

"I saw you there with her," the woman explained.

"Oh . . . I see."

"I'm Polly Berendt." She extended her hand.

DeDe shook it. "DeDe Halcyon."

"Is that . . . uh . . . swarthy woman your lover?"

DeDe nodded, wondering how closely they'd been watched. "This is our first festival," she said, moving artfully from the specific to the general. "How 'bout you?"

"First one," said Polly, toeing the ground again. "Got off work for it, even."

"What do you do?"

"I work in a nursery. Plant Parenthood."

"Oh," said DeDe. "Michael Tolliver's place."

"You know him?"

"Well, he's sort of a friend of a friend. His lover delivered my kids."

"Jon?"

DeDe nodded. "Sweet guy. Did you know him?"

"No," said Polly. "He was . . . before my time." She paused. "You don't shop there, though. I would've remembered."

DeDe wondered if she was blushing. Even before this strategic compliment, she'd been mildly distracted by Polly's freckled cheeks and white teeth, the sun-gilded down on her forearms. "Actually," she said, "we don't live in the city. We're down on the Peninsula. In Hillsborough."

Polly nodded slowly, taking it in. "That's pretty swanky, isn't it?"

"Well . . . parts of it."

"Are you a Dowry Dyke?"

DeDe laughed. "Not if I don't go to that workshop."

Polly smiled at her. "Wanna go for a walk instead?"

Their hour-long odyssey took them through most of the subdivisions at Wimminwood, through the chemical-free and chemical-tolerant communities, through the zone for the loud-and-rowdy, the zone for the differently abled, the zone for sober support. "God," said Polly when they reached the riverbank, "it's a wonder they don't issue us fuckin' visas or something."

"I suppose it makes things easier," said DeDe, paying lip service to D'or's argument. She wasn't used to dealing with someone so unapologetically incorrect.

Polly's brown eyes wandered to the end of the beach, where a woman was sunning in the nude. "You ever take your shirt off?" she asked.

"No," said DeDe. "Not really. No."

"Why not?"

DeDe shrugged. "My lover and I discussed it. We just don't

think it's necessary. We don't need to prove anything to any-body."

Polly looked at her sideways, then skipped a flat stone on the water. "Chicken," she said.

Having lost track of the time, DeDe left Polly in haste just before noon. She ran the last hundred yards to her appointed duty post, a large open-sided tent near the entrance to Wim-minwood. It was crawling with efficient women in black T-shirts.

She approached the one she recognized, the cheerful black woman who had greeted them at the gate. "Excuse me, please."

The woman swung around. "I know you. Uh . . . big Buick full of brats."

DeDe laughed. "Don't rub it in."

"I'm Teejay, and you're . . . ?"

"DeDe."

"Right. What can I do for you?"

"I'm looking for the security chief."

Teejay looked around. "I think she's gone out for . . . No, there she is . . . over there, next to the butt cans."

"I'm sorry . . . the what?"

"Butt cans, precious. You know . . ." She made a cryptic motion, encircling her waist with her hands. "Her name is Rose. The one with the haircut."

DeDe felt her face drain. Rose with the haircut. The hateful Rose. The monster who'd deported Edgar to the boys' com-pound.

Unmistakably the chief, she was leaning against a tent post in loose green fatigue pants. Her breasts, which were bared today, had turned Spam-pink in the broiling sun.

DeDe approached warily, berating herself for not choosing Garbage Patrol, or even Health Care, for heaven's sake. Rose looked at her and said: "We meet again."

"Looks like it," said DeDe.

"You the noon relief?"

135

"Uh-huh."

"You're not in uniform, then." Rose reached into a box on the ground and produced one of the black T-shirts, handing it to DeDe. "I need you at the gate," she said. "I usually handle it myself, but there's been some trouble over in chem-free."

DeDe nodded. "Will somebody show me . . . uh . . . what I'm supposed to . . ."

"Right. That's my job." Rose winked at her almost amiably, and DeDe felt a little surge of relief. If all the woman wanted was to be in charge, DeDe was more than willing to oblige.

Leading her out to the gate, Rose explained the intricacies of the job. "Mostly you answer questions. Stuff about the various zones, where they should park. *Don't* let any cars onto the land unless they've got a pass."

DeDe was still a little uneasy. "The zones. I don't really know where . . ."

"Here's a map," said Rose, handing her a dog-eared pamphlet. "It's all there."

"Good."

"Oh, yeah. You'll probably have to deal with the Porto-Jane men."

"I'm sorry . . . the what?"

"We call the toilets Porto-Janes," said Rose.

Wouldn't you just? thought DeDe. "Then . . . I let these guys come onto the land?"

"Yeah," said Rose. "They're the *only* men we allow onto the land. They clean out the Porto-Janes and leave. It takes about an hour total. They've got a truck and ID badges, so ask to see 'em."

"Gotcha," said DeDe.

"There's a walkie-talkie at the gate. You can always call for reinforcements if there's anything you can't handle on your own. It's been quiet so far."

"Thank God," said DeDe.

"Don't you mean Goddess?" said Rose.

*   *   *

The shift turned out to be far less threatening than DeDe had imagined. She spent most of her time chatting with friendly women in overloaded cars. When they groused about the parking regulations, they did it with good humor, and one or two of them had even sent wolf whistles in her direction.

Twenty minutes before the end of her shift, an enormous white limousine pulled up at the gate. The windows were the one-way kind, so she couldn't see a soul until the front window hummed open.

A redheaded woman in a chauffeur's cap leaned out and asked: "Which way to the stage?"

"Well," said DeDe, "it's down this road and to the right, but I'm afraid you can't drive there."

"Why not?"

"It's the policy. No cars on the land. You can park in this lot, if you like. There's a shuttle to the land every fifteen minutes."

The chauffeur looked peeved. "We were told to go to the stage."

"Well, if you're a scheduled performer . . . I mean, if whoever . . ."

"Nothing is scheduled. My customer is a friend of the festival organizer."

"Do you have a pass?" DeDe asked.

"No. We were told we wouldn't need one."

"Gosh, I'm really sorry. My instructions are to make sure that no one—"

"I'll speak to her!" This was a voice from the back seat, raspy but resonant. It was followed by the whir of another shiny black Darth Vader window as it descended into the door. The face revealed was pale and without makeup, framed by a shock of black hair with a white skunk stripe down the middle.

DeDe felt her heart catch in her throat. It was Sabra Landauer, the legendary feminist poet-playwright, whose one-woman show, *Me Only More So,* had been the rage of the last two seasons on Broadway.

"Oh . . . Miss Landauer," said DeDe. "Welcome to Wimminwood."

"Thank you. Is there a problem here?"

"Well, a bit. If they'd told me you were performing . . ."

"I'm *not* performing. I'm visiting my friend Barbara Farrar, the *founder* of this festival."

"Ah . . . well . . . of course." Her resolve crumbled. When it came to catching hell from Rose or catching hell from Sabra Landauer, there was no contest. "So anyway, the stage is down this road, then off to the left. It's the only big clearing. Anybody with a blue wristband can help you."

"Thanks," said the chauffeur.

"And Ms. Landauer," DeDe added hastily, touching the limo to make it wait, "I have to tell you . . . *Medusa at the Prom* is my favorite book of poems *ever.*"

Sabra Landauer made a pistol barrel out of her forefinger and fired it rakishly at DeDe. "Read my latest," she said. "There's something in it just for you."

Before DeDe could respond, the dark window ascended. The limousine sped off down the road in the proverbial cloud of dust. Left standing in it, DeDe felt mildly disgusted with herself.

Why on earth had she said that? She had never even read *Medusa at the Prom.* Why had the mere sight of a famous woman made her lose it completely?

Muddled, she flagged on two other cars, only to be jolted back into reality by the sight of two rough-hewn men in a pickup truck. Remembering their mission, she stepped forward crisply and said: "Porto-Janes?"

"Yo," said the driver, showing a snaggletooth smile. Poor guy, she thought. To have such a job!

She flagged him on, giving him a thumbs-up sign by way of moral support. The pickup moved on, slowly at first; then it scratched off amidst a barrage of maniacal laughter. Both men reached out the window to flip her the bird.

"Dumb-ass lezzie!" one of them shouted.

She stood there for a moment, paralyzed by shock, her head ringing with Rose's admonition to ask for an ID badge. Stupid, stupid, stupid! Those weren't the Porto-Jane people at all!

She lunged for her walkie-talkie, but couldn't remember

what people always said in the movies. All she could think of was "Roger," and that, she felt certain, was patently sexist.

"Hello, Security," she said at last, all but shouting into the walkie-talkie. "Security, this is DeDe. . . . Come in, please. . . . This is an emergency."

No reply.

She checked the talk button to see if it was set correctly. Who knew? She tried again: "Emergency, emergency . . . This is DeDe at the gate. Men on the land! Men on the land!"

Still no answer. She shook the machine vehemently, then threw it into the ditch in a fit of pique.

Coming to rest in a blackberry patch, it startled her by talking back: "Security to gate, Security to gate . . . Come in *immediately*. . . . "

She climbed into the ditch and made her way gingerly through the treacherous tendrils, holding them at arm's length like dirty diapers. As she reached for the walkie-talkie, a bramble sprang out of nowhere and pricked her hand. "Damn!" she muttered.

"DeDe, this is Security. . . . Come in."

She fidgeted with the button again. "Men on the land, Rose! Men on the land!"

"Tell me!" Rose replied, just as the renegade pickup roared out of Wimminwood, occupants still cackling, spewing a cloud of reddish dust over everything.

Numb with terror, she stared at the departing marauders, then turned back to the walkie-talkie. "Is everybody O.K. down there?"

A damning silence followed. Finally, Rose said: "Wait there, DeDe. *Do you read me?* Wait there!"

The wait was almost half an hour, reducing DeDe to a nervous wreck. When Rose appeared at last, her jaw was rigid, her eyes chillingly devoid of emotion. A thin white icing of sunscreen now covered her breasts. "O.K.," she said. "What happened?"

DeDe spoke evenly. "I thought they were the Porto-Jane men."

"Did you ask to see their IDs?"

"No. I asked them if they were the Porto-Jane men, and they were driving a pickup like you said."

"I didn't say pickup. It's a big truck, DeDe. It sucks up the shit."

"Well, how was I supposed to know?"

The security chief shook her head slowly. "You are something else. You reeeally are."

"O.K. I made a boo-boo. I apologize."

"Made a boo-boo?"

"Fucked up, then."

"Do you have any idea what those assholes just did?"

DeDe caught her breath. *Please God, don't make it gross.* She shook her head warily.

"They drove past the Aura Cleansing Workshop, screaming 'Fucking dykes' at the top of their lungs—"

"I realize I—"

"Wait a minute. Shut up. On their way out, they knocked over a Porto-Jane."

"God."

"With somebody in it, DeDe."

DeDe pressed her fingers to her lips as her stomach began to churn. "Was she . . . hurt?"

An excruciating pause followed. "She was severely traumatized," Rose said at last. "We had to hose her down at the Womb."

Racked with nausea, DeDe looked away from her accuser. "If I'd had any idea . . ."

"You didn't follow instructions," said Rose. "It's as simple as that."

DeDe nodded. "You're right . . . you're right." She couldn't help wondering, though, what would have happened if she'd refused entry to the marauders. Would they have obeyed her? Her children certainly never did.

"I'd think you'd want to prove yourself," said Rose. "Considering your background."

"My *background?*" said DeDe.

"You know what I mean."

"No, I don't. Please tell me."

"I know about your father, O.K.?"

"You know *what?* My father is dead."

"Your stepfather, then. Whatever. I've known all about his fascist Reagan connections."

DeDe's face burned. "So what does that make me, then?"

Rose shrugged. "You tell me."

Hesitating a moment, she considered several retorts, then handed Rose the walkie-talkie. "It's past two," she said. "My shift is over."

She walked back to her tent in a daze, tormented by an issue far more troublesome than a toppled Porto-Jane: How could Rose—or anyone else—have known about Booter, unless D'or had said something?

And why would D'or do that? Why?

Broken Date

BOOTER'S LAKESIDE TALK HAD BEEN A RESOUNDING success. So far, at least a dozen Bohemians had pulled him aside to congratulate him, comparing him favorably to Chuck Percy and Bill Ruckelshaus, who had also addressed the multitudes that week. Sure, he had scrambled his notes once or twice, but no one seemed to notice, and the ovation afterwards had verged on thunderous.

He was walking now to burn off energy, filling his lungs with the pungent afternoon air. On the road above Green Mask, he passed a shirtless young man in his late twenties. His age and musculature suggested that he was an employee, so Booter felt duty bound to say something.

"Hot one, isn't it?"

The young man made a sort of whinnying noise to indicate that it was.

"You work here?" Booter asked, doing his best to sound pleasant about it.

"Yessir."

"Well, there's a rule about shirts, you know."

The young man looked at him blankly.

"You have to wear them," said Booter.

"Oh." He reached for his shirt, dangling from the back pocket of his khakis.

"It's fine by me," said Booter. "But . . . somebody else might give you trouble about it."

The young man slipped on the shirt, buttoned it up.

"I'd say the same thing to a member," Booter added, not wishing to seem a despot. "It's just the rule."

"Right."

"It's a hot one, though, isn't it?"

"Yeah."

Booter smiled at him and continued on his way back to the river road.

Order. Mutual respect. This was why the Grove was his favorite place on earth.

He found Jimmy Chappell in his tepee at Medicine Lodge. "There he is," piped Jimmy. "The William Jennings Bryan of the SDI."

Humility was in order, so Booter grunted disparagingly and sat down on the cot next to him.

"You want a drink?" asked Jimmy.

"Nah."

Jimmy poured cognac into a plastic cup, downing it with a satisfied smack. "Low Jinks sounds good," he said.

Christ almighty. Was that tonight?

"It's called 'I, Gluteus,' " Jimmy added, picking up a Grove program to read: " 'Bohemians and guests will thrill to love duets by Erotica and Testicus, shiver at the plot hatched by Castrata against Fornicatio, giggle at the airy antics of Flatus, and feel tension mount between Nefario and Intactica, leader of the Restive Virgins.' "

"Fart jokes," said Booter. "Can't we do better than that?"

"Well . . . you laughed your ass off at that song I did for . . . What the hell are you talking about? You helped me write it."

"I was drunk," said Booter.

Jimmy snorted.

"I can't go tonight, Jimmy."

"Why not?"

"I'm . . . going into town."

"Town?" said Jimmy.

"Yeah."

"Monte Rio?"

Booter nodded.

"Why the hell would you leave the Grove on the night of the Low Jinks?"

"You're not gonna be in it," said Booter.

"Well, I know, but . . . what the hell, forget it."

"I'll be at the Grove Play, Jimmy. Wouldn't miss it."

"Yeah, yeah."

Booter felt the weight of his guilt. He and Jimmy hadn't missed a Low Jinks together for at least a decade. Jimmy was a born annotator, a bantamweight Boswell who loved nothing so much as the act of explaining. Without a listener, he was lost.

"Look," said Booter. "If you keep your trap shut, I'll tell you the real reason."

Jimmy's scowl slackened. He scratched himself under his arm. "Go on," he said.

"It's George," said Booter. "He's coming in tonight."

Jimmy blinked at him.

"The Vice-President."

"Yeah. So what? I knew that." He scratched again and frowned. "What does that have to do with Monte Rio?"

"Nothing," Booter replied. "Forget I said that. There's gonna be a reception up at Mandalay." This was a much safer lie, since Jimmy had never been invited to Mandalay.

"A reception?" Jimmy said quietly. "During Low Jinks?"

The truth, Booter decided, might have been preferable to this tangled web. "It's very small," he said at last. "They don't wanna make a big noise."

Jimmy nodded slowly, taking it in.

"You know I wouldn't miss the Jinks with you if there wasn't a good reason."

Jimmy ran his fingers through his wispy hair. "Yeah, well, that's a reason, all right."

Booter could tell he was hurt.

Jimmy looked up dolefully. "Tell him I said hello, will ya?"

Betrayed

STINGING FROM THE INCIDENT AT THE GATE, DEDE RE-
turned to her campsite, to find it empty. D'or and
Anna were gone, apparently still on their shopping
spree at the Crafts Tent. In her current state, she
found solitude unendurable, so she doubled back to
the boys' compound and asked for Edgar.

He arrived dripping wet, fresh from the swimming hole,
already the color of a new catcher's mitt. "What's up, Mom?"

"Oh . . . nothing in particular. Just thought I'd stop by and
say hi."

He nodded. "I'm O.K., Mom."

"I know that."

Gesturing behind him, he said: "There's this really major
water fight . . ."

"Go for it," she said, smiling at him. He smiled back, then
vanished into the undergrowth.

She headed inland toward the Day Stage. The walk and the
music would be just the thing for her blues. She was here to
have a good time, wasn't she? Why let somebody like Rose
Dvorak ruin her day?

Once out of the woods, she rejoiced in the feel of the sun

against her skin. Linda Tillery was on stage singing "Special Kind of Love." An endless line of women snaked jubilantly across the clearing, drunk on the music.

She had been there less than five minutes when she saw Sabra Landauer.

The first thing she noticed was the skunk stripe. The second thing was the tall, bare-breasted woman who stood at Sabra's side, deep in animated conversation with the poet-playwright.

It was D'or.

Her throat went dry. Her skin grew prickly with dread.

Before she could retreat, D'or spotted her and waved. "Come join us."

As if in a nightmare, she moved across the field.

"I want you two to meet," said D'or. "Sabra . . . this is DeDe Halcyon."

Not "DeDe Halcyon, my lover," just plain old "DeDe Halcyon," thank you very much. Sabra, of course, didn't need a last name.

"Hello," said DeDe, shaking the large, bony hand of the poet-playwright. She was certain she wouldn't be remembered, and she wasn't. She turned back to D'or and asked: "Where's Anna?"

The accusation in the question wasn't lost on her lover, but she remained breezy. "Over in Day Care, bless her heart. She wanted to show off her treasures to the other kids."

She's not the only one, thought DeDe.

"This is Sabra's first time at Wimminwood," D'or added. "I'm giving her the grand tour."

Sabra smiled obligingly. "It's truly wonderful," she said.

"Isn't it?" said DeDe.

"Can you join us?" asked D'or.

"Not really."

"Oh . . . O.K." D'or's insistent smile finally faded. "See you back at the homestead, then."

"That's up to you," said DeDe.

* * *

Twenty minutes later, when D'or returned to the tent, DeDe was waiting for her. "One of us should go get Anna," she said coldly.

"She's meeting us at the chow hall," D'or said, kicking off her boots. She turned and gazed at DeDe. "I wouldn't have believed it."

"What?"

"You are actually jealous."

"I'm embarrassed, D'or. I'm embarrassed for you."

"Oh, really?"

"Yes."

"Do you mind if I ask why?"

"C'mon. Look at you. Flashing your tits all over the place as soon as a famous woman—"

"Now, wait just a goddamn minute."

"It's unworthy of you," said DeDe. "That's all."

"It was hot today."

"I noticed," said DeDe.

D'or drew back. "Oh, boy . . . ohboyohboyohboy."

"I also don't appreciate your blabbing it all over camp about Booter working for Reagan. If you can't respect our privacy—"

"Wait a fucking minute."

"Well, did you or did you not tell Rose?"

"*Who?*"

"The one who deported our son."

D'or looked totally dumbfounded. "I haven't even seen her since—"

"Well, you told *somebody!*"

D'or's brow wrinkled. "I may have *mentioned* it to Feather at the Salvadoran workshop."

"And Feather told that runty, big-mouthed lover of hers. . . ."

"DeDe . . ."

"O.K., forget runty. . . . Vertically challenged. How's that?"

D'or shook her head slowly. "It was just a lighthearted remark. I can't imagine how . . ."

DeDe rose. "I'm sure you get plenty of mileage out of it. Why don't you try it on Cruella de Vil?"

Slack-mouthed, D'or observed her, then broke into raucous laughter.

"Keep laughing," said DeDe as she charged out of the tent. She was heading for the loud-and-rowdy zone.

Adoring Fan

AS NIGHT FELL, WREN DOUGLAS FOUND HERSELF ON
the deck at Fife's, a gay resort on the outskirts
of Guerneville. The evening was so balmy that
several dozen people were still gathered outside. Shaking the rocks in her Scotch and water,
she stood at the rail and watched as a blond man in parrot
green shorts swam laps in the pool.

She felt crisp and glamorous tonight in serious makeup and
a turquoise-and-white sailor suit, fresh from a country Marti-
nizing. She'd expected to be recognized—hoped for it, in
fact—and she was.

"Excuse me," he said. "You're Wren Douglas." He was
brown-haired and brown-eyed, mustachioed. The mischief
and sweetness in his expression would have betrayed him as
gay at a PTA meeting in Lynchburg, Virginia.

"Yes," she replied.

He stuck out his hand. "I'm Michael Tolliver. I was in the
audience when you did *Mary Ann in the Morning*. You were
fabulous. You're always fabulous."

She smiled and squeezed his hand. She was used to this
kind of homo hyperbole, but it never failed to please her.

"You didn't see me on *Donahue*," she said with a rueful expression.

"No. What happened?"

She shrugged. "Some large lady from Queens called me . . . let's see . . . 'an insult to *decent* fat people everywhere.' "

"Oh, no."

"It was a big breakthrough for me, I'm tellin' ya. I wasn't just fat anymore . . . I was a *fat slut.* What a revelation! A minority within a minority, and getting more specialized all the time."

He laughed, but it sounded a little lame, carrying the weight of dutiful fandom. She wondered if he'd heard her tell the same story on the Carson show.

"What . . . uh . . . brings you here?"

"Where? This place?"

"Well . . . the river."

"I'm staying over in Monte Rio," she explained. "A friend of mine rented a house there."

"Same here," he said. "We're in Cazadero. Know where that is?"

"Mmm. Love their general store."

"Well, we're not very far from there."

"And 'we' means . . . ?"

He pointed down to the pool. "The guy who's swimming laps, and . . . over there, under the trees . . . the one in the plaid shirt."

"Well . . ." She raised an eyebrow artfully. "How nice for you."

He laughed. "The one in plaid is straight."

She nodded soberly. "Gay guys haven't worn plaid for years."

Another laugh. "As a matter of fact, he's married to Mary Ann Singleton."

"Who?" she asked.

"The woman who interviewed you."

"Oh, God, yes. Miss Terminally Perky. Poor guy. He's *married* to her?"

He looked a little upset. "She's O.K. once you get to know her."

"I'm sure."

"She just hasn't . . . responded well to being famous."

Right, thought Wren. World famous in San Francisco. She glanced over at the man in the plaid shirt and admired his dimpled chin with a sudden twinge of déjà vu. "Oh, *him,*" she exclaimed. "We've met. I tried to pick him up at the general store."

He laughed. "Seriously?"

"You bet. I *seriously* tried. He didn't mention me?" She made a hurt face. "I'm crushed."

"Well, he's been kind of under the weather lately."

I could cure him, she thought.

"This is such an honor," said Michael.

She cocked her head at him. "Thanks."

"Would you . . . uh . . . possibly care to have dinner with us?"

"Thanks, but . . ." She checked her watch. "I'm meeting my friend back at the house."

"Oh."

Her eyes perused the man in plaid again before returning to Michael. "He's leaving about ten o'clock, though. You could come up for a nightcap."

"Really?" He seemed genuinely elated. "Are you sure?"

"Sure I'm sure."

"All of us?"

"By all means," she replied.

Trouble in Chem-Free

DARKNESS HAD COME EARLY TO THE LOUD-AND-rowdy zone, a loose configuration of tents and RVs near the gate at Wimminwood. After less than half an hour there, DeDe had come to feel curiously comfortable, like a child who'd been kidnapped by gypsies and had grown to like it. Or maybe like Patty Hearst; she wasn't sure.

"Pour that girlie another drink!" This was Mabel, apparent high priestess of the Party Animals. "She's lookin' all mopey again."

"No," said DeDe, covering her tin cup with her hand. "I'm fine, really."

"Pour her a damn drink. Ginnie, get some more rum out o' the tent. Get your ass in gear and fix this sweet thing a drink."

Ginnie, who'd been absorbed by her own bongo music, stopped playing and looked at DeDe.

"Well," said DeDe, "maybe a little one." She'd been holding back out of some sense of obligation to the kids, but it seemed silly at this point. Edgar had his own life now, and Anna was at the chow hall with D'orothea.

Oh, God. Was Sabra with them?

"Smile," barked Mabel.

DeDe smiled.

Mabel winked at her. "Attagirl." She was reclining on an air mattress in front of her Winnebago. With her short gray hair and lumpy gray sweatsuit, she bore an uncanny resemblance to a plate of mashed potatoes.

"I know that bitch," said Mabel. "Her and me go waaay back."

For a moment, DeDe thought she meant Sabra. Then she remembered her other nemesis, the one she'd told them about. "You mean Rose?"

Mabel grunted. "She confiscated my crossbow at the Michigan festival. Fuck her."

DeDe tried to look sympathetic, but had a hard time of it. Mabel with a crossbow? Mabel *drunk* with a crossbow in the midst of a thousand people? Please.

"All that shit about Goddess this and Goddess that. I told her: 'I'm gonna get you back, I swear to God.' And she said: 'Anybody who swears to God is only bowing to the patriarchy.' And I said: 'I'm gonna patriarchy your butt all the way to East Lansing, if you don't get the hell out o' my Winnebago.'"

One of the other rowdies let out a whoop. "Go get her, Mabel."

"I've been beatin' men at their own game for sixty years. You think I need some sorry-ass little drill sergeant tellin' me how to talk like a dyke? Tellin' me I'm a threat to the general welfare because of a harmless little crossbow?"

DeDe watched as the bongo player swapped smirks with a lanky woman seated on an ice chest next to Mabel's air mattress. Mabel and her trusty crossbow had obviously become a central motif in their shared familial lore.

"And now," Mabel added, "she's treatin' *you* like dirt too. Small damn world, huh?"

"I guess so," DeDe said.

"Somebody should have a talk with that girlie."

"Oh, no," said Ginnie wearily. "Here we go again."

Puffing a little, Mabel hefted her weight onto her feet.

"Somebody should just go tell her it's time to stop pushing my friends around."

DeDe glanced nervously at Ginnie. This wasn't for real, was it?

"You should be flattered," said Ginnie, smiling sardonically. "Your honor is about to be defended."

DeDe turned back to Mabel. "Mabel, really, I appreciate your concern, but I don't . . ."

Mabel lumbered past her toward the Winnebago. "Yessir-ree-bob," she said as she climbed inside.

Panic-stricken, DeDe turned to Ginnie and asked: "The crossbow?"

Ginnie laughed. "It's back in Tacoma. Don't worry."

Thank God, she thought.

"She gets like this," offered the woman on the ice chest. "She was with the Post Office for thirty-seven years."

Mabel emerged from the Winnebago, gave DeDe a rakish salute, and began marching down the road toward the chem-free zone.

"You don't even know where she is," yelled Ginnie.

Mabel maintained a determined gait. "The hell I don't."

"She's doing this for you," said the woman on the ice chest, addressing DeDe. "She's showing off."

DeDe felt utterly helpless. "What's she gonna do?"

Ginnie shrugged. "Kick butt."

"Look," said DeDe, "the last thing I want is some horrible fight over . . . Can't somebody stop her?"

"She's not gonna do anything," said the woman on the ice chest. "She's blowin' smoke."

"Don't be so sure," said Ginnie. She turned to DeDe with a look of gentle concern. "Maybe you'd better go after her, huh?"

"Me? I don't even know her. Why should I be the—?" She cut herself off, suddenly envisioning Mabel and Rose locked in woman-to-woman combat. She leapt to her feet and bounded down the road after Mabel.

She caught up with her as they approached the border of the chem-free zone. "Mabel, listen . . ."

"Comin' along for the fun?"

"No! If you're doing this for me . . ."

"I'm doin' this for *me,* girlie."

DeDe strode alongside her, breathing heavily but keeping pace. "But if she thinks that I sent you down there to . . ."

"Who the hell cares?"

"*I* care, Mabel. I'm here with my lover and kids, and . . . I'm just trying to have a good time."

Mabel slowed down a little and smiled at her. "How's it been so far?"

"Shitty," said DeDe.

"Well, see there? It's time we had us some fun."

"Mabel, a rumble with the security chief is not my idea of a good—"

"Shhh," Mabel ordered, whipping a forefinger to her lips. "There it is."

"What?" DeDe whispered.

"Her lair." She seized DeDe's arm with a grip of iron, pulled her into a thicket of madrone trees, let go suddenly, and flung herself to the ground like an advancing infantryman.

Rose's tent was beneath them, at the bottom of a gentle slope. A lantern burned inside, making it glow like the belly of a lightning bug.

"Mabel, I want no part—"

"Get down!"

DeDe dropped to the ground, her heart pounding furiously. Mabel gave her a roguish wink and made another silencing gesture with her finger. There were sounds coming from Rose's tent. Not voices exactly, but sounds.

First there was a kind of whimpering, followed by heavy breathing, followed by: "Yes, oh yes, uh-huh, you got it, all right, O.K., *there* . . . yes ma'am, yes ma'am . . ."

DeDe tugged on Mabel's sweatshirt, making a desperate let's-get-out-of-here gesture. Mabel used her palm to stifle a snicker, then peered down the slope again, obviously enthralled by the drama of the moment.

The sounds continued: "Uh-huh, oh yeah, oh yeah, mmmmmm, oh God, oh God please . . . oh Gawwwddd . . ."

Mabel shot a triumphant glance at DeDe, then sprang to her feet, cupped her hands around her mouth and shouted, *"Don't you mean Goddess?"*

All sounds ceased in the tent.

DeDe tried to shimmy away on her belly, but the underbrush enfolded her. She lurched to her feet and stumbled frantically away from the scene of the crime. Behind her, Mabel was cackling victoriously, thoroughly pleased with herself.

"Come *on!*" DeDe called, suddenly worried about Mabel's safety.

Mabel savored the scene a moment longer before effecting her own escape. She crashed through the madrones, puffing noisily but still cackling. "Was that *perfect,* girlie? Was that the best damn—"

She tripped and fell with a sickening thud.

"Are you O.K.?" DeDe called. "Mabel? . . . Mabel?"

Mabel wasn't moving at all.

Sick with fear, DeDe made her way back to the grounded figure, knelt, touched the side of her face. "Please don't do this to me. Please don't."

Mabel's nose wiggled.

"Thank God," said DeDe.

The old woman emitted a sporty growl and hoisted herself to her knees. DeDe was pulling her the rest of the way when Rose emerged from the tent and peered up at the two invaders.

She locked eyes with DeDe for an excruciating eternity, then went back into the tent. Mabel shrugged and flopped her arm across DeDe for support. "You think she was alone?" she asked.

"I'm done for," said DeDe as they made their way back to the Winnebago.

"No you're not."

"I am. You don't know. She hated me already. Now . . ."

"I'll protect you," said Mabel.

"Right," said DeDe.

They passed a group of tents near the edge of chem-free. She distinctly heard someone say the words "Junior League," followed by a chorus of harsh laughter.

They knew, they all knew. Her debacle at the gate had entered into the lore.

It was time she got out of there.

Making Up

JIMMY LOOKED MOODY AND DRUNK WHEN BOOTER RE-
turned to his tepee. "How was the Jinks?" Booter
asked.

No answer.

"Bad, huh?"

"I didn't go."

"Why not?"

Jimmy shrugged. "How was the Vice-President?"

"Fine," said Booter. "Optimistic."

"About what?"

Booter was thrown for a moment. "Well . . . economic
indicators . . . the Contras. That sort of thing."

"Oh." Jimmy nodded, then looked down at the empty plastic glass in his hand.

"You should've gone to the Jinks," said Booter.

"Why?"

"I dunno. To give me a report. I was kinda curious."

Jimmy grunted.

"Sounded like your kinda show." Why was Jimmy acting
this way? Because Booter hadn't gone to the Jinks? Because
Booter hadn't invited Jimmy to meet the Vice-President? Be-

cause Jimmy turned maudlin after three drinks?

Applause came clattering through the woods like lumber spilling from a truck.

"There's the end of it," said Booter.

"Of what?" asked Jimmy.

"The Jinks."

"Oh."

Booter hated it when he got like this. "I thought I'd wander down to Sons of Toil . . . have a drink with Lester and Artie."

Another grunt.

"You wanna come along?"

"You go ahead," said Jimmy.

Booter frowned and sat down on the cot next to him. "Jimmy, ol' man . . ."

Jimmy rose, fumbling in his shirt pocket for a cigaret.

"You don't need that," said Booter.

"Hell with it." Jimmy lit the cigaret and tossed the match out into the night. He took a drag, then expelled smoke slowly, forming a contemplative wreath over his head.

"I wasn't up at Mandalay," Booter said at last.

"Oh, yeah?" said Jimmy. "Where'd you meet him?"

"I didn't."

"You didn't have drinks with George Bush?"

"No."

"Then what the hell . . . ?"

"I was with a woman, Jimmy."

Jimmy cocked his head slightly, like an old retriever inquiring about the prey.

"I rented a house in Monte Rio," Booter added. "She's been . . . staying there for a few days."

Jimmy looked dumbstruck for a moment, then started to laugh. As usual, his laughter deteriorated into a coughing jag. Booter clapped him on the back several times.

When Jimmy had collected himself, he said: "Why didn't you tell me it was just a woman?"

Booter shrugged. "You're a thespian. You've got a big mouth."

"Then . . . you didn't see Bush at all?"

"No."

Jimmy smiled and shook his head in amazement. No, in relief. "A woman," he said.

Booter gave Jimmy's leg a shake. "C'mon. Let's go see Lester and Artie."

"Is she . . . uh . . . long-term?"

"No," said Booter.

"You buy one of those whores down at the Northwood Lodge?"

"No."

Jimmy's eyes grew cloudy with reminiscence. "I bought a whore once. Nothing spectacular. Just this . . . nice little gal from Boulder during the war. Her name was . . . damn, what was it?" He sucked in smoke, then expelled it slowly. "Funny name . . . not like a whore's name at all."

"Let's go," said Booter.

"I always figured there'd be more just like her . . . or better. I had time for everything. Hell, five or six of everything." He was mired in memory again.

Booter found Jimmy's jacket and handed it to him. "We gotta hurry," he said. "Lester wants to play his saw for us."

Jimmy struggled into his jacket. "She have big titties, your girlfriend?"

Booter chuckled. "You ol' whorehound."

"I'm not as old as you," said Jimmy. "God damn, where do you get the energy?"

Booter shrugged and smiled.

"The only big titties I ever see are around this place." Jimmy sighed elaborately. "Old men and their big titties. It's so depressing. Where the hell is my hat? Some of those fellows out there could use a brassiere, Booter. Ever notice that?"

Booter found Jimmy's hat, a model he'd worn since the fifties, when he'd seen a similar one on Rex Harrison in *My Fair Lady.* He handed it to Jimmy and said: "You look as young as I've seen you in a long time."

In point of fact, Jimmy's bypass had whipped at least thirty pounds off him, imparting a sort of crazed boyishness to his face. "What is it that happens, Booter? Why do we all start looking like old women? What the hell is it? Revenge?"

161

Booter preceded him out of the tepee, merging with the tide of returning Jinks-goers. A screech owl heralded their exit. Jimmy caught up with him and said: "My wife's Aunt Louise had a full mustache by the time she was seventy."

Booter kept walking.

"There's a message there," said Jimmy, sighing again. "There's a terrible message there."

Midnight Quartet

THE ROAD ABOVE MONTE RIO WAS RUTTED AND UNLIT, deadly after dark.

"Are you sure this is right?" asked Thack.

He thinks I'm a flake, thought Michael. Useless with a hammer and useless in a car. "Well," he said evenly, "she said it was the very last house on the road."

"Yeah," said Brian, "but is this the road?"

"That's what I was wondering," said Thack.

Now they were ganging up on him. "What other road could it be?" he asked.

"That last turnoff," said Thack.

"Yeah," said Brian.

"But it was heading down, wasn't it?"

"Hard to tell," said Thack.

There was nothing to be gained by capitulating now. "I'm gonna keep on," said Michael.

"Whose place is this, anyway?" This was Brian again.

"I dunno," said Michael. "Some friend of hers rented it."

"Male, female, what?"

Michael chuckled. "Male, probably. Didn't you read her book?"

"I looked at the pictures," said Brian.

"I can't believe you didn't recognize her."

"She looked different."

"I wouldn't have recognized her," said Thack.

"She's a big star," said Michael, irked with them both for not understanding the honor they'd been afforded. "And she's so accessible."

"I noticed," said Brian dryly.

Thack laughed.

"You're both pigs," said Michael.

The crumbling road became a driveway, which led them up the steepest incline yet.

"This is crazy," said Thack.

"Yeah," said Michael, "but I think this is it." Ahead of them, caught in the headlights, lay an enormous moss-flecked chalet.

"Jesus," said Thack. "It looks like a Maybeck."

"A what?" asked Brian.

"He was an architect," Michael explained. "Early twentieth century."

"You know his work?" asked Thack.

"Very well," said Michael. Take that, Mr. Butch-with-a-Hammer.

He parked next to a white sedan behind the chalet. There were broad stairs leading to the second floor, where the living quarters seemed to be. The ground floor was shingled-over storage space.

The three of them climbed the stairs as a phalanx. Halfway up, Brian turned to Michael and said: "Let's don't make this long, O.K.?"

"O.K.," Michael whispered.

As they reached the top, Wren flung open the door. "Hi, boys."

"Hi," said Michael.

"Your timing is perfect," she said.

"Really?"

"Really. I'm ready to party." She sailed ahead of them like a galleon, listing here and there to turn on a lamp. When they

164

reached a big stone fireplace, she stopped and stuck her hand out to Thack. "I'm Wren," she said.

"Thack Sweeney."

"You're quite a swimmer," she said.

"Thanks."

"Are you another San Franciscan?"

"No," said Thack. "Charlestonian. South Carolina."

"Ah." She turned to Brian. "And we've met."

"Yeah," said Brian sheepishly. "I guess so. I'm Brian Hawkins."

"Charmed." She dipped coyly, smiling at Brian. Michael thought she looked fabulous tonight in her pale pink sweatsuit. A satin ribbon of the same shade secured her sleek dark hair behind her head.

"Michael, my love, how 'bout a hand?"

"Sure," he said instantly, seduced by the way she'd made them sound like old friends. He followed her into a dimly lit kitchen with an industrial sink, a sloping wooden floor, and a pair of cobwebby antlers over the stove. She gathered glasses and dumped ice into a bucket. "Glad you could come," she said.

"Glad to be here," he replied stupidly. "Has your . . . uh . . . friend gone?"

"Oh, yes." She opened the liquor cabinet. "There's some grass in the bedroom. The cigar box on the dresser. Roll us a couple, would you?"

"Sure." He made his way down a redwood-paneled hallway to a cozy bedroom. There, he sat on a rumpled bed and rolled joints while an owl hooted outside the window and Thack and Wren laughed over something in the living room.

When he returned, Wren was seated in an armchair next to the fireplace. Thack and Brian were on the sofa.

"There's drinks on that tray," said Wren, as he handed her the joints.

"Thanks," said Michael. "I'm fine." He sat on a tapestry cushion next to the hearth.

"In that case . . ." Wren struck a kitchen match against the fireplace and lit a joint. She took several dainty tokes before offering it to Michael.

"No, thanks," he said.

"C'mon."

"I'm on the wagon for a while. Cleaning out my system."

She made a face at him, then offered the joint to Brian. He shook his head, smiling dimly.

"I'll take some," said Thack.

"Thank God." She leaned over and handed Thack the joint. "These Frisco boys are a lot of fun, aren't they?"

Thack laughed.

"So," said Wren, turning to Michael. "What's there to do in this neck of the woods?"

"Well . . . we've been walking a lot, swimming in the creek."

"Swell."

Michael shrugged. "You came to the wrong place if you wanted action. There are one or two discos. . . ."

"Forget it."

"I agree," said Thack, returning the joint to Wren.

"What about your friend?" said Michael.

"What about him?" She took another hit off the joint.

So, thought Michael, we've established the gender. "Well, hasn't he shown you around?"

"No, not really. He's gone most of the time." She gave him a crooked, faintly knowing smile, telling him to mind his own business. Was she being kept? Was it somebody famous—like half the men in her memoirs?

"Michael says you're gonna make a movie with Sydney Pollack." This was Thack, jumping in.

"Well . . . Michael knows more than I do."

"I read it somewhere," said Michael defensively.

" 'Inquiring minds want to know,' " said Wren.

"No," said Michael, grinning at her. "It was . . . maybe I saw it on *Entertainment Tonight.*"

Wren gave him a teasing smile. "Oh, well, then . . . it must be true."

"C'mon," he said.

"We're just in the talking stage," she told him. "I don't wanna jinx it."

"It's such a fabulous idea," said Michael.

"Brian's wife is gonna be on *Entertainment Tonight.*" This was Thack.

"Is that right?" said Wren, turning to Brian with the dimmest of smiles. Michael braced himself.

Brian nodded. "They're taping this weekend, as a matter of fact."

"My," said Wren, "that's quite a coup for . . . you know, someone local."

There was a definite edge to this remark, but Michael found it forgivable. Mary Ann, after all, had bad-mouthed Wren on the air.

"She's pleased about it," said Brian.

"You should be there," said Wren. "Can't they use a husband?"

"She wanted me there," he replied.

"What's the matter? Afraid of the camera?"

"I dunno."

"Shouldn't be," she said. "That chin would look great on camera." She turned to Michael for a second opinion. "Doesn't he have a great chin?"

"Great," said Michael, deadpanning.

Thack laughed and exchanged glances with Brian, whose embarrassment was evident.

"It's like a little tushie," she said. "Two perky little hills." She squeezed her own chin in an effort to create the same effect. "A plastic surgeon could make a fortune."

They all laughed.

Wren winked at Brian, granting him clemency, then turned to Thack. "So . . . are you two . . . you know?"

Thack looked puzzled. "What . . . me and Michael?"

"Yes."

Thack hesitated so long that Michael took over. "We're buddies," he said.

"Yeah," said Thack. "We just met."

"I see," said Wren, nodding slowly. "You guys are worse off than I am."

* * *

167

They drove back to Cazadero an hour later. Their arrival was heralded by a sally of yaps from a neighbor's toy poodle. The people in the pink trailer had built a fire, from which sparks ascended like fireflies into the blue-black velvet sky. There seemed to be more stars than ever.

"I'm gonna take a walk," said Thack, as they climbed out of the VW.

"Oh," said Michael. "O.K."

He and Brian entered the cabin, flipping on lights, kicking off their shoes. Brian went to the kitchen sink and began washing the dishes from lunch.

"I'll get that," said Michael.

"No problem," said Brian.

Michael sat down at the kitchen table and watched Brian for a moment. "You feel O.K.?"

"Fine."

"All day?"

"Yeah. I feel much better, actually."

"Good," said Michael. "Must've been a bug."

"Yeah."

"Wren's nice, isn't she?"

"Yeah," said Brian. "She is."

"Is there more of that lemon cake in the fridge?"

"I think so."

Michael went to the refrigerator and found the ravaged Sara Lee tin. "She likes you," he said, plunging a fork into the cake.

"I know," said Brian.

When Thack returned to the cabin, Brian was fast asleep; Michael was pretending to be. Through half-lidded eyes, he watched as Thack shucked his clothes and shimmied under the covers on his studio couch.

Thack rolled over once or twice, then threw back the covers and got up again, crossing the room to Michael's bed. He knelt and brushed his lips softly across Michael's cheek.

"Good night, buddy," he said.

Michael opened his eyes and smiled at him. "Good night," he said.

A piney zephyr passed through the room. Down by the creek-bank, a frog was making music with a rubber band.

Red Alert

EELING ACHY AND COTTON-MOUTHED, DEDE AWOKE AT
first light, to find D'or sitting by the river's edge.
"There's coffee if you want it," said D'or, barely
looking up.

"Is Anna awake?" asked DeDe.

"No."

DeDe sat down next to D'or in the sand. High above them,
a huge black bird was circling Wimminwood in a sinister
fashion. She had seen these birds before, but this one struck
her as an omen, a harbinger of horrors to come.

"I wanna go home," she said.

"Why?"

"I just do, D'or. I don't like what it's doing to us."

D'or hesitated, then said: "You're overreacting."

"I am not."

"You're letting that . . . business at the gate get to you."

DeDe looked at her and frowned. "Who told you about
that?"

D'or shrugged.

"It's all over Wimminwood, isn't it?"

D'or looked away.

"Why are they blaming *me?* That's what I wanna know."

"Nobody's blaming you. It's over, hon. Put it behind you."

"O.K., fine," said DeDe. "It's behind me. Let's go home."

D'or heaved a forbearing sigh. "Hon, I promised the kids we'd stay a few more days."

"Why did you do that?"

"Because they *like* it here, O.K.?"

"When did they tell you that?"

"Last night, DeDe. When you were out getting drunk."

"I didn't get drunk."

"Whatever."

"I drank. There's a big difference. Why were you getting the kids on your side?"

"What?"

"You never ask their opinion unless you want their support. What's the big deal about staying here?"

D'or dug a little trench in the sand, then patted the sides methodically. "There's lots we haven't done."

"Like what?"

D'or shrugged. "The Holly Near concert. Sabra's doing a poetry workshop this afternoon."

"A poetry workshop," echoed DeDe.

"Yes."

"Since when have you been interested in poetry?"

She felt the whip sting of D'or's eyes. "Since when have you asked?"

"Oh, c'mon."

Using her palm, D'or smoothed over the little trench. "If you wanna take the car, go ahead. The kids and I are staying."

DeDe and Anna were still sunning when D'or returned from Sabra's workshop. It was almost four o'clock, and the willows were awash with gold.

"Don't burn yourself, hon." D'or sat down on the sand next to Anna.

Anna held up her Bain de Soleil bottle. "I'm wearing number eight," she said.

"Yeah, but you've had enough."

Anna turned to DeDe. "Mom," she intoned, elongating the word until it sounded like a foghorn. "Do I hafta?"

"I think so, precious. Go on. Hit the showers. I'll be up in a little while."

As the child scampered away, DeDe turned to D'or. "So," she said. "How was it?"

"Interesting," said D'or. "You should've come."

DeDe shrugged. "I know what she's all about."

"Oh, you do, huh?"

"Or *not* about, as the case may be."

D'or shifted irritably. "Meaning?"

"Well, she's not talking about being a lesbian, is she?"

"She talked about it plenty."

"Sure. *Here*. Just not on *The Today Show*."

"She's a feminist," said D'or. "She'd lose her effectiveness if people knew she was gay. Get real."

"You're the one who's not being real."

D'or picked up a pebble and flung it into the river. "Since when did you get to be such a radical?"

"Is that radical?" DeDe asked. "To expect people to tell the truth?"

"When didn't she tell the truth?"

"All the time. O.K. . . . When she was on Merv Griffin. She kept talking about the kind of man she likes."

"Well . . . a lesbian can like men."

"But she doesn't say that, does she? She deludes people, D'or. It's the same as lying. She's a tired old closet case."

"She's a great poet," said D'or.

"Well," said DeDe. "Did you learn anything?"

"Do you really care?"

"You must've written something," said DeDe.

"No."

"You just listened?"

"If you must know, I assisted her during the reading."

"Assisted her?" said DeDe, gaping. "Turned the pages? What?"

"Very funny."

"Well, tell me."

D'or raked her fingers through her hair. "One of the pieces required . . . interpretive body work."

DeDe blinked at her. "Dancing?"

"Yes."

"You danced while she read?"

"Yes."

"Oh, swell," said DeDe.

"I considered it an honor."

"Who wouldn't?" said DeDe.

D'or rose, dusting off the seat of her pants. "I don't need this."

DeDe followed her back to the tent. "You see what she's up to, don't you?"

"She enjoys my company," said D'or.

"She enjoys your tits," said DeDe.

D'or's eyes flashed again. "She relates to my energy. She thinks we knew each other in a past life."

"Oh, please."

"Back off, DeDe, O.K.?"

"Fine."

"I like talking to her. She likes talking to me. It's as simple as that."

DeDe snorted. "You think she wants you for *conversation?*"

D'or spun around. "Is that so hard to believe?"

"Oh, for God's sake, stop acting like such a . . . ex-model. Wake up and smell the hormones, D'or. The woman is in heat."

D'or crawled into the tent. "I'll keep that in mind." She grabbed her knapsack and crawled out again. "I'll certainly keep that in mind."

"Where are you going?"

"Use your imagination," said D'or.

Night fell, and D'or did not return. Anna and DeDe ate dinner together at the chow hall, then went to visit Edgar at Brother Sun. He showed them a wallet he'd stitched and a knee wound he'd incurred during a wrestling match. He seemed happy enough, DeDe decided; her escalating misery would find no company at the boys' compound.

On their way back to the campsite, they passed a large tent where two women in mime makeup were entertaining kids with "a festival of non-violent, non-sexist cartoons." Recognizing two of her playmates inside, Anna asked if she could join them, so DeDe left her there and continued the trek on her own.

She was taking a shortcut across the hearing-impaired zone when she saw her tomboy friend from the bulletin board. Polly something.

"Hey there," said Polly, waving merrily. "How's it been goin'?"

DeDe rolled her eyes. "Don't ask."

Polly smiled. "That was you on the gate, wasn't it? When the men got in."

Jesus. Had there been a press release?

"I remembered you were heading for your work duty," Polly explained, "so I just figured . . ."

"Well, it's over now," said DeDe, maintaining her stride.

Polly walked alongside, swinging her arms, bouncing on the balls of her feet. "I thought I might see you at that emergency meeting. That's the only reason I went."

"What emergency meeting?"

"You know . . . the one ol' baldie called."

"Rose Dvorak?"

"Yeah."

"She called a meeting?"

"A major one," said Polly.

DeDe's stomach constricted. She wondered if they'd discussed her—her ineptitude, her Neanderthal stepfather, her dubious loyalty to Womankind.

"They've beefed up security something fierce," said Polly. "Rose thinks it's gonna happen again."

"Bullshit," said DeDe.

Polly shrugged. "Seemed pretty random to me."

"It *was* random," said DeDe.

"They're getting off on it. That's what I think. Rose just

creams at the thought of declaring martial law. Slow *down*, DeDe."

"Sorry."

"Why are you so wound up?"

"I don't know." She stopped suddenly and looked at Polly. "Yes I do. My lover is messing around with Sabra Landauer."

Polly blinked, then emitted a long, low whistle. "You *know* that?"

"I suspect it."

"Well, that's different."

"She'd like to," said DeDe. "I can tell you that."

"Who wouldn't? Sabra gets more offers than Rita Mae Brown."

DeDe glowered at her. "If you think you're being comforting, Polly . . ."

"All I know is, this wife swapping isn't fair. If you're gonna have an affair, have it with a single girl. That's what we're here for."

DeDe thought for a moment. "Does Sabra have a lover?"

"She did," said Polly. "She dumped her last month."

"Great," said DeDe numbly.

They began walking again. When they passed a stern sentry brandishing a walkie-talkie and a nightstick, Polly tugged on DeDe's arm. "See what I mean?" she whispered. "The troops are on Red Alert."

Jimmy's Big Entrance

THIS YEAR, JIMMY CHAPPELL WAS TO PLAY A SISTER OF Mercy in the Grove Play, an epic called "Solferino," about the founding of the Red Cross. Another adventure in tedium, no doubt, but Booter showed up anyway, to keep peace with his old friend. Ten minutes before curtain time, he scaled the slope of the great outdoor stage and found Jimmy waiting in "the wings"—a bark-covered screen disguised as a redwood tree.

"Christ," said Booter. "I hope you look better from down there."

Jimmy's wig and nurse's cap, a single macabre unit, were hanging next to him on a nail. His few strands of real hair were matted and sweaty, and his white uniform was already streaked with makeup. "It's all illusion," said Jimmy.

"It better be," said Booter. "What's your first scene?"

"Well . . . I call for more tourniquets."

"Is that all?"

Jimmy looked annoyed. "It's a speech, Booter. It's an important moment."

"I'm sure it is."

Jimmy plucked a cigaret from the pocket of his uniform and

lit it with his lighter. He took a long drag, then said: "It gets more substantive later on."

"What happens then?"

Jimmy smiled a little and tapped his cigaret. "I call for more plasma."

Booter chuckled.

"It's not my finest role," said Jimmy.

"What the hell," said Booter.

"I don't care. It's theater." Jimmy gazed down on his fellow Bohemians, filing in to the log benches. "God, I love it." He cast a pensive glance in Booter's direction. "What the hell am I doing in real estate?"

"Making a damn good living," said Booter.

"Yeah, I guess."

A stage manager rushed past them with an armful of prop rifles. "Places, Jimmy. Two minutes."

"O.K.," said Jimmy.

"I'd better hightail it," said Booter.

"Where are you sitting?"

"Toward the back. With Buck Vickers and the rest of that gang."

"Well . . . stay if you want."

"Here?"

"Sure. Keep me company. I sit right here most of the time."

"Won't they throw me out?"

Jimmy made a stern face. "I'll raise hell if they do. I might not be the star of this extravaganza . . ."

Booter laughed. "You get a pretty good view up here." He peered through a fist-sized hole in the bark screen. Below, a lilliputian stagehand scurried across the main stage, scattering bloodied bandages in preparation for battle. The audience in the redwood amphitheater spoke with a single voice, whiskey-charged and jovial.

The lights dimmed suddenly. The audience fell silent as the orchestra plunged into the overture.

"Too late now," said Jimmy. "You're stuck with me."

"What the hell," said Booter. As a matter of fact, he rather liked the idea of staying here in Jimmy's lair—like a couple of

177

schoolboys playing hooky in a secret tree house.

Jimmy snatched his nurse wig off the nail and plopped it onto his head. Squatting a little, he faced a triangle of broken mirror and made final adjustments. His face exuded the humorless concentration of a man devoted to his craft. He gave Booter a thumbs-up sign, then marched into the public eye, his jaw set with the now-or-never determination of a paratrooper.

A blue spotlight followed him as he descended the long switchback trail to the main stage. A fifty-voice chorus sang about the rigors of war, the nobility of dying. After two or three minutes of this, Jimmy confronted Hubert Watkins (who was dressed as a general) and recited a list of casualties, making a desperate but eloquent plea for sterile dressings.

He returned five minutes later, breathless from the climb. He leaned against the bark wall and slid to a sitting position. "Whew," he said.

"Brilliant as usual," said Booter.

"You're not just saying that?"

"No. It was very moving."

"Nobody laughed, at least."

"No," said Booter. "You could've heard a pin drop."

Jimmy took off the wig and mopped his brow with a Kleenex. "Stupid ol' Lonnie Muchmore missed two light cues."

"Didn't show," said Booter.

"It didn't?" Jimmy glanced up hopefully.

"Looked fine from here. The audience liked you."

"Yeah," said Jimmy, grinning. "They did, didn't they?"

Jimmy's plasma scene went without a hitch. Back in the wings again, he unwound with Booter. "I forgot to tell you," he said. "I met George Bush."

"Oh, yeah?"

The bewigged face smiled. "I guess you could say I met him. I peed on a tree next to him."

Booter nodded soberly. "Congratulations."

Jimmy laughed. "When I joined this outfit fifteen years ago, all I ever heard was: So-and-so peed on a tree next to Art Linkletter or John Mitchell. . . ."

"Henry McKittrick peed on a tree next to J. Edgar Hoover."

"There you go," said Jimmy.

"You're not really a Bohemian until you've peed on a tree next to somebody."

"So there I was, answering the call of nature." Jimmy spun his yarn with histrionic relish. "And I look over, and who's standing there not five feet away but ol' Number Two himself."

"Doing number one," said Booter.

Jimmy ignored this witticism. "Right, and I look at him big as life and say: 'What's the matter? Don't they have toilets up at Mandalay?' " He laughed at his own joke, then began coughing violently.

"Take it easy," said Booter. "You O.K.?"

Jimmy nodded, gasping. "Never better." He hoisted himself to his feet. "I gotta change for the finale."

"Another costume?"

"Well, there's a different sash, at least. I put this red cross on the front of . . ." For a moment, it seemed he was considering something, then he fell back against the wall, clutching his chest.

"Jimmy, for God's sake . . ." Booter lunged for him, but Jimmy collapsed into a heap on the floor, thrashing his legs about like an injured thoroughbred. "Jimmy, is there medicine? Where the hell is your . . . ?"

Jimmy's eyes looked up at him, blinking. Then he registered another jolt, groaning between clenched teeth, clamping his palm against the pain. In another instant, his body went slack again and there was no movement of any kind.

Booter knelt next to him. "Jimmy, damnit . . . don't do this, ol' man." He checked Jimmy's heart, his pulse. Nothing. "You're gonna miss the big number, fella. . . ."

Down below, the orchestra was piling strings upon trumpets upon drums, thundering toward the finale. Roman candles burst above the hillside in a festive facsimile of warfare.

The chorus was singing angelically about the formation of the Geneva Convention.

The stage manager rushed up, out of breath. "Wake him up, will you? He's missing his entrance."

"No he's not," said Booter.

The stage manager looked exasperated and left, issuing orders to other nurses behind other trees. The music soared, the sky burned with pink phosphorescence, the forest reverberated with applause.

When it was over, Booter removed Jimmy's wig and hung it back on its nail. Then he took a Kleenex and—slowly, meticulously—removed Jimmy's lipstick. It wouldn't do for him to look like this when they came to take him away.

Goodbye and Hello

WREN WOKE AT EIGHT THIRTY-EIGHT WITH A vague sense of being behind schedule. Her limousine from the city was due to arrive at ten, which left—what?—three hours or so before the departure of American Airlines flight 220 to Chicago. Her head was already cluttered with numbers again. The wilderness had lost its hold on her.

She ate a farewell breakfast on the porch, gazing down on the cruising vultures, the ancient forest, the diamond-bright landscape of bluest blues and greenest greens. She would miss it, she decided. She would miss the exquisite *texture* of being alone in such a place.

Rolando would be waiting for her at O'Hare—seven-fifteen Chicago time—overflowing with candy and wilted carnations, looking dear and out of it in a suit. She had welcomed this respite from his boundless energy, his excruciating attentiveness, the ardor which bordered on priapism. Now she couldn't wait to be back. Her heart tap-danced at the thought of him.

After breakfast, she did the dishes for the last time, then

dragged out her suitcases. She decided against packing a bird's nest she had found in the woods, picturing how forlorn it would look amidst the chrome and whitewash of her loft. Vacations, she had learned, hardly ever survived transplanting.

As she gathered her loose receipts and paperbacks, she looked at Booter's check and smiled. He had originally made it out for ten thousand, but she'd insisted that he change it. Five thousand, after all, had been his first offer, and there was no point in being greedy.

The phone rang. What now? Was her driver lost?

"Wren Douglas," she purred, reassuming the mantle of an incorporated woman.

"It's me," came a weak voice. It was Booter, but he didn't sound like himself.

"Oh, hi."

"I have to see you again."

"Are you O.K.?" she asked. "You sound like a truck just hit you."

"Something has happened," he said quietly, his voice drained of color. "I have to see you."

"Booter, my flight is at one o'clock."

"Cancel it. Please."

"I can't. There's a driver coming from the city."

"He can stay here overnight. I'll pay for it."

"Look," she said, "if I flake out on my boyfriend one more time . . . What's the problem, anyway? Tell me about it."

"No," he said quietly. "Not now."

"Well, then, if . . ."

"I'll pay you more, of course."

That made her mad. "Damnit, Booter . . ."

"Well, what do I have to do?"

"Nothing," she said wearily, resigning herself to another shouting match with Rolando. "If it's really important . . ."

"You can catch the same flight tomorrow. Tell your driver he can stay at the Sonoma Mission Inn. It's very nice. I have an account there. I'll call ahead and arrange everything."

"Well . . . O.K."

"I'll be there this afternoon."

"When?"

"No later than three," he said.

His Own Mischance

WHEN SOMEONE DIED AT THE GROVE, THE NEWS of it rumbled through the encampment like the drums of the Navajo. Jimmy's death had been no different from the rest, electrifying Bohemia for a few uncertain hours until banality came along to put the horror in its place. Discussing it over breakfast fizzes the next morning, Jimmy's campmates had spoken with a single voice: "He loved performing more than anything. He died a happy man."

Booter knew better. He had been there. He had seen the look on Jimmy's face. These fond farewells were too damn facile, if you asked him. When *he* went west, by God, he wanted serious mourning. If not weeping and wailing, at least a little gnashing of teeth.

Most of this occurred to him during Jimmy's impromptu memorial service at Medicine Lodge, Father Paddy Starr officiating. Booter knew the priest only slightly (he was a member of Pig'n' Whistle), but the fellow struck him as a little too swish for his own good.

"He was one of the greats," Father Paddy told him afterwards.

"Yes," said Booter.

"I loved him in that Egyptian thing."

Booter nodded.

"I suppose his wife has been notified."

"His wife is dead," said Booter.

"Oh." The cleric clucked sympathetically. "What about children?"

"I dunno," said Booter, walking away. "I think there's a son in the East."

He downed two Scotches at the Medicine Lodge bar and walked back to Hillbillies by himself. On the way, he passed one of the Grove's infamous "heart-attack phones." Housed in their own miniature chalets, these infirmary hot lines had been installed for the sole purpose of saving lives.

Sometimes they did the job; sometimes they didn't.

Bohemians made grim jokes about the phones, the worst of which Booter had heard from Jimmy.

Poor bastard, he thought, as he stumbled into the compound at Hillbillies. I know damn well you weren't ready.

He had two more drinks at Hillbillies, but left shortly thereafter, finding the camaraderie oppressive. He walked down the river road past the Club House, then decided to forsake this eternal gloom for the sunshine of the riverbank.

The sentry at the guardhouse gave him a funny look. The old codger had always struck him as slightly impertinent.

"Havin' a good mornin'?" he asked.

"Not particularly," said Booter.

"Well . . . hope it gets better."

Booter grunted at him and kept walking. He wondered where they had kept Jimmy overnight. Was there a morgue in the infirmary? The funeral people had arrived from the city this morning, so Jimmy must've stayed somewhere in the Grove, away from his brothers, alone in the dark. . . .

He crossed the footbridge above the gorge leading down to the beach. Laughter drifted up from the water, but it sounded callous to him, disrespectful of the dead. Didn't they know what had happened to Jimmy? Didn't all of Bohemia know?

Descending the slope to the river, he checked out a canoe at the dock and padded it with one of the thin cotton mattresses they issued for sunbathing. Snug in this waterborne nest, he paddled away from the cruel mirth of the swimmers, intent upon solitude.

When he was fifty yards or so downriver, he pulled in his paddle and leaned back against the mattress. There was virtually no current, and the sun felt good against his skin. He thought of Wren for a moment, welcoming the comfort she could offer in only a matter of hours.

He took his flask from his hip pocket and wet his whistle. Where did that come from—wet your whistle? He had heard it all his life without actually stopping to think about it. Jimmy would know, damn him. Why wasn't he here?

Jimmy would like this a lot. Jimmy was a real kid in a canoe. Naming all the birds, spinning yarns. He could tell his story about the narrow-gauge railway that ran along the river road in the 1890s . . . how the old-timers had come to the Grove using public transportation, starting with the Sausalito ferry, then taking the old Northwestern Pacific . . .

A huge, hungry-looking creature was patrolling the sky above the canoe. *Nothing dead down here, fella. Beat it.* It was a predatory bird of some sort, probably an osprey. Or was it a turkey vulture? Jimmy would know. . . .

But Jimmy wasn't there, was he? He had marked out his life in encampments, summer to summer, and now he was gone, rocketing down the freeway, stiff as a board, robbed of his finale.

Just like that, Jimmy, just like that.

He closed his eyes and let his fingers trail in the water. For some reason, this pose struck him as vaguely Pre-Raphaelite, like that painting of the Lady of Shalott, supine in her boat, drifting off to her death.

Tennyson. How did it go?

"And down the river's dim expanse, / Like some bold seer in a trance, / Seeing all his own mischance,—/ With a glassy countenance / Did she look to Camelot. . . ."

It was his mother's favorite poem. He had memorized it four or five years after she died, for an English lit project at Deerfield.

"And at the closing of the day / She loosed the chain, and down she lay: / The broad stream bore her far away, / The Lady of Shalott."

He opened his eyes. The great bird of prey was a dark smudge against the sun. The brightness was too much for him. His eyelids caved in under the weight.

"And as the boat-head wound along, / The willowy hills and fields among, / They heard her singing her last song, / The Lady of Shalott."

Her last song . . . Mother's last song . . . Jimmy's last song . . .

The canoe found the current and swung around as he melted into the mattress and entered a realm of sweet release. His progress down the river was marked only by the vulture, who made several lazy loops in the air and returned to her nest in the forest.

The Honeymoon Period

MICHAEL AND THACK HAD DRIVEN OUT TO THE ocean that afternoon. From Cazadero they had followed a crumbly one-lane road which snaked through the dark green twilight of the redwoods before climbing to a mountain meadow the color of bleached hair. There were gnarly oaks here and there, and Wyeth-gray fences staggering down to the sea.

"Look," said Michael, pointing to the roadside. "Naked Ladies."

Thack blinked his pale lashes once or twice.

"Those lilies," Michael explained. "Pink, see? And no leaves. Naked Ladies."

"Oh," said Thack.

"You don't have 'em in Charleston?"

Thack shrugged. "We might. I'm not good on flowers."

"Just houses, huh?"

"Yep." He smiled faintly and returned his hand to Michael's denimed thigh. It had been there for most of the drive, pleasantly warm and already familiar.

"This was nice of Brian," Thack said.

"What?"

"Giving us time to ourselves."

"Oh . . . well, actually he wanted some time alone himself." This was true enough, even though it *had* been Michael who'd broached the subject to Brian. "He's a good guy," he added, feeling vaguely guilty again.

"I like your friends," said Thack. "Was that Charlie who called this morning?"

"Yeah."

"Just . . . checking in?"

"Yeah," said Michael. "Wondering how the cabin was." This was a bald-faced lie.

"Has he been sick long?" asked Thack.

"A year or so," said Michael. "He came down with pneumocystis last month."

Thack made a little whistling sound.

"He's O.K. now," said Michael.

"He seems to be. I mean, aside from the lesion."

"It usually gets better," said Michael, "before it comes back. They call it the honeymoon period."

"Oh."

Michael gave him a rueful glance. "Isn't that a terrible expression?"

They passed a parched field, the carcass of a barn. The sea burned blue below them.

"Do you know anyone with AIDS?" Michael asked.

"A few."

"In Charleston?"

"No. New York, mostly."

"You have them in Charleston."

"I know," said Thack.

"Sometimes I think we're all gonna die."

Thack paused. "Have you thought about taking the test?"

"I've taken it," said Michael.

Thack looked at him.

Michael managed a rueful smile. "I was not amused."

Thack hesitated. "It doesn't really mean anything, you know."

"Promise?" said Michael.

189

Thack returned his smile, then faced the blinding blue of the Pacific. "I haven't taken it," he said.

Michael nodded.

"Are you sorry you took it?" Thack asked.

"No," said Michael. "I hate surprises."

They spent an hour or so roaming through the old Russian settlement at Fort Ross, then found a niche at the foot of a cliff where they leaned against each other and watched the waves. "Sometimes," said Michael, "I feel like Hermione Gingold."

Thack chuckled.

"You know . . . in *A Little Night Music*. What was the name of that song?"

" 'Liaisons,' " said Thack.

"Exactly." He gave Thack a teasing nudge. "Fags are so handy."

Thack smiled at him. "Why do you feel like Hermione Gingold?"

"Oh . . . everything seems like such a long time ago."

"Like what?"

"Just . . . the good ol' days. There used to be this beach up at Wohler Creek. Still is, I guess. It was a nude beach, only it was divided up into straight, gay and hippie. The hippies were a sort of buffer zone between the straight part and the gay part."

"That makes sense," said Thack.

"Somebody told me once that it belonged to Fred MacMurray."

"What? The beach?"

"Well, the land, I guess. People just showed up there by the hundreds, and he was nice about it. He just owned it, apparently. He was never there."

"Oh."

"The gay part was amazing. Dozens of naked guys, all stretched out on the beach, and *everybody* had a raft. You could lie on the beach and look out across the water, and it was nothing but a sea of beautiful butts." He smiled. "They called it the San Francisco Navy."

Thack laughed.

Michael looked out to sea. "That was nineteen eighty-one . . . the last time I went."

"Four years," said Thack.

"It seems like forty," said Michael. He turned and looked at Thack. "Does it bother you that I'm positive?"

Thack returned his gaze, then gave him a gentle, leisurely kiss on the mouth.

"Is that an answer?" said Michael.

"Well . . . it's the best I can do right now."

Thack pulled him closer and kissed him again. Beneath the burnished ribs of his old corduroy shirt, his back felt like warm marble. His lips were incredibly soft, tasting faintly of apple juice.

"That's more like it," said Thack.

"Uh-huh," said Michael.

Thack smoothed the hair over Michael's ears. "You know what?"

"What?"

"Our sleeping arrangement is fucked."

Michael smiled. "I know. I'm sorry."

"Stop being sorry," said Thack, kissing him again.

Shortly after four, they followed the wiggly road back to Cazadero. When they parked in front of the cabin, Michael spotted Brian in a lawn chair by the creek and gave him a wave. "Yo," Brian hollered.

"See you inside," Michael told Thack. "I'm gonna go talk to him."

He walked down to the creekbank in the slanting afternoon light. Brian looked healthier, more relaxed, with color in his face. "How was it?" he asked.

"Great," said Michael.

"Good. I'm glad."

"That drive is incredible."

"Maybe I'll take it," said Brian. "You guys need the car tonight?"

"Tonight?" asked Michael.

"Well . . . for the next three or four hours."

"I guess not."

"I thought I'd go look at the sunset, maybe eat dinner at that place in Jenner."

"By yourself?" asked Michael.

"Sure."

"Brian, listen . . ."

"I want to, Michael. I like being alone. I've had fun today."

"Are you sure?"

Brian nodded.

"Well . . ."

"So . . ." Brian rose, picked up his copy of *Jitterbug Perfume*, folded the lawn chair. "The drive was nice, huh?"

"Wonderful," said Michael.

"Great."

They walked back to the cabin together, Brian's arm across Michael's shoulder.

"Oh," said Brian, "I put fresh sheets on the sofa bed."

Michael looked at him and smiled.

"Just thought I'd mention it," said Brian.

He left in the VW twenty minutes later.

Thack turned to Michael and said: "Beer?"

"Hug," said Michael.

Thack obliged him, kneading the knots in Michael's back. "Shall we eat before or after?"

Michael laughed. "Anything but during."

"Right." Thack let go of him and headed for the bathroom. "I'm gonna shower."

"O.K."

Thack called from the bathroom. "Is it too warm for a fire?"

"Not for me," said Michael.

"Great. Why don't you build us one?"

Michael gazed at the freestanding fireplace—hooded, orange and hideous—and decided that it was easily the finest fireplace in the Western world.

His kindling had just begun to crackle when the phone rang. If this was Charlie again . . .

"Hello."

"Uh . . . Michael." The voice was velvet-gloved and unmistakable.

"Wren? I thought you'd gone."

"Well . . . that's sorta the problem. Something kinda weird has happened."

"What?"

"My friend has disappeared."

"Your friend. You mean . . . ?"

"Yeah, him."

"What do you mean, disappeared?"

"Well . . . it takes some explaining. Could you come up here?"

No way, he thought. "Gosh, I'm really sorry. Brian took the car, so Thack and I . . ."

"I could come get you."

"Now?"

"Yeah."

"Wren . . . this is really not a good time."

"Oh." She knew what he meant immediately. "I'm sorry."

"I hope you understand."

"Well," she said, "you told me to call if I needed anything." This was true, and he kicked himself for it. "Can't I help over the phone?"

"No," she replied. "I have to show you."

The bathroom door opened. Thack emerged towel-wrapped, on a cloud of steam. "What's the matter?" he asked, seeing Michael's grim expression.

"Wren's friend is missing."

"What?"

"Tell me where you are," said Wren. "I'll come get you."

Michael heaved a sigh and told her. He couldn't help wondering if she always got what she wanted.

The three of them stood on her deck above the river. "That's where he's supposed to be," said Wren, pointing to a distant chunk of water. She was wearing voluminous white Bermuda shorts and a pink cotton blouse with the collar turned up.

"What's down there?" asked Thack.

"The Bohemian Grove. Ever heard of it?"

Thack shook his head.

"It's a club," said Michael. "For society people."

"Not people," said Wren. "Men."

"Right," said Michael.

"When did you last talk to him?" asked Thack.

"This morning. I canceled my flight for him. He called and said he wanted to see me. He sounded really out of it and desperate."

Thack's brow furrowed. "In what way?"

"I dunno. He made me cancel my flight, for one thing."

"Made you?" asked Michael. He was still a little angry with her.

"Asked me. He sounded desperate, so I did it. He said he'd be here no later than three, and I know Booter well enough to know that he would never—"

"Booter?" said Michael. "His name is Booter?"

"No jokes, all right?"

"No. . . . I think I know him."

"Oh, God."

"Booter Manigault?"

"Jesus," said Wren. "How small is that town, anyway?"

"Small," said Michael. "Microscopic."

Thack turned to Michael. "He's a friend of yours?"

"No," said Michael, "but I know who he is. My lover delivered his . . ." He thought for a moment. "Step-grandchildren."

"Oh, well," said Wren dryly, looking at Thack. "Clears it right up, doesn't it?"

"Why don't you just go down there and ask?" said Michael.

"Where? The Grove? I did, darling. It's strictly Tubby's playhouse. No Girls Allowed."

"Couldn't you leave a message?" asked Thack.

"I did. They said they'd write it on the chalkboard at the Civic Center . . . whatever *that* means."

Michael chuckled. "I picture them walking around in togas or something."

"The thing is," said Wren, "the whole damn place is designed to protect them from women. If you haven't got a pecker, they don't wanna hear from you."

"I still don't get it," said Michael. "Why don't you just take off? If he didn't show, he didn't show. What's the big deal?"

"Because," said Wren, "I feel an obligation."

"How long have you known him?" asked Michael.

"Not very."

"How long is that?"

"A week, ten days."

"Well, maybe this is the kind of stunt he pulls."

"No," she said. "I don't think so."

"O.K.," said Michael. "Then maybe he got called home on an emergency or something. You could call his house in Hillsborough."

"No way," she replied.

"I'll do it," he said.

After at least eight rings, an ancient-sounding maid answered the phone. He asked to speak to Mr. Manigault, deciding that he could either hang up or make a landscape gardening pitch if Manigault should be at home. The maid, however, reported that he was "up at the Grove" and that Mrs. Manigault had "gone to a fashion show in the city."

Michael thanked her and hung up. "He's still here, apparently."

Wren looked troubled. "Something's the matter, guys. There's no way I can fly home without knowing . . ."

"We could go down there," said Thack.

"Would you?" asked Wren.

Michael frowned. There went their evening at home.

"Maybe," said Thack, obviously getting into it, "we could talk to the guard, tell him we're friends of Booter."

"No," said Wren. "The gate's no good, if they don't have your name on a list."

"Then what?" asked Thack.

"Well . . . there's another way in." She turned to Michael and asked: "Are you as good a swimmer as Thack?"

Foreign Shores

BOOTER AWOKE TO FIND HIMSELF STARING AT THE stars. They were bright tonight, brighter than ever, pulsing like the light bulbs in the cellars of his childhood. He felt oddly peaceful in his mattress-lined cocoon, even though it was night and he was sunburned and the canoe had beached itself on the shores of God-knows-where.

How long had he slept? Three hours? Four? And how far had he drifted?

He gazed up the moonlit river for some reassuring point of reference—the Monte Rio bridge, a neon-trimmed road-house, an A-frame bathed in the blue light of television.

But there was nothing.

Only bone-pale sand and gray shrubbery and black trees pricking the blue-black sky.

And drums. And the song of sirens.

It was a dream. That was his first thought.

He remembered the whiskey (tasted it, in fact) and remembered his sleeplessness after Jimmy's death. He had needed sleep and it had come to him, so he was still asleep, that's all. And whiskey invariably made him dream.

The breeze, though, seemed real enough as he climbed out of the canoe. So, too, did the ache in his limbs and the rodent squeak of aluminum against sand as he pulled his craft ashore and tried to get his bearings again.

So why were the drums still beating, the sirens still singing?

The voices were female, certainly. And lots of them.

He moved in their direction, shaking the stiffness out of his joints. There were Christian retreats in the area, he remembered. Baptist Bible camps. These girls could easily be part of such a place.

He headed into the underbrush somewhat warily, fearful of frightening them. Beet red and rumpled, he knew he must look like a wild man, but he had no choice but to ask for their assistance.

They could lead him to a phone, and he could call the Grove. Someone would send a car for him. He'd be back in time for the Campfire Circle, no worse for wear and no one the wiser. Hell, he might even tell them about it, make it into a story. The way Jimmy would have done.

Following the music, he threaded his way through a dense thicket of madrone trees. There was a campfire up ahead—quite a large one—and he caught glimpses of swaying figures and faces made golden by the fire.

The drums stopped abruptly as he approached. Spurred by this primeval sign of danger (or the memory, perhaps, of Tarzan movies), he ducked behind a redwood, then chuckled at the absurdity of his reaction.

He emerged again, to see something extraordinary:

A tall, full-breasted woman, naked but for slashes of blue and green body paint, lifting her arms toward the heavens.

He hid himself again, collecting his wits as the woman began to chant:

"We invoke you, Great One . . . in the memory of nine

million women executed on charges of witchcraft . . ."

What on earth . . . ?

"We invoke the name of the Great Goddess, the Mother of all living things . . ."

Peering incredulously around the tree, he saw that the other women were naked too. Some held bowls of fruit or bunches of flowers. Others were draped with amulets or holding amethyst geodes in their cupped hands.

"We invoke you, Great One . . . you whose names have been sung from time beyond time. You who are Inanni, Isis, Ishtar, Anat, Ashtoreth, Amaterasu, Neith, Selket . . ."

There was nothing to do but retreat. As quickly and quietly as possible. He would find help elsewhere, but not here, for God's sake, not here.

". . . Turquoise Woman, White Shell Woman, Cihuacoatl, Tonantzin, Demeter, Artemis, Earthquake Mother, Kali . . ."

He crept away from the tribal fire, but Nature took note of him and acted accordingly. Dry branches crackled underfoot, young tendrils caught hold of his limbs, night birds screamed warnings to anyone who'd listen. . . .

And something large and terrible leapt from the shadows to strike a blow to the back of his head.

Night Crossing

SETTING THEIR SCHEME IN MOTION, MICHAEL AND THACK took Wren's car and drove to the Guerneville Safeway, where they bought a box of heavy-duty Hefty bags. When they returned to the hilltop lodge, Wren was smoking a joint on the deck, her eyes on the dark river below.

"Any word?" asked Michael.

She shook her head. "He's not gonna call. I've got this gut feeling."

Michael wasn't so sure about her gut feelings, but he kept his mouth shut. "What do you want us to do?" he asked. "Once we get there."

"Just find out where his camp is. Hillbillies, it's called. Ask around for him. If he's there, or somebody at least knows where he is, then I can go home."

"If we find him," said Thack, "what do you want us to tell him?"

Wren rolled her eyes. "Tell him to call my ass."

"He'll wonder how we got in, won't he?"

She shrugged. "Tell him. He won't report you. I can promise you that."

"And if he's not there?" asked Michael.

"Then," said Wren, "we figure out something else."

"How do we get back?"

"Through the gate. You'll be O.K. on the way out. It's a mile or so down to Monte Rio. Call me from that greasy spoon at the bridge and I'll come get you."

"Got it," said Thack.

"I'm glad *you* do," said Michael.

Ten minutes later, she drove them to the river's edge, parking in a neighborhood that seemed disturbingly suburban. Why, Michael asked himself, do people move to the redwoods to build mock-Tudor split-levels with basketball hoops over the garage?

The nearest house was dark, so the three of them scurried burglar-like across the side yard until they found a sandy path leading down to the water.

"See?" whispered Wren, pointing across the river. "There it is."

The Bohemian swimming platform and dressing rooms were a dark jumble of geometry in the distance. Michael estimated the swim to be no more than fifty yards. Easy enough, assuming the absence of crocodiles or unfriendly natives with blowguns.

"According to Booter," said Wren, "there's a bridge above that ravine and a guardhouse a few yards beyond that. You can probably avoid both of them if you follow the ravine up from the beach."

"Are you sure?" asked Michael.

She shook her head with a wry little smile.

"Great," he said.

"They won't shoot at you," she said. "It's just a club. If worst comes to worst, you can use Booter's name, and they'll send for him."

"They're gonna know we're not members," said Thack.

"Nah," she replied. "There's a thousand men in there. Nobody knows everybody."

Thack sat down on the sand and began to strip, stuffing his clothes into a Hefty bag. "If you want," he said to Michael, "put your things in here with mine. No, forget it. It'll be too heavy with the shoes."

Michael sat next to him and began to stuff his own bag. Thack had stripped all the way, so he did the same, willing away the last vestiges of his Protestant self-consciousness.

Pale as moonlight, Thack waded into the river with his bag of clothes. When he was knee-deep, he turned and spoke to Wren. "Wish us luck."

"More like a bon voyage." She laughed. "Shall I break some champagne across your bow?"

Michael followed Thack into the water, which was warmer than he expected, but his skin pebbled anyway. The silt of the river bottom oozed up between his toes. "If we're not back by sunup," he said, "send in the Mounties."

"Ha!" said Wren. "Think I'd trust you with a Mountie?"

"Keep your voices down," said Thack.

Wren clamped her hand to her mouth, then came to the water's edge and whispered: "I'll be waiting for your call. You have the number, don't you?"

"No," Michael replied.

"I do," said Thack.

Michael looked at him and said: "God, you're organized. I bet you alphabetize your albums."

"Wait," said Wren. "I forgot." She poked through the high grass until she found the terry-cloth towels she'd brought, then handed them to Michael, who stuffed them into his Hefty bag.

"You're such a doll to do this," she said.

He shrugged. "Life's been boring lately."

"It's Hillbillies," she said. "Don't forget."

"I won't." He waded out to join Thack again. They commenced a sort of tortured sidestroke, dragging their bags beside them.

When they reached midriver, puffing like steamboats, they looked at each other and burst into laughter.

Wren was still watching from the shore, a dead giveaway in her white Bermudas.

A Debutante Reason

RECLINING TOPLESS ON HER COT, POLLY BERENDT folded her hands behind her head and said: "Something weird is happening down in chemfree."

Also topless, but sitting on the ground, DeDe asked: "What do you mean?"

"Well, when I went out to pee, I saw this huge huddle of those black-shirt girls. I mean, more than I've ever seen in one place. They clammed up when I walked by, like I'd just walked in on a cabinet meeting or something."

"I don't even wanna know," said DeDe. She was finished with Security and their nasty little intrigues.

Polly chuckled. "They probably found somebody with a Stevie Wonder tape."

DeDe didn't get it. "What's the matter with Stevie Wonder?"

"What else?" said Polly. "He's male."

"C'mon."

"Sure. It's a violation of women-only space. No records with male singers. Read your regulations." Polly rolled over, propping her head on her elbow. "You know what I want?"

"What?"

"A burger. With lots of cheese and pickles and blood pouring out of it. . . ."

"Yuck," said DeDe.

"Well, it beats the hell outa this place," said Polly. "Did you try that phony meat tonight?"

DeDe smiled grimly. "Sloppy Josephines."

"When are these girls gonna drag their asses out of the sixties? That's what I wanna know."

DeDe turned and gave her a big-sisterly smile. A lucky combination of sunshine and lantern light had turned Polly's taut little tummy the color of the rivets on her 501's. DeDe observed this effect with appreciation but without passion, like an art-conscious matron perusing a Rembrandt.

And she *was* a matron, compared to this kid.

"You don't remember Kennedy, do you?"

Polly rolled her eyes. "They always, always ask that."

"Well, *excuse* me."

"Why was he such a big deal, anyway? He made it with Marilyn Monroe. Big deal. Ask me if I remember the first moon landing."

"O.K. . . . Do you?"

"No."

DeDe groaned and threw a sweat sock at her. "You little turd."

Polly cackled triumphantly. She reminded DeDe of Edgar somehow. After he'd dropped a worm down Anna's back.

"The thing about the sixties," said DeDe, feeling older by the minute, "is that it wasn't so much a time as it was . . . a transformational experience. Some people did it then. Others waited until later."

"Like, wow," said Polly, mugging shamelessly. "Heavy."

"Fuck you," said DeDe.

Polly smiled at her. "So when did you transform?"

DeDe thought about it, then said: "The spring of nineteen seventy-seven."

"So specific?"

"I joined the People's Temple. In Guyana."

Polly looked stunned. "Jesus," she said.

"We got out, of course . . . before . . . all that."

"You and your lover?"

"Mmm. And the kids."

"They must've been babies," said Polly.

"They were. They don't remember anything."

There was a long silence. Then Polly said: "Why did you go?"

"I don't know." DeDe gave her a rueful glance. "It was D'or's idea."

Polly digested that, then said: "Like this, huh?"

DeDe nodded vaguely. "I guess so. I have a mind of my own, believe it or not."

"I believe you."

"She's strong, so I let her be strong. I like it that way. Most of the time."

Mischief flickered in Polly's eyes. "Is she the one who lights the charcoal and grills the steaks?"

DeDe wasn't sure how to take that, but she laughed, anyway. "The tuna," she said, correcting her.

"Oh. Right. No red meat. I forgot." Polly nodded solemnly. "And she's the one the kids obey?"

"What is this?" asked DeDe.

"I'm just curious."

"Yes, you are."

"Well, we're friends, aren't we? I just wanna . . . share." Polly smiled. "Like in the sixties."

DeDe popped the top on a Diet 7-Up. "You're incorrigible."

"Don't say that," said Polly.

"Why not?"

"It sounds like my seventh-grade English teacher."

DeDe took a sip. "You hated her?"

"No," said Polly. "She turned me on."

"Don't make me self-conscious, O.K.?"

Polly stared at her for a moment, then shook her head slowly and said, "Boy!"

"What?" asked DeDe.

"DeDe the Debutante."

This irked her. Why did everybody get to fire off this potshot? Debutantes—no, *reformed* debutantes—were probably the last oppressed minority on earth. "Look," she said, "I took off my shirt, didn't I?"

"You did," said Polly quietly, "and breast fans everywhere are grateful."

DeDe groaned at her.

"But," said Polly, "you took it off for a debutante reason, not because you're really comfortable that way."

"C'mon. What the hell does that mean—a debutante reason?"

Polly shrugged. "You took it off because D'or took hers off, and you're afraid that Sabra's gonna take hers off pretty soon. So you beat her to it."

"Oh, please," said DeDe.

"It's so obvious," said Polly. "It's the Pillsbury Boob-Off."

"Will you stop? In the first place, Sabra Landauer would never take hers off in a million years."

"O.K. . . . So you took yours off to prove that you're better than Sabra."

"I did not."

Polly picked up an apple, polishing it against the leg of her 501's. "So where is she now?"

"Who?"

"D'or."

"At the Holly Near concert."

"Is she with Sabra?"

"Probably," said DeDe.

"You think they've been doing it?"

DeDe thought exactly that, but she refused to give shape to her fears.

Polly took a bite of the apple, chewed and swallowed. "You know what?"

"What?"

"You should fake her out, pretend to be fucking around yourself."

DeDe gave her a doubtful look. "With you, I suppose."

"Sure. I could be real convincing."

"I'll bet."

Polly turned and grinned at her.

"I could never be that petty," said DeDe.

"Force yourself," said Polly. "There are big stakes here. Sabra's wrecked a few marriages in her time."

DeDe didn't want to hear this. "She's not all that good-looking," she said.

"Yeah, but she's rich."

"I'm rich," said DeDe.

"She's rich and famous," said Polly. "And she gets to do everything. Broadway openings, limos all over the place, personal friends with Lily and Jane . . ."

"Thanks," said DeDe. "Thanks a lot."

Polly studied her a moment, then sat up and pulled on a celadon sweatshirt.

"Where are you going?" asked DeDe.

"I'm outa here," said Polly. "There's a burger out there with my name on it."

DeDe felt deserted again. What would she do? Go back to her tent and wait for Anna to return from her quilting class? Should she be there, looking useless and alone, when D'or returned?

And what if D'or *didn't* return?

Polly hopped to her feet and began searching the tent for her socks. "Come with me," she said. "I won't be gone that long."

"Well . . ."

She handed DeDe her shirt. "C'mon, Mama. Let's get dressed and go to town."

Name-Dropper

ACCORDING TO JIMMY, THE MOST IMPOSING SPIDERS were female, and this one certainly fit the bill. Fat, furry and crimson-bellied, she dangled from a fragile trapeze, weaving her macramé only inches from Booter's sunburned face.

He was in a tent; he could tell that much. His mouth tasted foul, and his head was throbbing. His feet were bound together, and his hands were tied behind his back. He was lying on his side, facing the spider.

His first thought was: "Weaving spiders come not here."

That was the Bohemian motto, but he drew no comfort from it now. At the Grove, the phrase meant dealmaking was prohibited, no business on the premises.

Here, it meant nothing.

Here, that spider could weave where she wanted.

He'd been conscious for almost five minutes when he heard a woman's voice outside the tent.

"Where is he?" she asked.

Someone hissed for quiet.

"We have to call the police."

"Sure. Turn him over to men."

"I don't care, Rose. We have to."

He heard boots scuffing against earth, then saw the tent flap move, revealing a woman in a black T-shirt. She held a walkie-talkie in one hand, and her head was shaved to varying degrees, forming a sort of topiary garden on her scalp. She squatted on her haunches to examine him.

"Listen," he said, "whatever you think I did—"

"I don't think. I saw."

"I was in a canoe," he said.

"I know that."

"I fell asleep. I must have drifted."

"Did you enjoy the show?" she asked.

So they had seen him watching.

"Answer the question," she said.

"It was an accident," he said. "I didn't know where I was. I went up there to ask directions."

"You're lying," she said.

"Don't tell me I'm lying!" How dare she talk to him like that? Who, after all, had clobbered whom?

"What's your name?" she asked.

He hesitated. What if she called the police? He could clear himself, of course, but what sort of indignities would he be forced to endure? "I don't have to tell you that," he said at last.

She appraised him coolly for several seconds before dropping the tent flap and walking away. He hollered, "Wait!" but got no response.

She came back about fifteen minutes later.

"Thirsty?" she asked.

He was and said so.

"I'll have some water sent by for you."

"Wait a minute," he said. "Don't go."

"What?"

"You're making a very big mistake, young lady."

"Yeah?"

"I know how it may have looked to you, but I'm no Peeping Tom."

"O.K. Then who are you?"

"I'm a member of the Bohemian Club. We're up the river a bit. I don't want to make trouble for you, but—"

"I asked your name."

"Manigault," he muttered.

"What?"

"Manigault. Roger Manigault."

"Sure."

"Well . . . I don't have my wallet with me."

"As in Pacific Excelsior?"

"Yes!" He literally sighed with relief. Thank God she knew about business! "That's me!"

"That's you?"

"Yes! I'm not the sort of man who—"

She cut him off with a wild bray of laughter. "Booter. They call you Booter?"

"Yes. Now will you please untie—"

"Reagan's friend?"

"Well . . , I know him. . . . I wouldn't exactly say—"

She dropped the tent flap and went howling into the night.

A Dream Come True

THANKS TO BOOTER, DINNER HADN'T HAPPENED TO-night, so Wren postponed her journey home, stop-ping off at the greasy spoon near the Monte Rio bridge. Michael and Thack wouldn't call for at least an hour, so why not settle her nerves with a basket of fries and a chicken-fried steak?

The greasy spoon was a "family restaurant," replete with squawling brats, cracked plastic menus and redwood room deodorizers for sale next to the cash register. She was debat-ing dessert when a teenaged girl approached, wearing an expression of tentative fandom. "O.K.," she told Wren. "If you're not, you might as well be."

Wren put her fork down and stuck out her hand. "I guess I am, then. What's your name?"

The teenager, on closer inspection, seemed more like a young woman. She was short and wiry, with freckles and a sparkling pink-gummed smile. "Polly Berendt," she replied. "I really can't believe this."

"What?" said Wren. "That you found me eating?"

Polly laughed. "You look just like you look on TV. Better. This is the most amazing thing. This is so great."

"Sit down." Wren winked at her and patted the place mat across from her. "We're frightening the nuclear families."

Polly cast a glance over her shoulder, than sank into the chair. "Sorry," she said. "I get loud."

"Yeah," said Wren. "Me too." She popped open her compact mirror and began to repair her lipstick. "You on vacation or something?"

Polly didn't answer for a while, lost in her amazement. "What?" she said at last.

"You on vacation?"

"Oh . . . yeah. I'm down at Wimminwood. Know what that is?"

"Uh . . . well, a women's music festival, right?" She'd read about it on the bulletin board at the Cazadero General Store. She'd figured the kid for a lesbian.

"Yeah, that's right."

"So what are you doing here? Playing hooky?"

Polly chuckled. "Yeah, more or less."

"All by yourself?" O.K., she was flirting a little, but what harm could it do?

"No. I'm here with a friend. I mean, here at the restaurant. That blonde lady over there."

Wren dropped her lipstick into her purse and gazed across the room. Caught in the act of watching them, the blonde looked decidedly uncomfortable. Wren gave her a little smile, which induced even more embarrassment.

"She's against this," said Polly.

"Against what?"

"Me coming over here."

"Why?"

Polly shrugged. "She says it's tacky."

"Nah," said Wren. "I think she's jealous."

Polly cast a quick glance at the blonde, then looked back at Wren. "No shit?"

Wren gave her one of her Mona Lisa smiles.

"That would be wonderful," said Polly.

"What?"

"If she would be jealous. I don't think she likes me that much."

"Well . . ."

"Could I get a lipstick print from you?"

Wren blinked at her.

"I collect them," said Polly. "It's a hobby. I already have Diana Ross and Linda Evans and Kathleen Turner."

"Sure. Fine. What do I do?"

Polly beamed at her. "I can't believe this."

"What do I do?" Wren asked again. "Blot on a napkin?" Her eyes wandered across the room. The blonde woman was staring straight down into the remains of her hamburger. She was obviously mortified.

"Or," Wren added, "I could pucker up and really smooch on it." She looked back at Polly and grinned conspiratorially. "Your friend would like that."

Polly giggled.

Wren picked up a napkin and settled on something between a blot and a smooch, giving the results to Polly. "Happy summer," she said.

"Same to you," said Polly, shaking Wren's hand briskly. "Same to you."

Into the Grove

MICHAEL AND THACK HAD CROSSED THE RIVER without a hitch, drying off and dressing in a dockside room erected for just that purpose. They'd followed the ravine up the forested hillside until they found the footbridge Wren had told them about. It loomed above them, huge and skeletal, like an abandoned railway trestle.

"What now?" whispered Michael.

"We go under it," Thack replied. "Up that hill."

"Wait!"

"What?"

"I heard something."

Thack cocked his head. There were rustling sounds, then the resonant thump of footsteps on the bridge. Michael flattened himself against a support post, pulling Thack back into the shadows. The moon was traitorously bright.

A voice called: "Who goes down there?"

Michael held his breath, glancing at Thack. Wren's words reverberated in his head. *They won't shoot at you. . . . It's just a club. . . . They won't shoot at you. . . .*

Thack pressed his finger to his lips, clearly intent upon going through with this madness.

The footsteps commenced again, then stopped at mid-bridge. A flashlight beam probed the underbrush only yards away from their hiding place. Michael hugged the post and prayed for release. Or at least leniency.

"Who goes?" yelled the guard.

Michael looked at Thack. Enough was enough.

Thack shook his head emphatically.

The guard stood there for half a minute, then began to walk again. Away from them. Off the bridge and up the hillside.

Thack's eyes flashed triumphantly. Michael expelled air and whispered: "Let's get the fuck outa here."

"What? Swim back?"

"Sure."

"C'mon. The worst is over."

"How do you know?" asked Michael. "What if he comes back?"

"Well, we've come this far. Don't be such a pussy."

"I'm being practical," said Michael.

Thack gave him a friendly goose. "Then don't be so practical, Maude."

They waited another five minutes, then continued up the hillside until the lights of a road led them into the Grove. Men passed them in boozy clumps, singing and jostling, hooting hello as if they, Michael and Thack had been there all along, making merry under the redwoods.

Manhood, it seemed, had been their only requirement, their only badge of identity.

"This is so unreal," said Michael. "It's like a hologram or something."

"*Pinocchio,*" said Thack.

"What?"

"You know. Those wicked boys on Pleasure Island."

They were walking through a gorge, apparently, with ferny

forests climbing the slopes on either side. The redwoods along the road were as fat around as Fotomats, clustered so tightly in some places that they became walls for outdoor rooms, foyers for the camps that lay behind them.

The camps were wonders to behold. Giant tepees and moss-covered lodges and open-air fireplaces built for the gods. Strings of lanterns meandered up the canyon wall to camps so lofty that they seemed like tree houses.

And everywhere there was music. They heard Brahms for a while, then Cole Porter. Then an unseen pianist began tinkling his way through "Yesterday."

Thack asked: "There are no women at all?"

"Nope," said Michael. "They've been to court over it."

"How do they defend it?"

Michael shrugged. "Women make 'em nervous. They can't be themselves."

Thack chuckled and slipped his arm across Michael's shoulder.

"I wouldn't do that," said Michael.

"What?"

"This is the straightest place on earth, Thack."

"Oh." Thack removed his arm, looking vaguely wounded. "Plenty of *them* are doing it."

"Yeah, but . . . you know . . . it's different." Michael knew how gutless this sounded, but he was still feeling incredibly paranoid.

A hawk-faced old man was catching his breath against a tree. Thack approached him, somewhat to Michael's alarm.

"Excuse me, sir. We're kinda lost."

The old man chortled. "New here, eh?"

"Yeah."

"Where ya wanna go, podnah?"

"Well . . . Hillbillies, we were told. Booter Manigault's camp."

"Ah." He nodded slowly. "You guests of Booter?"

Thack hesitated ever so slightly, so Michael said: "Right."

"Good fella, Booter."

"Yeah, he is," said Thack.

"The best," Michael added, perhaps a little too eagerly.

"I tell you what you do," said the old man. "You keep on down the river road . . . this road right here . . ."

"O.K.," said Thack.

"It's a few camps down, on the left. You'll see the sign."

"Thanks a lot."

The old man said: "What'd ya do? Pass it and double back?"

"Uh . . . yeah, I guess we did."

"Well, you just keep on down this way. You're on the right track now."

"Great," said Michael.

"On the left," added the old man. "You can't miss it."

"Terrific."

"Sign's over the entrance. Big bronze one."

As they withdrew, both nodding their thanks, Michael wondered why old men take such a long time to give directions. Was it senility or a yearning for company?

Or just the unexpected exhilaration of feeling useful again?

The Hillbillies plaque depicted Pan with his pipes and a naked female spirit rising from the steam of a caldron. "Would you look at that?" said Thack, standing back to admire it. "Pure Art Nouveau."

Michael, who still felt like an impostor, refrained from a telltale display of aesthetic appreciation.

Thack led the way into an enclosed compound dominated by a two-story redwood chalet. Half a dozen men of varying ages were gathered around a fireplace in the courtyard. One of them stared hard at the newcomers, then sailed in their direction at great speed, wearing a phosphorescent smile.

"Michael, my child!"

It was Father Paddy Starr, the television priest who presided over religious affairs at Mary Ann's station.

"Oh, hi," Michael said feebly, panicked at the sight of a familiar face.

"What a lovely surprise!" Father Paddy clamped his chubby hands together. "Have you been here the whole time?"

It was probably an innocent question, but Michael got flustered, anyway. "Well . . . uh . . . no, actually. We just got here. We're guests of Booter Manigault."

Father Paddy's brow wrinkled. He began to cluck his tongue and shake his head. "The poor old dear," he said.

Thack shot Michael a quick glance.

"Has something happened to him?" Michael asked.

"Well," the cleric replied. "I expect you heard about Jimmy Chappell?"

"No . . . uh . . . not really."

"Oh. Well, Jimmy died last night."

"I'm sorry. I don't think I know who . . ."

"No, of course not. How silly of me. He was one of Booter's oldest chums."

"Oh," said Michael.

Father Paddy heaved a sigh. "I think it's been hard on him, poor dear."

"You haven't seen him, have you?"

"No. I expect he's gone home."

"No," said Thack. "We were supposed to meet him here."

"Ah . . . well, then he must be up at Lost Angels. He has friends up there."

"Lost Angels?"

"C'mon," said Father Paddy. "I'll show you." He turned to Thack and extended his hand, palm down, as if to be kissed. "I'm Father Paddy . . . since Michael's forgotten his manners."

Thack shook the cleric's hand. "Thack Sweeney," he said.

"An Irishman! I might have known."

Thack pointed to the Hillbillies plaque. "What can you tell me about the artist?"

"Not a blessed thing," said Father Paddy, "but isn't it ador-able?"

As the priest sashayed out, leading the way, Thack spoke to Michael under his breath. "So," he said. "The straightest place on earth."

The Escape Plan

OOTER HEARD FOOTSTEPS AGAIN. THE TENT FLAP opened, to reveal a Negro girl wearing gym shorts and a bright blue T-shirt. "Hi," she said, with surprising cheerfulness. "I'm Teejay."

He wasn't about to swap nicknames with her.

"The water girl," she added, holding up a canteen.

"You know," he said, "you can all be arrested for this."

Kneeling in front of him, she lifted him to a sitting position. "Are your wrists uncomfortable?" she asked.

"What do you think?" he replied.

She examined his bonds for a moment. "I can't loosen it without taking the whole thing off."

"Then do it," he said.

"Sure." She smiled at him. "And let you bop me on the head." She lifted the canteen to his lips, tilting it slowly, wiping away the overflow with a blue kerchief.

When she was done, Booter said: "I don't bop people on the head."

She tightened the top of the canteen. "Rose says you make instruments of war."

"I make aluminum honeycomb," he said.

"She says you went to Bitburg and laid wreaths on Nazi graves."

"That was a *reconciliation* gesture. Look . . . what's going on here? You can't just hold me indefinitely. I didn't do anything."

The girl used her fingers to comb the hair off his forehead. "We've had . . . some harassment. Rose thinks you're part of it. She wants to hold a tribunal."

"A tribunal? What? Here?"

She nodded.

"She's crazy," said Booter. "She's a complete lunatic. If she thinks she can humiliate me . . ." He collected himself and tried to sound as reasonable as possible. "Look . . . I don't have anything against you or anybody here. I'm a man of my word. If you let me go, I promise I won't lay a finger on you."

"No," she said. "You have to."

"What?"

"We have to make it look that way."

"Like what?"

"Like you overpowered me. Otherwise I'll catch hell."

He grasped her meaning with a rush of relief. "O.K. Fine. However you want to do it."

Leaning closer, she said: "The best way out is the way you came. Your canoe is still there."

"Are you sure?"

"I've already checked," she said.

"Are we near the river?"

"Oh, God," she said. "You don't know where you are?"

"No. How could I? That . . . whatshername—"

"O.K.," she cut in. "There's a dirt road just outside the tent here. Down a little and to the right. Follow it until you reach the river. Then . . ." She fell silent suddenly and cast an uneasy glance over her shoulder.

"What's the matter?" he whispered.

"Nothing," she said. "I thought I heard something." She

listened a moment longer, then continued: "The canoe is up the river about fifty yards from the point where the road meets the river. Got that?"

"I think so, but . . ."

"What?"

"Well, I can't paddle back to . . . my place. The current's against me."

She pondered the problem, then said: "There's a Baptist camp about a mile downstream. You'll be safe there." She knelt behind him and began to tug at the ropes around his wrists. "Just make it damn quick and don't look at anybody on your way out. This is women-only space."

"If they see me, though . . . ?"

"You'll be all right," she said soothingly. "We're not all like Rose."

"Is that right?" came a voice outside the tent.

There was no mistaking it, and no mistaking the sculptured scalp which burst into view through the tent flap.

The girl let go of the ropes and spun around to face her superior. "Rose . . ."

"This'll go on my report," said Rose.

"I was just loosening them," said the girl.

"I heard what you were doing."

"Rose, he's an old man."

"So was Mengele," said Rose.

Booter had heard enough. "Listen here, young lady—"

"Don't you call me that!"

"I'll call you anything I want!"

"Rose, we can't legally—"

"Get out, Teejay!"

The girl stood there a moment longer, saying nothing, then muttered under her breath and left.

"Please," Booter told her, "call the police. . . ."

The shaved woman began rummaging noisily through a pile of gear in the corner of the tent. Booter watched as she ripped open a cardboard box, then tore off lengths of masking tape. She leaned over him and clamped something white and gauzy against his mouth, binding it in place with the tape.

His eyes had begun to water a bit, but he could still discern the label on the box: *New Freedom Maxi-pads*.

Mrs. Madrigal's Lament

IT WAS ALMOST NINE O'CLOCK WHEN BRIAN RETURNED TO the cabin on Austin Creek. All he had done was drive, following the coastal highway as far as Elk, then swinging south again in time for dinner in Jenner at the River's End Restaurant. Having spoken to no one except a waitress and an Exxon attendant, he welcomed the prospect of company.

But Michael and Thack were gone. They weren't in the cabin and they weren't by the campfire, and they didn't have a car. Had they walked into Cazadero for dinner?

He lit a fire and tried to get back into *Jitterbug Perfume*, but his mind began to wander. On an impulse, he picked up the phone and called Mrs. Madrigal.

"Madrigal here."

"Hi. It's Brian."

"Oh . . . yes, dear. Are you home?"

"No. We're still here. Just thought I'd check on things."

"Oh . . . well . . . good."

"Has Puppy been a problem?"

"Don't be silly. As a matter of fact . . . Puppy dear, come

say hello to Daddy. Go on. That's right, it's Daddy. Say 'Hello, Daddy.' "

"Hello, Daddy," came a small, familiar voice.

"Hi, Puppy. Have you been good?"

"Yes."

"I miss you a lot."

Silence.

"Do you miss Daddy?"

Silence.

"Puppy?"

Mrs. Madrigal came back on the line. "The telephone throws her. She thinks you should be on TV."

"What do you mean?"

The landlady chuckled. "When Mommy's away, Mommy's on TV. So when Daddy's away . . . well, it makes sense, doesn't it?"

"I suppose."

"She misses you, dear. Take my word for it."

"Is Mary Ann O.K.?"

"Fine," she said evenly. "I haven't seen her that much, but she's been so busy lately. Did you try to reach her at The Summit?"

"No."

"Well, she's at some big gala tonight, but she should be home by ten."

"O.K."

"She was lovely on that Hollywood show. Did you get a chance to watch?"

"No." he said.

"Well, she was . . . very poised. What's the name of that show?"

"Entertainment Tonight," he said.

"Yes. She was just splendid. I'm sure she taped it. You can watch it when you get home."

He couldn't think of anything to say.

"Dear, are you all right?"

"Yeah. Fine."

"No you're not."

"I'm just a little tired tonight."

"Well, put your feet up. Have some chamomile."

"O.K."

"When are you coming home?" she asked.

"Tomorrow."

"Good." She paused. "We lost our appeal, by the way."

"Oh . . . the steps, you mean?"

"Yes."

"What does that mean exactly?"

"Well . . . they tear them down on Monday."

"So soon?" said Brian. "How will we get up to the lane?"

The landlady sighed. "Apparently on some horrid temporary thing. Aluminum. Until the concrete sets." She was quiet for a moment, then added: "It's too awful to contemplate."

He murmured in agreement.

"Am I being silly?"

"No. Not at all."

"You know . . . I sit there with my tea in the morning. The wood gets warm in the sun. The very *feel* of it under my fingers . . ." She sounded like someone remembering a love affair.

He asked: "Couldn't they build a new one in redwood or something?"

"That's exactly what I proposed. They can't be bothered. *Maintenance,* they said."

"Those assholes," said Brian.

"All of life is maintenance, for heaven's sake. That's the *pleasant* part. Taking care of things."

He thought about that for a moment. "Have you spoken to Mary Ann?"

"Yes, but . . . you were right. It's not really suited for her show."

"Maybe so, but she could . . . I dunno . . . talk to the people in News, at least."

"Well, I mentioned that to her, but she said they would need . . . a hook, I believe she called it."

"A hook!" All of a sudden he was mad. "They're tearing down the steps! There's the hook!"

"I know, but . . . she's the professional."

227

"That's for goddamn sure! What does she want you to do? Chain yourself to the steps?"

"Dear . . . calm down."

"Well, she pisses me off sometimes."

Mrs. Madrigal paused. "Why are you so cross with her?"

"I'm not cross with her," he said.

He was back on the sofa, buried in his book, when the phone rang.

"Yeah?"

"Brian?"

"Yeah."

"It's Wren Douglas."

"Oh, yeah."

"If you're wondering about your roomies," she said, "I made off with them."

"Oh. That explains it."

"They asked me to call you. They've gone on a little mission for me."

"They're not there, you mean?"

"No. I'm gonna meet 'em down in Monte Rio in an hour or so. I'm just here, waiting for their call. I thought you might wanna join me."

After a moment's hesitation, he said: "Uh . . . sure. Great."

"We can hang out . . . talk. Whatever."

"Terrific."

"You remember the way?"

"How could I forget?" he said.

Friends Are One Thing

THEIR STOMACHS AGLOW WITH FORBIDDEN FOOD, DEDE and Polly returned to the Halcyon-Wilson campsite, to find Anna reading comic books in her pup tent.

"Hey," said DeDe, "did you cut your quilting class?"

Her daughter shook her head. "We got out early."

"You've been here all alone?"

"Yeah."

DeDe felt a twinge of guilt. "Have you been O.K.?"

"Mom."

"Polly and I just . . . took a walk." She wasn't quite sure why she lied about this, why her trip to the greasy spoon had felt so much like going AWOL. Polly was just as puzzled, apparently, giving DeDe a funny sideways look.

"This lady was looking for you," said Anna, turning back to the ThunderCats.

"When?" asked DeDe.

"Little while ago."

"What sort of lady, Anna?"

The child shrugged, but didn't look up. "A black lady."

"Did she tell you her name?"

"No . . . yeah. Two letters."

"Two letters?" DeDe gave her daughter the evil eye. "Put that down and look at me."

Anna did so begrudgingly. "What?"

"What do you mean, two letters? Was it Teejay?"

"Yeah. Teejay."

"Did she say what she wanted?"

Anna screwed up her face. "She said . . . meet her behind the Womb as soon as possible."

Polly snickered.

DeDe glared at her and turned back to her daughter. "Why, Anna? Did she say?"

"There's gonna be a tri-something."

"A tri-something?"

"A triathalon," said Polly.

"Shut up," DeDe muttered. "A tri*bunal*, Anna?"

"Yeah. That's it."

"I'm supposed to meet her?"

"Yeah. Behind the Womb."

"Dear God."

"What is it?" asked Polly.

"Nothing," said DeDe, her heart rising to her throat.

She left Anna's tent and walked back to her own, Polly nipping at her heels. "C'mon, DeDe, what is it?"

"They're gonna nail me," she said. "They're gonna burn me at the stake."

"*Who?*"

"Rose Dvorak . . . and the rest of 'em."

"I don't get it."

"Teejay *works* for Rose."

"Oh." Polly wrinkled her nose. "So what are they gonna do?"

"I dunno. Whatever they do at tribunals."

"C'mon. They're gonna *try* you? What for? Letting those rednecks in? That was a mistake."

"It isn't just that," said DeDe.

Polly looked at her, slack-mouthed. "What else have you done?"

"It wasn't me. It was this woman named Mabel. I was with her when . . ." She ducked into her tent and collapsed on the sleeping bag.

Polly sat across from her. "When what?"

"It doesn't matter," said DeDe.

"Aren't you gonna see her?"

"Who?"

"This Teejay person."

"No. Hell, no. I'm gettin' outa here first thing in the morning."

"What about . . . you know . . . D'or?"

"What about her?" asked DeDe.

"What if she doesn't wanna leave?"

DeDe shrugged. "She can stay. The kids and I are going."

Polly looked at her wistfully. "What if *I* don't want you to leave?"

"You're sweet," said DeDe. "You're really nice."

Polly slid closer on her denimed butt, then leaned down and gave DeDe a clumsy peck on the mouth. "D'orothea is nuts," she said, her voice turning husky. "I'd be with you all the time."

"Polly . . ."

"All the time."

DeDe backed off a little. "It's not that way when you've been together for a while. Not for anybody."

"I dunno."

"Well, I do."

Polly gave her a crooked grin. "Whatever you say, Deirdre."

This rattled her. "Where did you hear my real name?"

"Anna told me yesterday. When you were swimming."

For some reason, this struck her as vaguely conspiratorial. "She just . . . volunteered that?"

"No. I asked her. I wanna know all there is to know about you."

DeDe fidgeted with the zipper on the sleeping bag.

"I'm really gonna miss you," said Polly.

"And I you." She hated people who said that, but it just tumbled out in her embarrassment.

"Will you come visit me at the nursery sometime?"

"Well . . . D'or does most of the gardening."

"I can call you, can't I?"

DeDe avoided her gaze.

"O.K., forget it."

"Polly . . ." DeDe took her hand. "Friends are one thing. What you want—"

"You don't know what I want."

DeDe chose her words carefully. "Maybe not, but . . . c'mon, I'm a stuffy old married lady."

"I don't care," said Polly.

DeDe drew back. "You're supposed to say I'm not stuffy, I'm not old."

"I like 'em old," said Polly.

DeDe groaned and lobbed a sneaker at her. Polly deflected it, grinning impishly. "O.K.," she said. "I'm outa here."

"No," said DeDe. "Stay and play Pictionary."

"We need three people for that."

"Well . . . practice with me, then."

"Your lover might come back," said Polly.

"So what?" said DeDe. D'or could certainly use a dose of her own medicine. Besides, Rose was on the rampage, and DeDe hated the thought of being alone.

Divine Intervention

FATHER PADDY LED THEM INTO THE WILDERNESS, CHAT-tering incessantly.

"By the way," he said as he charged up a winding trail. "I'm aware the dress is a bit much."

He meant his cassock, obviously, but Michael refrained from comment.

"I wore it for poor Jimmy's memorial service, and I haven't had a *moment* to change. Please don't think me ostentatious."

"No," said Michael.

"Usually," added the cleric, addressing Thack, "I'm content with a simple turtleneck and crucifix—especially at the Grove—but the deceased was a theatrical sort, so I felt a little pageantry was in order."

Michael detected a puckish gleam in the priest's eye. He was testing Thack, apparently, trying out his time-proven shtick on an unwitting neophyte.

"How did he die?" asked Thack.

"Oh, you know . . . the ticker. Happens fairly often here."

"I can imagine," said Thack, dryer than usual for Michael's benefit.

Now well above the floor of the gorge, Father Paddy turned

off the main trail and led them across an elevated boardwalk spanning a dry creekbed. At the end of it lay a tented pavilion, vibrant with lights and laughter. Three or four similar camps were visible beneath them, clinging to the side of the hill.

"Lost Angels," said the priest, gesturing toward the pavilion. "Booter's bound to be here."

"Why do they call it that?" asked Thack.

"Well . . ." Father Paddy leaned closer and spoke from behind his palm, as if imparting a shameful secret. "Some of them are from Los Angeles." He approached a fortyish man near the end of the boardwalk. "Evening, Ollie."

"Evening, padre."

"Haven't seen Booter, have you?"

The man shook his head. "Not since the funeral."

Scanning the revelers in the pavilion, the priest said: "I thought perhaps . . ."

"Look around," said the man. "Help yourself to some chow while you're at it." He turned to Michael and Thack. "You fellows look like you could use a drink."

Michael glanced at Thack.

"Go ahead," urged Father Paddy. "Belly up. That's what it's there for."

"I'll get 'em," said Thack, addressing Michael. "What do you want?"

Michael pondered. "Uh . . . gin and tonic."

Thack turned to the priest. "Father?"

"Oh, thanks, no. I only drink on duty."

Thack grinned and headed for the bar. When he was gone, Father Paddy pulled Michael aside and said: "He is absolutely adorable."

"I know," said Michael.

"Are you two . . . together?"

"Not really."

The priest looked stern. "Don't be coy, my child."

"Well," said Michael, "it hasn't been that long. He's just visiting from South Carolina."

"Oh."

Uncomfortable, Michael glanced around and tried to change the subject. "Do you think maybe Booter . . . ?"

"You look just perfect together."

Michael shrugged.

"Just for the record, I have a marvelous little solemnization ceremony."

"What?"

"It's not a marriage, mind you. The Holy Father will have none of that. But it's a blessing of sorts, and it's very sweet."

"Father."

"All right. I'll shut up. Forget I mentioned it."

"It's a deal," said Michael.

"I've never done one, and I've always wanted to. *But* . . ." His hand made several wistful loops in the air.

"He's going back to Charleston," said Michael.

"Very well."

"And we're both very independent."

"Mmm."

"Plus, you forget . . . I'm not even Catholic."

"Oh, really," said Father Paddy. "Picky, picky!"

Later, when they'd retreated to a bench above Lost Angels, Thack asked: "What do we do now? He's obviously not here."

"It's impossible to tell," said Michael. "There are so many camps."

"Yeah, but we could spend all night looking."

"I guess we should call Wren."

"You think something's happened to him?" Thack asked. "I mean, like . . . foul play?"

"Not really."

"I don't, either."

"I think Wren's overreacting."

"Yeah," said Thack.

They were quiet for a moment, then Thack asked. "What were those eye signals all about?"

"What eye signals?"

"You know. Down there. Between you and Sister Bertrille."

"Oh." Michael rolled his eyes. "You're not gonna believe this."

"Try me."

"He's matchmaking."

Thack gave him a blank look.

"He offered to marry us." Michael widened his eyes to emphasize the frivolous nature of the idea.

"What?"

"To perform the ceremony," said Michael. "Cute, huh?"

Thack frowned a little. "Where did he get that idea?"

"Beats me. He just liked the way we looked together."

Silence.

"I told him we were buddies. That you didn't even live here."

"Here" wasn't right somehow, considering their location. Softened by woodsmoke, the tiny tent villages beneath them seemed more dreamlike than ever. It was hard to imagine *anyone* living here.

"Fuck him," said Thack. "Who needs the church for that?"

His vehemence was a little surprising. "Are you Catholic?" Michael asked.

"Ex. I belonged to Dignity for a while, but I quit."

"Why?"

Thack shrugged. "Why should I keep kissing the Pope's ass when he doesn't even *approve* of mine? I don't call that dignity. I call it masochism." He smiled suddenly. "I've got a great idea."

"What?"

"Wait here." He shook Michael's leg and ran off down the trail, darting into the undergrowth near the lights of Lost Angels. He returned five minutes later, dragging a twin-sized mattress behind him.

"Where did you get that?"

"One of the cabins," said Thack.

Michael frowned.

"An empty one. We'll return it."

"Yeah, but what if . . . ?"

"C'mon," said Thack.

236

*　*　*

Michael followed him up a slope through a tangle of pesky undergrowth. When they reached a ledge about twenty feet above the path, Thack dropped the mattress.

"I wonder if we should be paranoid?" said Michael.

"That's easy," said Thack. "We shouldn't."

"Yeah, but we don't really know how private . . ."

"Look, we can see the path from here. They're too old and drunk to make it up this far." He sat down on the mattress and dug into his shirt pocket, removing a joint and a matchbook.

"Where did you get that?" Michael asked, sitting next to him.

Thack lit the joint. "Wren. Our reward." He toked a couple of times and offered it to Michael.

"No, thanks. . . . Oh, to hell with it." He took the joint and filled his lungs with the stuff. He'd been careful all year. Tonight, his immune system could just go fuck itself.

"Listen," said Thack. " 'The Trail of the Lonesome Pine.' "

"How wonderful." Michael tilted his head to hear pianos and banjos rambling through the old tune.

"That was Gertrude Stein's favorite song," said Thack.

"It was?"

"I think so."

Michael returned the joint. "Where'd you hear that?"

"I don't remember, really."

"It's a great song," said Michael.

Thack stretched out, arching his ivory neck. "Look at that fucking moon. Is that beautiful or what?"

It was full and fluorescent, a real troublemaker. Michael stretched out next to Thack, leaned back on his elbows. There was something supremely sexy about a man who planned ahead like this, who wore his options like a tool belt, ready for any emergency.

Thack took another toke, then stubbed out the joint. He

rolled his head over lazily and gazed at Michael. "I thought this would never happen."

Michael smiled at him.

"You're a great guy," said Thack.

"You too." Michael turned on his side and flicked open the pearly snaps on Thack's denim shirt.

His mouth went straight for the left nipple, pink and proud as a tiny cock.

Afterwards, they lay there motionless, listening to the music. A snail's trail of semen still glimmered on Thack's stomach. He kept his hand cupped gently around Michael's cock, as if it were a wounded bird trying to escape.

Michael said: "Where's a priest when you really need one?"

Thack chuckled and nuzzled Michael's shoulder.

"Was that really Gertrude Stein's favorite song? Did you make that up?"

"Why would I do that?" asked Thack.

"I dunno. To get me in the mood."

"Gertrude Stein is a turn-on?"

"Well . . . it worked for Alice."

"You were already in the mood," said Thack.

"This is true," said Michael.

Further down the gorge, another piano began to play. Joyful male voices floated toward them on the breeze. For some reason, Michael thought of a faded daguerreotype he had seen in an antique shop on Union Street: a dozen lumberjacks with huge mustaches and vintage Levi's, straddling a fallen redwood tree.

"Brian would have loved this," he said.

"Think so?" said Thack.

"Yeah. He's a big kid."

"Like you."

"Yeah. I guess so."

Thack snuggled closer and slid his hand up to Michael's belly. "You're kind of a couple, aren't you?"

"Who?"

"You and Brian."

"Well . . . yeah . . . in some ways."

"How long have you known him?"

Michael thought about it. "Nine years, almost ten."

"Have you always been friends?"

"Not at first," said Michael. "But we . . . you know, swapped stories."

"About what?"

"Oh . . . getting laid."

Thack chuckled.

"He'd come bounding down the stairs after breakfast—he lived on the roof then, so he could see anybody who crossed the courtyard. He'd say something like: 'Michael, my man, how dark was it when you dragged that one home?'"

"Nice guy."

"Oh, I'd get him back. You know . . . tease him about the dog he took to bed. It was just a game."

"Yeah, but . . ."

"O.K., objectifying other people. But it brought us closer, and we never hurt anybody. I loved dishing with him. He loved sex as much as I did."

"Did?" Thack nipped at his ear.

"Do," said Michael, smiling.

"That's better."

"He was a big romantic, really. Mary Ann wouldn't date him for years, because she thought he was such a pig. When he finally fell in love with her, he courted her like crazy. He spilled his guts to me whenever the slightest thing went wrong. Meanwhile, I was having this on-again-off-again thing with my lover, and lots of other people. So Brian and I just kept on coming back to each other."

"I see," said Thack.

"It's funny," said Michael. "When I look back, he was the only constant."

"Mmm."

"He was there in the room with me when my lover died.

Holding my hand." Tears welled up in his eyes, blurring the moon. He wiped them away with two efficient strokes of his fingertips.

"Was it AIDS?" asked Thack.

"Yeah. When Jon got sick, I was so angry, because nobody really gave a fuck. They pretended to be concerned, but these were just faggots dying. They were sick to begin with. I remember thinking . . ." He couldn't find the right words for this.

"What?" asked Thack, stroking his arm.

"Just . . . that nothing would ever happen, no one would ever care until straight people started getting it."

"I know the feeling."

"But I prayed for it. I actually prayed for it."

"You didn't mean it."

"Does that make a difference?" asked Michael.

Nothing Romantic

WREN APPEARED AT THE TOP OF THE STAIRS when Brian parked the VW behind her hilltop chalet. "Bring a few logs," she hollered. "We're almost out."

He looked around him in the dark.

"To the left," she said, pointing. "Next to that bench. There's a woodpile."

He found it and loaded his arms with redwood logs. Most were green enough to be oozing sap, and their weight surprised him, causing him to stagger a little. His clumsiness embarrassed him. He was grateful for the cover of darkness.

When he reached the top of the stairs, he was out of breath. Holding the door for him, Wren said: "Dirty trick, huh? Didn't know you'd have to work."

"No problem," he said, making his way to the fireplace.

"They're so gunky," she said, following him. "I hate getting them, but I adore having a fire."

He dumped the logs on the big stone hearth. "They're awfully green."

"They do O.K.," she said, "once it gets hot enough." She picked up several of the smaller logs and tossed them onto the flames. "Now," she said, brushing off her hands. "A drink, a joint . . . what?"

"I'm fine," he said.

"Sure?"

"Yeah."

She gestured toward an armchair. "Sit down."

He did so, as she curled up on the sofa. She was wearing a pink blouse and white shorts. Her big friendly knees were as pale and round as a couple of honeydew melons. She cocked her head and smiled at him. "I saw your wife on *Entertainment Tonight.*"

"Oh . . . yeah."

"Did you watch it?"

"No."

"She was all right."

"So I heard. My landlady told me. My ex-landlady."

"Did you watch her show the morning I was on?"

No, he thought perversely, but I jerked off to the book. "Actually, I didn't," he said.

"She didn't like me," said Wren.

He nodded. "Sometimes she does that. Just to get a rise out of people."

Wren snorted. "She got one."

He smiled at her. "Good."

She studied him for a while, then rose and plucked a joint from a box on the mantelpiece. She lit it with a kitchen match and returned to the sofa, where she took a toke and held it, observing him again.

"If this is tacky," she said, "tell me."

He shrugged. "Go ahead."

"Do you usually take vacations without your wife?"

He laughed uneasily. "You mean with gay guys?"

"No," she said. "I mean without your wife."

He felt his head jerk reflexively. "I think we both . . . needed a little breather."

"I know just what you mean," she replied.

"You're married?"

"No, but I have a lover."

"Well," he said. "I guess he couldn't exactly go on a book tour with you. . . ."

"The tour was over last week."

"Oh."

"I needed time alone." She smiled mysteriously. "Well, mostly alone."

There was her "friend" again.

"But now," she added, "I really miss Rolando." She took a puff on the joint and held it for a while. "I even miss his snoring."

He chuckled. "You *do* miss him."

"Are you a snorer?"

"Mary Ann," he said. "She's the worst."

"She snores? I love it."

"She'd kill me if she knew I told you."

Wren made a zipping motion across her lips. "And you don't blab to Rolando."

"What could I tell him?"

"Well . . . he thinks I'm still on tour, for starters."

"A-ha." He felt much more at ease now that their conversation involved four people instead of three.

"He'll be all right," she said. "Once I'm home."

He looked at her for a moment, then said: "I wish I could say the same thing."

"She's . . . uh . . . on your case?"

He shook his head. "It isn't her."

"Oh," she said.

"I was seeing this girl. Nothing romantic. Just . . . friends who had sex from time to time."

She smiled sleepily. "I can relate to that."

"She has AIDS," he said.

Wren blinked at him.

"I saw her last week. She looked like someone else."

"Christ." She put the joint down.

"I took the test, but the results won't be back for another week."

"And your wife . . . ?"

"Doesn't know. I couldn't tell her until . . ." He made a lame gesture, unable to finish.

She jumped into the breach. "You're O.K., though. You look just fine."

He shrugged. "My stomach kinda burns. My energy is gone."

"That could be lots of things."

"That's what the doctor said."

"Well, there you go."

An awkward silence followed. Then she asked: "Are you scared?"

He nodded.

"Don't be," she said.

He shrugged again, afraid of crying.

"You're too nice a guy to be hurting."

He couldn't look at her. "Does a nice guy do this to his wife?"

"Hey," she said gently.

"If I've . . . passed it on . . ."

"You haven't. You don't know that."

"If I have, I deserve it."

"Stop that. Shut up. You shouldn't worry about that until . . . God, Brian, worry about yourself. That's who I'm worried about."

He felt himself unraveling. "Look . . . I'm really sorry. I should go."

"Oh, no," she said. "No way. That's hit and run, buster."

"I'm sorry if . . ."

"Come here," she said.

"What?"

"C'mon. Haul that cute ass over here." She patted the cushion next to her on the sofa.

He hesitated, then obeyed her.

She put her arm around him, easing him down until his head reached the expansive softness of her chest. "There," she said, stroking his hair. "Now just shut up for a minute."

When his tears surfaced, she began to rock him gently, humming a tune he couldn't quite place.

D'or Confesses

PICTIONARY PRACTICE HAD OCCUPIED DEDE AND POLLY for almost an hour. DeDe had performed like a champ until Polly sketched a standing figure, with another figure stretched out on a table. DeDe had tried "doctor," "mortician," and "masseuse," to no avail.

"C'mon," said Polly.

"What else is there?" asked DeDe.

Polly groaned and drew a huge penis on the standing figure.

"Masseur!" DeDe shouted.

"Yes!"

They shrieked in unison.

DeDe said: "Call Kate and Trudy. I'm ready for the play-offs!"

They were still giggling maniacally when DeDe heard footsteps advancing through the madrone trees. The gait was unmistakably D'or's.

DeDe made herself wait for a count of ten, then turned and said, "Oh, hi," as casually as possible.

"Hi," echoed D'or. Her voice was flat as day-old Diet Pepsi.

"You've met Polly Berendt, haven't you?"

D'or shook her head. "Not officially." She nodded in Polly's direction but didn't extend her hand.

"I was just leaving," said Polly.

"No," said DeDe. "Stay. We'll make some cocoa." She turned back to D'or. "How was the Holly Near concert?"

"I didn't go," said D'or, stonier than ever.

Polly rose and slapped the seat of her jeans, knocking off the sand. "Past my bedtime," she said.

This time DeDe didn't bother to protest. "Thanks for the evening," she said feebly.

"No sweat," Polly replied, heading off into the dark.

D'or sat down on the sand, but didn't speak until Polly's footsteps had died out. "Sorry," she said grimly, "if I interrupted something."

"You're one to talk," said DeDe.

D'or stared out at the water for a while. Then she said: "I stopped off and saw Edgar."

"How was he?"

"Fine. He really likes it there."

"I know," said DeDe.

"He told me I couldn't come in. Said it was men-only space." D'or smiled at this, obviously trying to break the ice.

DeDe refused to thaw.

"They have their own hierarchy already. Little lieutenants running around. It's really funny."

DeDe grunted.

D'or turned and looked at her. "You wanna leave tomorrow?"

"I'm planning to."

"Good. I think it's time." She looked around. "Where's Anna?"

"Asleep," said DeDe.

D'or untied the laces on one of her sneakers, tightened and retied them. "Why are you doing this?"

"Doing what?"

"You know."

DeDe resisted a sudden urge to slap her. Why was she, DeDe, always the one whose behavior required explanation?

D'or added: "She's gone. If that's what's bothering you."

"She?" asked DeDe. There was no point in making it easy for her.

"Sabra."

DeDe muttered.

"You were right about her. She's a big phony."

It took some effort to conceal her relief. "How did you come to *this* brilliant conclusion?"

"I just saw," said D'or.

"Oh, yeah?"

"She was looking to get laid."

"Well . . . did she?"

D'or hesitated, then nodded.

"I see," said DeDe. "And then she left?"

Another nod.

"Just . . . wham, bam, thank you, ma'am."

D'or played with the sand under her legs. "Laugh all you want. I deserve it."

DeDe kept quiet.

Her lover looked truly pathetic. "For what it's worth, I really did think it was my mind she admired. I thought she respected my input."

Two minutes earlier, DeDe could have fired off a pithy rejoinder to that one. "Well," she said instead. "Maybe she really did."

D'or shook her head. "It was like . . . shut-up-and-lie-down time."

DeDe abandoned the role of hurt child and assumed the mantle of mother confessor. "I knew she was a shitheel," she said.

"I couldn't believe it," said D'or. "We'd just come back from a Holocaust workshop."

DeDe felt a smile flicker at the corner of her mouth.

"I was so mortified I just went through with it. I don't know why. I really don't know why." She paused a moment, throwing a pebble into the river. "I guess I wanted to show her there was . . . something I could do better than her."

Than *she,* thought DeDe.

"She was so *cold* afterwards. Like she'd been humoring me all along."

DeDe thanked God for making Sabra Landauer such a callous, manipulative and thoroughly undependable person.

D'or patted the sand between her legs. "I wish I'd finished college."

DeDe slipped her arm around D'or's waist. "C'mon . . ."

"I do. I feel so dumb sometimes."

"D'or . . . you made several hundred thousand dollars before you were twenty-five. You traveled, you met people. . . ."

"Yeah, but I don't know anything. I'm really illiterate."

"Come off it. Just because Sabra was so tacky as to . . . Listen, have you actually ever read *Medusa at the Prom*?"

"No."

"Well, I have," she said, telling D'or the same lie she'd told Sabra. "It's just plain awful. It's trite and . . . lugubrious."

"See?" said D'or. "I don't even know what that means."

"Ohhh." DeDe gave her a little shove.

D'or shoved her back, pinning her against the sand. "I love you so much," she said.

"You're a mess," said DeDe.

"Maybe."

"Definitely."

"O.K." She leaned down and gave DeDe a kiss. "I'm sorry. I'm really sorry."

"Can we get out of here tomorrow?"

"First thing," said D'or. "Do you forgive me?"

"Ask me tomorrow," said DeDe.

"Where did you go tonight?"

"Into town," said DeDe, "where I consumed mass quantities of animal flesh."

"Oh."

"And I don't want any grief."

"You won't get any from me," said D'or.

In a burst of hideous insight, DeDe realized the depth of her commitment to this marriage.

She had just traded adultery for a cheeseburger and an order of french fries.

The Littlest Pallbearers

SOMEWHERE OUT THERE IN THE DARKNESS, A CREATURE was skittering through the underbrush. It sounded larger than a rabbit or raccoon, but it seemed to move in fits and starts, as if pausing for reconnaissance. It was joined, eventually, by an identical sound on the other side of the tent.

What now? thought Booter. Should he attract attention or not? He could thrash about, maybe, make the tent move, create some sort of sound in his throat. What if it was just the bulldagger again? She could make things even worse for him.

"Cuckoo," came a call from the darkness.

"Cuckoo," came the reply.

Not a bird sound, but a human one.

Children?

He tilted his head to listen.

"Wait there," whispered one of them.

"Where?" asked the other.

"You know . . . where I said."

"Well, how come you get . . . ?"

"Just shuddup. I told you I'm Platoon Leader. What did you get?"

There was a rustling of paper.

"Big deal. Another granola bar. Gag me."

"Look, she almost saw me."

"Well . . . so? You volunteered for this duty."

"Yeah, but I don't—"

"Just shuddup . . . and keep your head down. I'll meet you back here in three minutes."

Moments later, he heard someone ease open the big zipper on the tent. A thin electric beam searched the space, splashing light on the orange polyester walls. He arched his neck and came face to face with a boy of eight or nine, fat-cheeked and ginger-haired.

Booter groaned at him and made a thrashing motion. The boy's jaw went slack. For a moment, before he dropped the flashlight, his startled face became a levitating jack-o'-lantern, comic yet terrible in its intensity.

Then he ran away.

Booter kept groaning through the gag.

He heard the boy go yelping through the underbrush like a scalded pup. Then the silence closed in again, and he was left panting and sore, indignant in defeat. What the hell was the matter with the stupid brat?

Then the voices came back.

"If you're lying, Philo . . ."

"I'm not. I swear. His face was like . . . the Mummy or somethin'."

"Oh, sure."

"I swear."

"Which tent?"

"That one."

"You better not be lying. I'll report you to the Brigadier." Only slightly less terrified than Philo, the tough one seemed to be stalling for time.

Booter awaited them in silence. Moaning and twisting would only scare them off again.

The tent flap opened. Another beam, this one brighter than the last, found its way to Booter's tape-wrapped head.

He decided to wiggle a little, just to show them he was alive.

"See?" said the redheaded boy. He was standing next to the flashlight-wielder, his eyes big as quarters, his jaw even slacker than before. "Maybe they're holdin' him captive, huh?"

"Who?"

"I dunno. The chem-frees or somebody."

The boy with the flashlight steadied the beam on Booter's face, blinding him momentarily.

The redhead added: "He could be really dangerous."

There was no reply from the other boy. He knelt and leaned forward slowly to examine Booter's features.

Booter blinked several times, then beheld the familiar face of a handsome half-breed child. When their eyes met, the boy made an expression like a clenched fist and leaned even closer. "Booter?" he said.

Just as amazed, Booter uttered a grunt and nodded.

The boy turned to his henchman. "It's Booter," he said.

"Who?"

"He's married to Gangie. My mom's mom."

"He's your granddad?"

"No, booger-brain. He's married to my mom's mom. That doesn't make him my—"

Groaning indignantly, Booter cut him off.

"You better do somethin'," said the redhead.

Edgar tugged a piece of tape off Booter's cheek. It stung like hell. He made a sound to say so.

"Be careful," said the redhead.

Seizing another piece of tape, Edgar tugged more gently this time, until the whole sticky webbing, gag included, came away from his face. He gulped air and licked his parched lips.

"You O.K.?" asked Edgar.

He nodded, still filling his lungs. Then he said: "Where's your mother?"

"At her camp," the boy replied.

"Where's that?"

"Down by the river."

"Get her for me."

Edgar shook his head gravely.

"Why not?"

"It's women-only space."

"What?" It was a madhouse, this place, pure and simple. "What the hell are you talking about?"

"I can't go," the boy said earnestly. "They won't let me."

"Untie me, then. Help me, you little idiot! Don't just stand there!"

The redhead frowned and peered at Edgar for the final word. Edgar, in turn, gnawed on his fingernail and pondered. "Did you do something bad?" he asked.

"No," thundered Booter. "Of course not!"

"We better go," the redhead told Edgar. "Somebody's gonna come back and—"

"No," Booter blurted. "Don't go. Just untie my hands."

Wrinkling his brow again, Edgar began to pick ineffectually at the knot.

"Hurry up," said Booter.

"I can't. It won't untie."

"Find a knife, then."

The redheaded accomplice tugged on Edgar's sleeve. "I'm gettin' outa here."

Edgar kept his eyes on Booter. "If you didn't do anything wrong, how come they tied you up?"

"I fell asleep in a canoe, Edgar. It drifted ashore. They tied me up because I'm a man."

The boy bit his lower lip.

For emphasis, Booter added: "I swear."

Edgar studied his step-grandfather a moment longer, then grabbed the redhead's arm as he tried to leave. "Philo," he barked, "get Jackson and Berkowitz and the two Zacks. Tell 'em I need 'em here. On the double."

"Hey, Edgar, I'm not—"

"On the double!"

253

"Isn't there a knife?" asked Booter.

Edgar shook his head. "We'll get you outa here. Don't worry."

As the other boy scrambled into the night, Edgar squatted on his haunches next to Booter's head. "You wanna sit up?" he asked.

"Yes, son. Please."

The boy helped him into a sitting position, propping bed-rolls behind his back. When he was done, he searched his blue quilted jacket until he found a chocolate bar. Breaking off a piece, he said: "Want some?"

"Please," said Booter, opening his mouth for the proffered chunk. Its dark sweetness tasted sacramental on his tongue. When it was gone, he said: "When will they be back?"

"Not long. Few minutes."

"Those women could come back at any time."

"I know." Edgar patted his shoulder. "Don't worry, O.K.?" He looked at Booter gravely, then plopped down next to him against the bedrolls. "Hey," said the boy, brightening. "What's blue and creamy?"

Booter looked at him, utterly confused.

"It's a riddle," said the boy. "Guess."

"Edgar, this is no time—"

"C'mon," urged Edgar. "What's blue and creamy?"

"I told you . . . no!"

Edgar looked crestfallen for a moment, then broke off another chunk of chocolate. "Want some more?" he asked.

"Yes," said Booter evenly. Like taking candy from a baby, he thought bitterly.

Edgar fed it to him in small pieces this time, licking his fingers when he was through. "Is your canoe still down there?" he asked.

"I don't know," said Booter.

"Where did you come from?"

Booter thought for a moment, then said: "The Bohemian Grove. Has your mother told you about that?"

"I don't think so," said Edgar.

"It's sort of a camp. Your grandfather Halcyon used to belong."

"I was named for him," said Edgar.

"Yes . . . exactly." The boy was quick, at least.

"What do you guys do?"

"Where?" asked Booter.

"At your camp."

Booter wet his parched lips. "Well . . . we talk a lot. We go to plays, concerts. Read books."

Edgar screwed up his face. "It's a camp?"

Booter nodded. "More or less. Look . . . are you sure your friends are coming back?"

"Positive. Was my grandfather your best friend?"

"Yes, he was."

"Who's your best friend now?"

Booter took the easy way out. "Well, of course, your grandmother and I . . . Gangie . . ."

"No," said Edgar. "Girls don't count."

Booter hesitated. "I guess I don't have a best friend right now."

The boy looked concerned. "Why not?"

Booter felt an unexpected little stab of pain. "What are you doing here, anyway? Pinching candy?"

Edgar's eyes narrowed.

"I won't tell them," said Booter.

"It's just a game."

"I know. Don't worry, son. We're on the same side."

Philo returned breathless, with four other boys in tow.

"Who brought the knife?" asked Edgar.

No one had.

"Goddamnit," Booter muttered.

"O.K.," said Edgar, "here's the deal. We carry him back to the compound."

"Sure," said one of them.

"It's easy," said Edgar. "We spread out this sleeping bag, and we put him on it, and we each grab some of it . . . three to a side."

Booter didn't like it. "Wait a minute . . ."

"We gotta," said Edgar, checking his watch. "The concert's almost over."

"What concert?"

"C'mon, Zack . . . gimme a hand. You other guys wait outside."

Edgar and Zack seized Booter under the arms and pulled him over to the sleeping bag. Then they dragged the bag out into the open air, where the other boys were already in position, ready for the hoist.

"Hey, Edgar," said Philo, "what if he hops instead?"

Edgar groaned. "He's an old guy, numbnuts. He can't hop."

Booter didn't argue. He was an old guy, all right. Hopping was out of the question.

Edgar surveyed his henchmen. "Jackson, swap places with Zack Two. He's stronger."

"He is not," said Jackson.

"Just shuddup," said Edgar. "O.K. . . . Lift when I say so. One . . . two . . . three . . . *lift.*"

As he ascended, Booter gazed up at six intent little faces and thought of them suddenly as his pallbearers.

"Where are we going?" he asked Edgar.

"Back to Brother Sun."

"Where?"

"The boys' compound. Brother Sun."

The boys began to walk, carrying him perilously close to the ground. The darkness was almost total; the terrain seemed strewn with obstacles. There were rocks and spongy spots, impenetrable thickets, prickly branches that swooped down without warning, thrashing the boys like vindictive schoolmarms.

"Is it far?" asked Booter.

"No," said Edgar.

One of the boys broke stride, then stumbled.

"Philo!" barked Edgar. "Stop spazzing out."

"I heard something," said Philo.

"Big homo," said someone else.

"I did. Hold up, you guys."

Amidst groans of protest, the boys came to a halt, still

256

holding Booter aloft. He could see the moon through the trees and not much else, but he didn't move for fear of upsetting the balance of their cargo.

The woods seemed quiet enough. An owl or two. Guitars and voices in the distance, dim and harmless.

"It's nothing," said Edgar. "What did you think it was? The boogeywoman?"

The other boys shared a laugh at poor Philo's expense as Booter's magic-carpet ride began anew, faster this time. They seemed to be going down a slight incline, and the foliage had grown more sparse.

"How much further?" asked Booter.

"Not far," said Edgar, puffing a little.

"What is this place, anyway?"

"What place?"

"Here. This camp. These . . . ladies."

"Wimminwood," said Philo, obviously eager to redeem himself.

"Aren't there any men here?"

Philo said: "You're lookin at 'em."

Philo's tormentor snorted derisively. "Big homo."

"Zack, shut up," said Edgar, slowing their pace a little. "I think I heard something."

"Now he hears it," muttered Philo.

"What the hell?" came a voice from the darkness. It was growly and female.

The boys shot panicked glances at one another and began to trot. Booter winced as the sleeping bag banged against a protruding stump.

"Stop right there," bellowed the voice.

"We'd better stop," whispered Zack.

"No way," said Edgar, picking up speed.

From Booter's viewpoint, the moon was caroming crazily off the treetops. Vertigo overwhelmed him, so he shut his eyes and set his jaw and waited for the worst. Their nemesis was so close he could hear her lumbering Sasquatch gait, the sound of her labored breathing.

One of the middle boys deserted his post, hightailing it into the woods.

257

"Hey," called Edgar, his reedy voice full of anger and despair.

The boy next to Edgar stumbled, dropping Booter's legs. The whole flimsy mechanism jerked rudely to a halt and Booter was deposited on the ground, his fall somewhat softened by the sleeping bag.

Another boy fled. Then another. Only Edgar was left, staring down into his step-grandfather's stunned face. "Get outa here," said Booter, giving the boy the absolution he sought. "You did your best."

Edgar regarded him gravely for a moment, then darted off into the forest. The same faint scampering sounds that had marked the arrival of this band now betrayed its departure. Booter swallowed hard and tried to right himself.

The growly voice said: "What the hell?"

Turning his head, he saw a short, heavyset woman emerge from the underbrush. She approached him warily, raking her fingers through the short gray hair over her ears. Even from here, he could tell she was drunk.

"Please," Booter began, "can you help me?"

She inched forward and regarded him in a pitcher's squat, legs spread, hands clamped on her knees. Her mouth hung slack for a moment before she said: "Well . . . if that don't beat all!"

"I won't hurt you," he said.

"Hurt me?" She threw back her head and hooted. Her voice was raspy with nicotine and whiskey. "Oh, yeah . . . please don't do that." Laughing again, she was seized by a sudden coughing jag, which threw her off balance and sent her tumbling ingloriously to the ground.

She rose slowly, but only to a sitting position. "Damn," she said.

He licked his lips and swallowed. "If you help me, I'll pay you anything. . . ."

"Who the hell are you?"

He remembered what had happened the last time he used his name. "I came down the river," he told her. "By canoe. I fell asleep, and I—"

"Who did this?"

He hesitated. "I don't know. She hit me on the head first. Look, I haven't done anything. . . ."

"She just tied you up and left your ass?"

"Yes."

"You see her? What'd she look like?"

He decided to risk the truth. "Her head was shaved. In patterns."

"Oh, hell." Catching her breath, she rose falteringly to her feet. "O.K. Ol' Mabel better get her ass in gear. . . ."

"No," he said, "please don't go."

"Sit tight," she answered, hulking away into the night.

Passions

I N THE KITCHEN AT WREN'S LODGE, BRIAN WAS POURING juice into Flintstones glasses. He bounced around jauntily, with self-conscious aplomb, like a television chef confronting his first national audience. Why, Wren wondered, do men always retreat a little after sex or confession?

"You think the guys got lost in there?" he asked. She had told him about Booter's disappearance, about their shack-up arrangement, even about the check Booter had left for her. One confession had seemed to merit another.

"Maybe it's a black hole," she said, leaning against the doorway.

"Yeah. Sort of a Bohemian Triangle." He handed her a glass of juice.

"You and Michael are pretty close, aren't you?"

"Yeah."

"I thought so."

"Why?"

"Well . . . he told me to call you, for one thing."

"When? Tonight?"

"When else?" Seeing his expression, she added: "I would've done it anyway."

"Did he tell you about . . . ?"

"No. Nothing." She looked him squarely in the eye to assure him that his revelation had, in fact, been a revelation.

The phone rang. "There they are," she said, setting her glass on the counter, heading into the living room.

"This better be you," she said.

"It is," said Michael. "Are we that late?"

"No. Never mind. Did you find him?"

"No. Not a sign."

She heaved a sigh. "Did they say if he'd gone home?"

"We asked at the gate," said Michael. "He hasn't checked out yet."

"He must be there, then."

"I guess so, but the place is like a small city."

She nibbled on a nail. "It just doesn't make sense. Why wouldn't he call me?"

"You got me," said Michael. "I don't know the man."

But I do, she thought, and something is horribly wrong. She imagined him lying dead somewhere in the dark, victim of a heart attack. Or suicide. His last phone call, after all, had been inexplicably forlorn, tinged with desperation.

"You tried his camp?" she asked.

"Yeah. And a bunch of the others. Nobody's seen him since this morning, when he went to a memorial service."

"Somebody died?"

"A friend of his," said Michael. "You think that's got something to do with it?"

"God . . . I dunno."

He waited, then said: "What do you want us to do?"

"Are you at the greasy spoon?"

"No. We're still in the Grove."

"Are you swimming back?" She was teasing, of course.

"Oh, please. Nothing but the gate this time. We're practically members."

"They like you, huh?"

Michael chuckled. "Thack got cruised by a priest."

She heard Thack laughing in the background. "I'll bet he did," she said.

"People keep pouring us drinks, inviting us in. It's amazing what just having a dick can do for you."

"Tell me," she said. "I haven't had one lately."

Another chuckle. "Poor thing."

"Never mind. I can cope."

"You'll be home to Rolando in no time."

That threw her. "How do you know about him?"

"You talked about him," he answered. "On the air. Mary Ann's show."

"Oh, yeah. A girl's got no secrets."

He laughed. "Not when the girl sells them."

"Fuck you," she said. "I'll meet you in half an hour at the greasy spoon."

"Fine," he said. "Is Brian with you?"

"None of your business," she replied, and hung up.

"Who died?" asked Brian.

"Died? Oh . . . a friend of Booter's."

He frowned, taking it personally.

"I'm not gonna worry about it," she said. "I've worried enough."

On the way into Monte Rio, Brian said: "You're flying out tomorrow?"

She nodded, pulling on the wheel. They were rounding a treacherous curve, drastically eroded on one side, obscured on the other by an almost perpendicular slope of dusty ferns. She knew it well, this curve. She had been here long enough for it to seem grimly familiar.

"I'm leaving," she said. "Come hell or high water."

He stared out the window for a moment, then asked: "Would you like company tonight?"

She turned and smiled at him.

"Just to cuddle," he said. "I really don't feel like . . ."

"I know. Shut up. Give me credit for a little versatility."

His eyes turned back to the road. "What about . . . you know . . . Booter?"

"What about him?" she asked.

"Well . . . if he comes back tonight."

She chuckled. "He doesn't *sleep* with me, sweetie."

"Oh."

"I'm just his afternoon delight. He sleeps with his buddies. Back at the Grove."

"I see."

"I'm just pleasure. The Grove is his passion." The road became asphalt finally, and there were random yellow porch lights to lead the way. "What about you?" she asked. "What are your passions?"

He seemed to think it was a trick question.

"What do you do?" she asked. "I know what your wife does, of course. . . ."

He looked more stricken than before.

"Sorry," she said. "That was grossly un-Californian of me."

"No," he said finally, "it's O.K. I take care of our daughter. I manage the house."

"Well, that's a lot." It sounded patronizing, she realized, and it was. The man thinks he's dying, so she reminds him he has no purpose in life.

"It's not a lot," he said quietly.

"Raising a child? Are you kidding?"

"It's not enough." He gazed out at the lights of Monte Rio. "It's not . . . a manhood thing with me. It just isn't enough. It used to be all I ever wanted . . . having a kid, being a husband." He turned and looked at her. "I was a lawyer once. Does that count?"

She laughed, determined to keep it light. "What I meant was . . . what are your hobbies?"

He didn't seem to hear her. "The person I really envy is Michael."

"Why?"

He shrugged. "He loves his job. He's outdoors a lot, not

263

shuffling paper. He makes stuff grow." Another shrug. "Seems like a good life."

"You have a good life," she said.

"Do I?" he asked.

The Wayward RV

BRANDISHING A HUGE SERRATED HUNTING KNIFE, THE gray-haired woman had returned. She knelt by Booter's inert body and began sawing at the ropes around his wrists. "Dvorak did a job on this," she said, breathing heavily.

"Yes," was all he could manage.

He rubbed his wrists and swung his arms while she went to work on his legs. "I brought my Winnebago around," she said, "but we gotta haul ass. It ain't s'posed to be here."

When she'd pulled free the last bit of rope, he tried to stand up. His knees were exceptionally weak, but they did the job. He sucked in air and stretched his arms. The next signal he received was from his bladder.

"I'm sorry," he said. "Would you mind . . . I haven't been able . . ."

"Go over there," she said, getting the message. "I won't look. You think I wanna see that ol' thing?"

When he was done, she led the way through a thicket to a narrow dirt road where a green RV was parked. He climbed into the front seat, sinking gratefully into the embrace of its cracked green vinyl.

"Get in back," said the woman.

"What?"

"We're gonna pass the gate. Get in back and keep your head down."

He did as he was told.

"If there's trouble," she added, "I can handle it. I'm packin' heat."

She pointed to an unmade bunk and laughed. There, amidst the zebra-patterned sheets, lay a gleaming steel crossbow.

"Hold on," he said.

"Joke," she said, starting the engine. She gazed at him over her shoulder and winked. "You're gullible, aren't you? What's your name?"

"Uh . . . Roger."

"Mine's Mable," she said, handing him a pint of Jack Daniel's. "Be my guest, Roger."

He accepted without protest. The whiskey stung his throat like iodine, then seeped into his aching limbs, warming them. He wiped off the bottle on the sleeve of his Viyella shirt and handed it back to her.

"Take another," she said.

"No, thank you."

"Go on. If Dvorak didn't kill you, a little Jack Daniel's sure as hell won't."

It reassured him to learn that his captor had such a reputation for heinousness. His subjugation had been the work of a mastermind, at least, not just some random woman. He returned the bottle to his cracked lips and took another swig.

"Who is she?" he asked, handing back the bottle.

"Security chief," she said. "They're all alike."

His knowledge of female security chiefs was woefully deficient.

"I believe in law and order," she added. "I voted for Reagan. But Dvorak is something else." She swatted the air in his direction, her eyes still fixed on the road.

"What?" he asked.

"Get down!" she ordered darkly. "The gate."

He flattened out on the shag-carpeted floor. There were

266

cigaret butts amidst the shag. Dust balls the size of gophers.
A Debbie Reynolds album. His heart beat wildly.

Someone outside the RV said: "You checking out?"

Mabel said: "Nah. Takin' her for a spin."

"It's a little late, isn't it?"

"Listen, girlie," said Mabel. "Don't mess with me."

Somewhat more meekly, the guard said: "Well, it's not like
it's a car."

"You through?" asked Mabel.

"Go ahead," said the guard.

The RV lurched when Mabel hit the gas. "Stupid spic," she
muttered.

Booter pressed against the yarny carpet to keep his equilib-
rium. They had reached asphalt and were barreling along at
a disarming speed.

"C'mon up," called Mabel. "It's over."

Grabbing the side of the bunk, he hoisted himself to a
sitting position. "You're going awfully fast," he said.

"Nah," she said. "Jus' seems that way from back there."

He rose on uncertain legs and hunched his way to the front,
collapsing into the seat. The scrubby moonlit landscape flew
past them like a painting on a freight train. It was freedom,
he supposed, but a shaky one at best.

"Where to?" asked Mabel.

How, he wondered suddenly, would he explain this vehicle
to the gatekeeper at the Grove? "Uh . . . Monte Rio," he told
her, resigning himself to another half mile on foot.

"You got it," she said, unscrewing the top on the whiskey.

They thundered down the deserted road in silence, civil
strangers sharing only a time and a place. He did his damnedest not to notice their speed, which was considerable, or
Mabel's expression, which was just this side of maniacal.

"You voted for Reagan?" he asked eventually.

"Damn straight."

"Then . . . you're a conservative?"

"Always have been. Hate welfare, hate communism, hate
all that stuff."

It made no sense to him. "But . . . that place?"

"What?" she asked. "Wimminwood?"

"Yes. It's . . . leftist, isn't it?"

She shrugged. "Mostly."

"Why do you go?"

Mabel gave a little snort. "That's easy. Pussy."

He was almost certain he had heard wrong until she began to guffaw exuberantly, slapping the dashboard with her flattened palm. When she turned to see his reaction, she lost control of the wheel, and he heard the sickening clatter of gravel as the RV slipped onto the shoulder.

"Watch out!" he hollered.

Her reaction wasn't nearly quick enough. The RV leapt a narrow ditch, then ripped through a curtain of brambles, plummeting willy-nilly into the darkness.

His hands shot to the dashboard. He gritted his teeth as she slammed on the brakes and the RV skidded to a stop in the underbrush.

"Good God," he murmured.

"Holy shit," said Mabel.

The RV was tilting dramatically, its two right wheels lower than the left.

"You O.K.?" she asked.

"Yes . . . I'm O.K." If she had been his wife, he would have yelled at her, but she was his rescuer, and a man doesn't yell at his rescuer.

She climbed down from the RV and inspected the damage. "It's gonna take Three-A," she said, returning. "Sonofabitch." She shook her head slowly, obviously annoyed with herself. "That's what I get for thinking about pussy."

He took the whiskey from the dashboard and offered it to her. Mabel accepted with a weary grunt, unscrewing the cap. "Ever have one of those days?" she asked.

"Yes," he answered dryly, feebly. "Yes, I have."

She blinked at him with red-rimmed eyes and began to chuckle. "Yeah, I guess so," she said, and took a swig of the whiskey, smacking appreciatively. Then she gave it back to him.

This time he tipped the bottle like a seasoned wino. "You on vacation?" she asked.

He nodded. "Supposedly."

"Yeah. Me too."

"Where are you from?" he asked.

"Tacoma," she said.

"Ah." There wasn't much he could say about Tacoma. He'd never even been there.

Mabel filled the silence by taking another nip from the bottle. When she had finished, she said: "Well, better get our tails in gear. There's a phone down at Duncans Mills. It's not all that far. You can wait here." She slapped the dashboard. "Keep an eye on the ol' girl."

Booter heard her, but just barely. His glazed eyes drifted toward the moon, which was dangling like an off-kilter ornament in the broken branches above the windshield. The night was uncannily still. He couldn't remember when he'd last felt so alone with someone.

"You O.K.?" she asked.

"Yes," he answered quietly.

She regarded him for a moment, then said: "That's Venus. The big, shiny one under the moon. The Greeks called it Lucifer in the daytime and Hesperus at night."

This odd footnote, imparted tersely and without provocation, reminded him instantly of someone else. Even the light in her eyes was right, the half-mad, tutorial glint which awaited his response like a child who had just told a favorite joke.

"You know much about that stuff?" he asked.

She squared her jaw in an eerily familiar fashion. "Nah. I watch that guy . . . whatshisname . . . the billions-and-billions man."

He nodded. "I know who you mean."

"Why the hell are you doin' that?"

"What?"

"Lookin' at me funny."

"I'm sorry," he said. "You reminded me of somebody. Just briefly."

"Who?"

"It's ridiculous. Somebody who knows a lot about . . . outdoor things. Knew, that is." He was embarrassed now; she was bound to take it the wrong way. "It's not a physical resemblance. He just enjoyed . . . explaining things."

Her brow wrinkled. "He's dead now?"

"Yes," he answered vacantly, feeling oddly relieved to be able to say it. "Last night."

She scratched her arm, staring at him.

"He was my best friend," said Booter, realizing how curious it sounded to him. He had never told Jimmy as much. Why was he telling her?

Mabel looked puzzled. "He was traveling with you?"

"No. We're members of the same . . . camp." He was wary of explaining Bohemia to a woman, even to one who'd befriended him. So far it had brought him nothing but trouble.

"Here?" she asked.

"Yes."

"He died at camp?"

He nodded. "During a play."

Sympathizing, Mabel shook her head dolefully. "Just sittin' there, huh?"

"No. He was performing in the play."

"What was it about?"

"Uh . . . the Red Cross, actually."

"I remind you of him?"

"Well . . . his spirit."

"What was he like?"

He thought for a moment, discarding any adjectives that might be loaded. "Well . . . interested in nature. Adventurous."

"Wild-ass," she said.

"Yeah." He smiled a little. "That too."

"So you got drunk, huh? And you passed out in that canoe."

He nodded in resignation.

"Then your poor ol' white ass just drifted on down into Lezzieland."

What was this woman's story?

"You get drunk much?" she asked, plucking a pack of Trues from the dashboard.

"No," he said.

"I do. I like it." She poked a cigaret into her mouth, then

flicked her Bic. Her red-veined face flared up in the darkness. "So," she asked, holding in smoke, "how did you like them dykes?"

He looked out the window to compose an answer. "It wasn't what I felt," he said at last. "What I felt had nothing to do with anything."

She nodded gravely. "I know what you mean." Holding the cigaret with her thumb and forefinger, she offered it to him.

"No, thanks," he said.

"Did you and your buddy live together?"

"No," he replied. "He lived in Denver."

"Huh?"

"It wasn't like that," he said. "I have a wife."

She narrowed her eyes a little, then asked: "Where do you live?"

"Hillsborough," he said.

"If he was your best friend"—smoke curled out of her and hovered overhead like a question mark—"when the hell did you see him?"

"Here," he said impatiently. "At the camp."

"How often?"

"Once a year."

"For how long?"

He thought about it. "Four or five days, usually. For twenty-seven years."

How many days did that make in all? As many as six months' worth? No, not even that many.

Mabel seemed to be doing the same arithmetic. "Was it mutual?" she asked.

"What do you mean?"

"Were you his best friend?"

He didn't look at her. "No. Probably not."

She nodded. "Never told him, huh?"

"No."

Another nod. Another drag off her cigaret. "Doesn't matter," she said.

"No. I guess not."

"It's just words," she said. "Doesn't matter." She stubbed

out the cigaret in a beanbag ashtray. "What kinda candy bars you like?"

"What?"

"There's a machine up in Duncans Mills."

"Oh . . . nothing, thanks."

"I'll be back in half an hour." She gave his knee a jovial shake. "Doesn't matter," she said.

She climbed out and made her way up to the highway, puffing noisily, cursing every villainous branch that got in her way.

Rearrangements

STILL ON FOOT, MICHAEL AND THACK CROSSED THE graceless iron bridge at Monte Rio and made their way to the greasy spoon. Ten minutes earlier, the midnight audience at the Rio Theater had been released from *Giant*. Now the movie-goers stood in circles, jabbering, like patrons at a cockfight.

When they entered the restaurant, Wren waggled her nails to get their attention. Brian was with her, looking a little sheepish.

"You're back in one piece," Brian said.

To confirm this, Michael held out his hands in a beatific pose. "How was your drive?" he asked.

"Great," said Brian.

"Sit down," said Wren.

Thack slipped into the booth next to Wren, leaving the spot next to Brian for Michael.

"What was the Grove like?" asked Brian.

"Beautiful," said Michael, "but weird."

"Too straight for you?"

"Too white," said Thack, frowning at a menu. "You guys eaten yet?"

"I ate here earlier," said Wren. "And I wouldn't recommend it."

"I'm starving, for some reason." Thack gave Michael a devilish sideways glance.

It wasn't lost on Wren, Michael noticed. "Go ahead," she said. "Eat. You've earned it."

"We ate at the Grove," said Michael. "We noshed our way through the place."

"You're right," said Thack, abandoning the menu.

"The coffee's O.K." said Wren.

"Actually," said Michael, "we just wanna crash. If you could drive us back to the cabin . . ."

"Fine," said Wren. "Your car is at my place, so we'll just all go back there."

"Oh . . . right," said Michael.

There was room here for a cheap shot, but the look in Wren's eyes told him not to take it.

In the car, she said: "I have a limo coming tomorrow, guys. I'd love company."

Thack said: "I thought you were going to the airport."

"Yeah, but we have to go through the city, anyway."

The prospect seduced Michael for a second or two, until he remembered. "What are we gonna do with the VW?"

"Oh, yeah," said Wren. "That's right."

"I could drive it," said Brian.

Wren gave him a funny look.

"No way," said Michael. "That's really nice, but . . ."

"Really," said Brian. "I like driving alone. I'd be glad to." He shrugged. "I've been in a limo. You seen one, you seen 'em all."

Thack chuckled. "Isn't that what Reagan said about redwoods?"

"It's no problem," said Brian.

Wren reached over and patted his cheek. "This man is such a doll."

"I could do it," said Thack.

Shut up, thought Michael. Leave well enough alone.

"I'm a troublemaker," said Wren. "I forgot all about the other car."

"I really don't mind," said Brian. "I prefer it."

"To our company?" asked Wren, pretending to be hurt. She turned to Michael and said: "Does he mean this or is he just being nice?"

"I think he means it," said Michael.

They made the bumpy ascent to the lodge in virtual silence. When they were all out of the car, Wren planted kisses on Michael and Thack. "You were so sweet to do this," she said.

"Hey," said Michael.

"Would you like . . . a nightcap or something?"

"No, thanks," said Thack. "It's late."

Good answer, thought Michael.

Wren turned to Brian and said: "Give the man his keys."

"Oh." Brian fumbled in his pocket and handed the keys to Michael. Even in the dark he looked embarrassed.

"The driver's coming at ten," Wren told Michael. "We'll swing by sometime after that."

"Fine," said Michael. He gave Brian an awkward little salute and climbed into the VW with Thack.

"Well, well," said Thack as they drove off down the hill.

One with Nature

A PECULIAR THING HAPPENED TO BOOTER AS HE LANguished there in the darkness, a virtual prisoner of Mabel's Winnebago: He found that he liked it. It was soothing, somehow, to be stranded this way, so thoroughly a victim of chance and circumstance that all decisions were moot, all responsibilities void.

Only twice during his forty-minute wait did a car whiz past on the narrow road, and the woods were seductively silent, except for owls and an occasional murmur from the leaves.

Briefly, but with startling drama, a raccoon had mounted a branch outside the window and studied him dispassionately through the glass. Booter had remained still, confronting the little bandit creature-to-creature, holding his breath like a child playing hide-and-seek.

When the raccoon padded away, curiosity sated, Booter made an appreciative sound in the back of his throat. An outsider might have mistaken it for a giggle.

One with Nature, he thought, tilting the bottle again. That was the expression, wasn't it?

Presently Mabel came loping through the broken branches.

He couldn't help thinking of one of those amiable, rumpled bears out of Uncle Remus.

"Half an hour," she said, climbing into the RV. "The tow truck's comin' from Guerneville." Wheezing a little, she caught her breath, then reached into her shirt pocket. "They only had Butterfingers," she said, handing him a candy bar.

He thought of the chocolate Edgar had given him, remembered the curious expectant light in his eyes. What did the boy want from him?

"I said no, thanks," he told Mabel.

"Well, I don't listen to what men say." She prodded him with the Butterfinger, like a new father proffering a cigar. "Take it, Roger."

He accepted.

"What are you grinnin' about?" she asked.

"Nothing."

"Well, eat your damn candy, then."

He peeled back the yolk-yellow wrapper. "We had these when I was a boy."

"Yeah," she said, working on her own wrapper. "Same here."

"They were bigger." He looked at the dark bar, then bit off a chunk.

She did the same. "How old are you?" she asked, crunching away.

"Seventy-one," he replied.

As if to match his fearlessness, she said: "I'm sixty-seven."

He nodded and hoisted his Butterfinger in a sort of salute.

"I don't look sixty-seven," she added.

"No," he agreed, "you don't."

In another gulp, she finished off the candy, wadding the wrapper. "So tell me about this camp of yours."

"Like what?"

She shrugged. "What do you do?"

He thought for a moment. "I made a speech a few days ago."

"Yeah? What on?"

"Well . . . the Strategic Defense Initiative."

She nodded with judicial dignity. "Good thing."

"Well, I certainly did my best to—"

"Damn good thing. If the Russians don't beat us to it."

"Well," he said, "there's certainly a danger of that."

"You can't trust them bastards."

"No, you can't. You're right."

They both fell silent. Mabel drummed her stubby red fingers on the dashboard. The night sounds grew louder, making talk seem alien.

"You wanna get out and stretch?" she asked eventually.

"No. Thank you."

"I'm sorry about your friend," she said.

"Thank you."

"You miss him?"

He nodded.

She heaved a noisy sigh and looked out the window for a moment. Then she said: "I got another bottle in back."

He turned and smiled at her. "Get it."

Pajamas without Feet

ACK AT THE CABIN, MICHAEL LAY ON THE SOFA BED, his head against Thack's chest. "What a night," he said.

"A-men, brother." Thack toyed idly with Michael's earlobe, like someone working dough. "Don't you feel a little guilty?"

"For what?" asked Michael with mild amazement. "Crashing the Grove?"

"No. Being an accomplice to adultery."

Michael hesitated. "I don't think that's adultery."

"You don't?"

"No."

"What would you call it, then?"

"I think it's more like . . . company."

"C'mon."

"I'm pretty sure of it," said Michael.

"You don't think they're up there banging each other's eyes out?"

"No."

"You're a rotten judge of lust."

"Maybe."

Michael lay there for a while, listening to the thump of Thack's heart. Outside, there were froggy choruses in the high grass along the creek. Someone in the pink trailer was playing Buddy Holly's "True Love Ways."

"I love that song," said Michael.

"Yeah."

They listened for a while, Thack humming along shamelessly.

"You're a corny guy," said Michael. He almost said "romantic," but the word struck him as dangerous.

"Well," said Thack. "We seem to get music every time we do this."

Michael chuckled. "That's true."

Thack traced Michael's shoulder with his finger, then laid his warm palm to rest on Michael's back.

"I'm corny too," said Michael. "It's not a bad thing."

"No, it's not."

"I mean . . . not if it's balanced. If both people are corny . . . then it's O.K."

Silence.

"You wanna know something funny?" asked Michael.

"What?"

"When I first met you, I tried to picture how you'd look in a jockstrap."

Thack smiled.

"Now," said Michael, "I wanna see you in pajamas."

"Pajamas?"

"Yeah. Flannel ones. Baby blue."

"Not the kind with feet in them?"

Michael laughed. "No. Just . . . the regular."

Thack stroked Michael's hair. "Maybe next time, huh?"

"Yeah, maybe so." He ran his hand across Thack's flat stomach. "When do you think that might be?"

"I dunno," said Thack. "Hard to say. Do you get back East much?"

"No, not really."

"I'd like to come back," said Thack.

"Would you?"

"Sure."

"We could work on this a little more."

"This?" asked Thack.

"Us," said Michael.

Thack said nothing, stroking Michael's hair.

Michael was pretty sure he had gone too far.

A Woman Scorned

U P AT THE LODGE, WREN ATTENDED TO BRIAN, WHO lay with his head against her chest.

"Will you call me?" she asked.

"When?"

"Oh . . . when the moon comes over the mountain. When the swallows come back to Capistrano." She gave his cheek a gentle whack. "When do you think, dummy?"

"O.K." he said.

"Promise?"

"Yeah."

"Just yes or no will do."

"O.K."

"If you don't," she said, "I'll call your house and embarrass the shit out of you."

He smiled.

Her fingers explored his springy chestnut curls. "You were sweet to let the boys take the limo."

"It's no big deal," he said. "What's gonna happen to your car?"

She began to fret again. "Well, Booter said to leave it here."

"Oh."

"I've done what I can do," she said. "I'm not his wife."

"Right."

Why the hell was she still issuing disclaimers? "I'll call his house when I get to Chicago. Somebody'll know something by then." She heaved a mother's sigh before adding glumly: "I hate being a whore. There are too many responsibilities."

"Don't talk like that," he said.

She smiled and slid her fingers through the swirly hair of his chest. "Thanks for the indignation, but I'm not ashamed of it. I wanted the experience, and I wanted the money. And Booter got his money's worth."

The bedside phone rang.

"Yell-o," she piped in her best receptionese.

"Wren," said the caller, "iss me."

"Booter?"

"Yeah, iss me."

If he wasn't shitfaced, he sure sounded like it. "Where are you, Booter?"

"Uh . . . Guerneville."

"Are you all right?"

"Yeah. I'm . . . I'm O.K."

"You could have called, for Christ's sake. Why didn't you call?"

"I couldn't. . . . Was in a canoe."

"What?" She heard a woman mutter something in the background. "Booter . . . who's with you?"

A pause and then: "Nobody."

"Oh, right." Now she was boiling mad.

"Iss juss somebody who—"

"You have one helluva lot of nerve, Booter." She turned to Brian and said: "He's ripped to the tits and he's got some woman with him."

"No," said Booter.

"What do you mean, no? I can hear her."

"Iss not like that."

"I'm leaving tomorrow, Booter. That check better be good."

"Iss good."

She could hear the woman cackling in the background. "I'm hanging up, Booter."

"Gobblesshew," he said.

"Right," she said, and slammed the receiver down.

She fumed in silence. Then Brian said: "I'm sorry you worried so much."

"I wasn't worried," she said.

"Well . . . still."

"Fuck him," she said. "I should've charged him the full ten thousand."

She went to sleep angry and woke up that way, rising before Brian to finish her packing. He made french toast for them both, then took out her last bag of garbage. When the limousine arrived at nine forty-five, they were waiting for it on the back steps. The driver was a new one (not, thank God, the one she had slept with), and he was openly curious as to why he'd been treated to a night at the Sonoma Mission Inn.

She let him wonder, determined to put the fiasco behind her.

They drove in silence to Cazadero, where Michael and Thack swapped places with Brian amidst coos of approval for the limousine. She gave Brian a quick hug at the door of his little cabin. "Call me," she whispered.

"O.K.," he answered.

She waved goodbye to him from the back window of the limo, but wasn't sure he had seen her.

Back in the city, at Michael's insistence, she told the driver to climb Russian Hill on its steepest slope. This turned out to be a street called Jones, a near-sheer cliff of a street which taxed the limo to the fullest and had them all whooping like idiots.

"Is this legal?" she gasped, clapping her hand to her chest.

Michael laughed. "It's even better going down."

"You're twisted," she said.

"I've never done this in a limo," he said.

She snorted. "There are better things to do."

"I'll bet," said Thack.

"Christ," she gasped. "Is that a stop sign up ahead?" She leaned forward and tapped the driver's shoulder. "Don't stop, O.K.? My system can't take it."

Another laugh from Michael. "Can it take a speeding Muni bus?"

The driver stopped where he was supposed to stop, then turned right and kept climbing, though far less precipitously this time. Taking another right, he inched his way down another nauseating drop-off. The bay lay beneath them in the distance, ridiculously blue.

"All right," she said, turning to Michael. "Enough with the Space Mountain."

"This is it," he said, wide-eyed. "Really."

"This is really what?" She was pressing her fingertips against the back of the front seat, as if this would prevent her from tumbling forward, out the window, down the hill and into the bay.

"Where I live," he replied. "That stairway beneath us. The wooden one."

"Sure."

"It is!" he said, beaming proudly. "You can park on the right there," he told the driver. "The rest is on foot." He turned back to her and added: "That big high-rise above us is where Brian lives."

"I can't look up," she muttered. "Or down. I'll blow lunch."

The driver parked on the right, using the emergency brake. Michael and Thack hastily assembled their stuff. Then Thack began collecting empty juice bottles in a paper bag. "Leave it," she told him. "That's part of the fun."

"He's compulsive," said Michael.

Thack gave them both a hooded glance and continued to gather trash.

"Just what you need," Wren told Michael.

This minimal shot at matchmaking seemed to embarrass Michael, so she thrust her hand into his and added: "It's been great."

"Same here," he said. "I can't believe I met you."

"Brian has my number," she said, wondering if he'd guess the reason.

Michael nodded.

"Take care of him," she said.

"I will," he replied, without meeting her eyes.

She turned and took Thack's hand. "Give my love to Charleston."

"O.K.," said Thack. "Thanks for the joyride." He climbed out and waited on the curb.

Michael regarded her for a moment, then gave her a quick peck on the cheek and bounded out of the limo. She watched as he and Thack crossed the street and began to ascend the ramshackle wooden stairway he had indicated. In the dry grass next to its base stood an off-kilter street sign bearing the word BARBARY.

"Is that safe?" she hollered, when they reached the first landing.

He cupped his hands and yelled back at her: "What the hell is?"

She was still smiling when he vanished into the dusty trees at the top of the stairs.

Her driver turned and said: "The airport, Miss Douglas?"

"Yeah," she replied. "Time to go home."

Prisoner of Love

WHEN THEY REACHED THE COURTYARD AT NUM-
ber 28, Michael found Mrs. Madrigal water-
ing her parched garden. The rigors of the
heat wave had forced her into an old ging-
ham sundress, which seemed far too Miss
Marpleish for her particular brand of rawboned grace.

"How was it?" she called, as they came through the lych-
gate.

"Terrific," said Thack.

She shut off the spray, dropped the hose, and tended to the
stray wisps at her temples. "It's been dreadful here, absolutely murderous. In the eighties every day."

"You're spoiled," said Thack.

She gave him a surprisingly coquettish glance and patted
her hair again. "Nevertheless," she said.

"The garden looks gorgeous," Michael told her.

"It's getting there. Did Brian come back with you?" There
was a purposeful glint in her eye which belied her breezy
delivery.

"No," said Michael. "We bummed a ride with somebody
else. He came home in my car."

"I see," said the landlady.

"Why?"

"Oh . . . well . . . Mary Ann asked."

Michael wondered how much Mrs. Madrigal knew. "He should be home soon," he said as blandly as possible.

She fixed her huge Wedgwood eyes on him. "He hasn't called her," she said. "He's been very naughty."

He made a helpless gesture. "What can I tell you?"

She looked at him a moment longer, then swooped down to pick up her gardening gloves. When she was upright again, she turned her attention to Thack. "Michael's showing you the sights, is he?"

"Oh, yes," answered Thack.

"Do you like it here?"

"Very much."

"I'm so glad. How much longer will we have the pleasure of your company?"

"Well," said Thack, "till tonight, I guess. My flight's tonight."

This was news to Michael, but he didn't look at Thack for fear of betraying his emotions. Mrs. Madrigal, he imagined, already saw the distress in his face, sensed the enormity of the cloud settling over him.

Up in his bedroom, after they had both showered and changed into clean sweats, Michael said: "What time is your flight?"

"Six-fifteen," Thack replied.

Michael went to the window and looked out. "I thought it was tomorrow, for some reason." His eyes fixed vacantly on Alcatraz, the cause of this pain, the scene of the crime. "I had sort of pictured us sleeping here."

Thack hesitated, then said: "It's a nice thought."

"But?" he asked, pushing the issue in spite of his better instincts.

288

Thack came up behind him, enfolding him in his arms. "They're expecting me at Middleton Plantation bright and early Tuesday morning."

"What for?" asked Michael, alienated by such an exotic excuse.

"To make a speech," said Thack, "to some Yankee preservationists."

"What about?" asked Michael.

Thack kissed him on the ear. "Funding, mostly. Boring stuff." He rocked Michael back and forth. "Sooner or later, real life comes crashing back in, doesn't it?"

This was much too glib, Michael felt, a ready-made coda to a shipboard romance. He lived here, didn't he? This was his ship. What hadn't been real-life about it?

"C'mon," said Thack, leading him to the bed. "Let's cuddle."

As they lay there, Thack's back against Michael's chest, Michael said: "I hate this. It seems like a Sunday afternoon."

"It *is* Sunday afternoon," said Thack.

"I know, but . . . I mean, like when you were a kid, when you knew that Monday was coming, and the clock was ticking away. Saturdays were perfect, because there was Sunday, which was sort of a buffer. But Sundays just got worse and worse."

Thack took Michael's hand and kissed it. "Hang on to the moment," he said.

To hell with that, thought Michael. "You know," he said quietly, "you're much more of a Californian than I'll ever be."

The late sun, slashing through the Levolors, turned them into prisoners again, striped by shadows. Michael slept for a while, waking when the stripes were gone. Thack was still asleep.

The clock said four forty-seven. For a six-fifteen flight, they should leave the house no later than five-thirty. If they overslept—and who was to say they couldn't?—the next flight might not be until God-knows-when. . . .

His deviousness under pressure was truly amazing. To repent for it, he slipped his hand around Thack's bicep and squeezed gently. Thack woke up smiling. How could he look so happy? For that matter, how could he sleep so soundly when the time—no, their time—was slipping away?

"You should pack," said Michael.

"Already am," said Thack.

Michael rubbed his eyes. "I'll drive you, of course."

" 'Fraid not."

"What?"

"Not unless Brian's back."

"Damn. You're right. Well . . . he must be." He grabbed the bedside phone and dialed The Summit. After three rings, Mary Ann answered with a glacial hello.

"It's Michael," he said. "Is Brian back yet?"

"I thought he was with you."

"No . . . I mean, he was, but we came home in separate cars."

"Why did you do that?"

"No special reason," he said, wary of mentioning Wren. "We met a friend there, and Brian said he'd enjoy being on his own."

"How long have you been home?" she asked.

"A few hours. Maybe he took the ocean road home."

"Yeah," she said distantly. "Maybe. I have no way of knowing. You saw him last."

This was clearly an attempt to assign guilt, and Michael would have none of it. "He said he was coming home," he countered tartly. "I'm calling because I need the car for an airport run. Just ask him to call me, O.K.? When he gets in."

She was silent for a while, then said: "Are you mad at me, Mouse?"

The nickname was as old as their friendship. She was using it, he realized, to signal her earnestness.

"No . . . I'm not."

"You sound furious. What have I done?"

"Nothing."

"I looked for you after the show the other day. You just took off."

"Sorry," he said, "if it looked that way. I had work to do, that's all."

"You said you wanted to meet Wren Douglas." A certain wounded tremolo, perfected in Cleveland, had come back into her voice. Michael hadn't heard it for a while, but it never failed to work on him.

"I didn't much care for her," he lied. "I changed my mind about meeting her after I saw the show."

"Oh."

"She wasn't that great," he added, somehow feeling traitorous to two women at the same time. "It had nothing to do with you, I promise."

"O.K. I just wondered."

"We'll talk later, all right? My friend'll miss his flight if I don't call a cab."

"I love you, Mouse."

"Same here, Babycakes. Bye-bye."

He hung up, racked with guilt, then called Veterans and ordered a cab for the foot of the Barbary steps. "We should go," he told Thack afterwards. "It won't take them long."

Thack's luggage in hand, they navigated the wobbly ballast stones along the lane. "I could go with you," Michael said suddenly.

Thack looked confused.

"To the airport," Michael added.

"Oh . . . well, you'd just have to pay the fare coming back."

Michael didn't argue with him. He pictured himself alone in that cab, and it seemed even worse than this.

"Besides," said Thack, "I like the idea of saying goodbye at the steps. I like the symmetry of it, a clean break."

It sounded like carpentry to Michael, precise and a little cold-blooded.

"Oh," Thack added. "Tell Mrs. Madrigal I'm sorry."

"For what?"

"Aren't they tearing down the steps tomorrow?"

"Oh, yeah." He hadn't thought about that for days. "I'll tell her."

Reaching the steps, Thack set his suitcase down. Michael did the same with the carry-on. Thack said: "It's been really great. Some great memories."

"Same here," said Michael.

Sadistically early, the cab appeared on the street beneath them. Thack waved authoritatively, then put his arms around Michael. "Gimme a kiss. We'll make him squirm."

"I don't think so," said Michael, seeing who the driver was. "Hello, Teddy," he hollered down.

"Hello, Michael," came the melodious reply.

"He's a friend of mine," he explained. "He must've recognized the address."

"Oh."

"He's a lord."

"Of what?"

"Of England," said Michael. "Lord Roughton. He married this lesbian friend of mine. Get him to tell you about it."

"All right," said Thack, smiling. "I'll do that." He kissed Michael lightly on the mouth. Twice. "Stay well," he said softly.

"I plan to," said Michael.

Thack grabbed his bags and headed down the steps, stopping only to reexamine his earlier handiwork. When he saw Michael watching him, he grinned sheepishly. "Our plank," he said.

"I know," said Michael.

There was nothing even close to comfort food in the house, so Michael ran down to the Searchlight and bought a quart of milk and a package of Oreos. He was tearing into them when the phone rang.

"Yeah," he answered flatly, faking civility for no one, least of all Brian, who should have called hours ago, if he was going to be this late.

But it was Charlie. "Well, how did it go?"

"It was fine," he said.

"Fine? What does that mean? What's that noise?"

"I'm eating," said Michael.

"Not cookies? Oreos?"

"Yes."

"Oh, shit. It's bad. Is he still there?"

"No. He left."

"There was a fight?"

"No, Charlie, no fight. He just went home."

"Well . . . you knew he was gonna do that."

"This is true," said Michael. "Now change the subject."

"Swell," said Charlie. "How 'bout going to a wake with me?"

Michael felt his skin prickle. "Whose?"

"You don't know him. Philip Presley. He worked on the Peninsula, I think."

"You think? Don't you know him?"

"Well, not exactly. His Shanti volunteer helped me out with Lou Pirelli's memorial service, so I kind of owe him one. Please, Michael, his parents are snake-handlers or something. I can't deal with Bible-thumpers without a little moral support."

"I'm running out of outfits," said Michael.

"Do the blazer," said Charlie. "The blazer is you."

"When is it?"

"Tomorrow."

"I should be at work, actually."

"It's during lunch hour. I'll pick you up. It won't take long. It's potluck, but I'll make my pecan pie, and it can be from both of us."

Michael capitulated with a weary laugh. "What time?" he asked.

"Noon," said Charlie. "You're a prince."

"See you then," said Michael.

"Bye-bye," said Charlie.

Michael hung up and continued ravaging the Oreos. He ate half a dozen of them and took the rest to the bathroom, where he soaked in the tub and waited for Brian to call.

Homesick at Home

FOR DEDE, THIS WAS THE VERY LANDSCAPE OF PEACE: the apple orchard, the swimming pool, the familiar line of bee-bristling lavender marching into the yellow hills. If Wimminwood had been D'orothea's Oz, here lay her own beloved Kansas, her eternal consolation, her Halcyon-only space.

Smiling, she sat up on her towel and watched as the sun sank like a hot penny into the buttery distance. A soft umber dust hovered over the orchard, motes dancing in the light, rendering the scene in sepia tones.

She called to her daughter, frolicking solo in the pool.

"What?" came the put-upon reply.

"Time to get out."

"Awww . . ."

"No lip, Anna. You'll shrivel up."

"No I won't. I gotta catch up. I've been pool-deprived."

DeDe mugged at her. "You poor little thing. You had a wonderful river right there in your front yard."

"A wonderful, yucky river," said Anna, climbing out of the pool.

To a certain extent, DeDe agreed with her, but she

wouldn't think of saying so. Anna ran to her, squealing, then did a little on-the-spot warpath dance, waiting to be dried. True luxury, DeDe decided, was only bestowed upon children.

"Where's Edgar?" she asked, toweling Anna's legs.

"In our room," said Anna.

Something about her daughter's tone made her suspicious. "You two aren't fighting again?"

"No," said Anna. "He says he feels crummy."

"He's sick?"

"No. He's homesick."

"Homesick?"

"For Brother Sun."

DeDe blotted Anna's face, then wrapped the towel around her like a sarong. "Well, I bet if you challenged him to a game of Parcheesi . . ."

Anna shook her head slowly. "He won't," she said.

DeDe scooped up her sunning stuff and strode across the terrace to the sun porch, where D'or was kitchen-knifing her way through the bills. "Your mother called," she said, looking up. "She wants us for brunch tomorrow."

"How did she sound?" DeDe asked.

"Good, actually. Cheerful. Not herself."

"Did you accept?"

"I did," said D'or. "Even more cheerfully."

DeDe smirked. "Look who's not herself."

Dropping her stuff in the kitchen, she swept through the house and up the stairs, then stopped outside the children's door, which was slightly ajar. He sat Indian-style in the window seat, his diary in his lap.

"Hi," she said.

He looked up gravely. "Hi," he replied.

"Lots to write about, huh?"

He shrugged.

"Sure," she said, sitting next to him. "You made lots of new friends, learned how to make wallets . . . lots of good stuff."

He nodded.

"It's all right to miss your friends, you know."

"I know," he said.

"I liked that one boy a lot. Philo? Was that his name?"

Another nod.

"Did you write about Brother Sun?" she asked.

"Yeah."

"Maybe if you read it to me . . ."

He shook his head.

"Why not?" she asked.

"It's just for boys," he replied.

"Oh . . . I see."

"No offense," said Edgar.

"I understand." She put her hand on his little knee, gave it a shake and got up. "D'or is grilling tuna tonight. Your favorite."

"With peanut butter sauce?"

"I think so," she said.

"Yum."

Stopping at the door, she looked back, to find him absorbed in his diary again. She felt an unmistakable pang of jealousy.

Geordie

ON A SAND DUNE AT POINT REYES, BRIAN WATCHED until the sun had been extinguished by the coastal fog. Then he trudged back to the car, past the secret inland sea called Abbott's Lagoon. He loved this spot—had loved it for years—for its desolation and drama, its pristine white knolls and sparkling water, a storybook Sahara rolling down to a Biblical shore.

The threat of death, apparently, was a last-minute eye-opener for some people, but not for him. He had known already how special this place was. He had said so a thousand times. On the proverbial path of life, there weren't many goddamn roses he hadn't already stopped and smelled.

Shouldn't that count for something?

He drove back to the city by way of the dizzying Stinson Beach road, then sat in traffic at the bridge while a wounded Saab was hauled away. It was after dark when he finally arrived at the doorstep of Geordie's cottage.

She checked him out through the little hatch, then opened the door. "Forget something?" she asked blandly. She looked less haggard than before. Rested, at least.

"I'm sorry," he said.

She shrugged.

"I shouldn't have run off like that."

"A week ago," she said, smiling wearily. "I've already forgotten about it."

"Can I come in?"

She shrugged again, then made a frivolous welcoming gesture. He stepped past her awkwardly into the low-ceilinged room. A half-eaten TV dinner, still steaming, sat on the coffee table.

"I'm interrupting supper," he said.

"So what else is new? Sit down." She raked newspapers off the sofa to make a place for him. "Want me to heat you one? It's Lean Cuisine."

"No," he said. "Thanks."

She could tell what he was thinking, and smiled. "It's not denial," she said. "I'm not dieting. I just haven't shopped since the diagnosis."

"Looks good," he said lamely.

"Did you take the test?"

"Yeah."

"When do you get your results?"

"Five days," he said.

She cut a piece of turkey with her fork and chewed it vigorously. "You're gonna be all right."

He didn't know what to say. It seemed selfish somehow to wish for something she had already been denied.

"How 'bout a beer?" she asked.

"No, thanks."

"You're a blast," she said, deadpanning.

He smiled back at her, then sat there tongue-tied, hands dangling between his legs. "How's your friend?" he asked at last.

"Not good," she replied. "Tubes . . . all that. He doesn't recognize me."

"I'm sorry." He looked down again, composing his

thoughts. "Look . . . I could shop. I'm a good shopper."

"For who?" She drew back a little.

"For you . . . whenever."

"Hey," she said. "So they found a lesion. I can still get around, Brian."

"You should eat better," he said. "Greens. Healthy stuff. Shiitake mushrooms."

"I loathe mushrooms," she said.

"Yeah, but these are great for the immune system. It comes in a powder. You put it in V-8 and it tastes just like pizza." He remembered Jon, sitting up in bed with a glass of the stuff, smacking his lips and saying: "What? No pepperoni?"

"That is dis-gusting," said Geordie.

He laughed. "Liquid pizza. Works for me."

"Thanks, but no thanks."

"You're gonna need somebody," he said.

She turned and stared at him.

"I have all sorts of free time," he added.

"You have a wife and a child."

"And a maid," he said. "Who does most of the work."

She studied his face a moment longer, then said: "My sister said she'd help."

"Good," he answered. "Then that makes two of us."

She cut off another piece of turkey, then asked: "Will your wife know where you're going?"

Tonight of all nights, he found a parking space at the very foot of the Barbary steps. When he reached the courtyard, he looked up at Michael's window, a bar of burnished gold embedded in the dark ivy of the second floor. Seeing a shadow pass, he almost called out, but changed his mind and pushed the buzzer instead.

Michael looked angry when he opened his door on the landing.

"I'm late," Brian said quietly. "And you needed the car."

Michael's face remained stony. "Thack wanted a ride to the airport," he said.

So that was it. He had robbed them of a decent send-off, a prolonged farewell. "Sorry," he said, as contritely as possible. "I didn't know he was leaving tonight."

"No big deal."

"I figured everybody would just . . . kick back."

Michael gave him a twisted little smile. "He's kicking back on a 747."

"Can I come in?"

"Sure," said Michael. He stood aside, then closed the door. "It's not your fault. I didn't know he was leaving, either."

Brian headed for the armchair and collapsed into it.

"I think he just freaked out," said Michael, sitting down on the sofa.

"About what?"

Michael plumped the pillow next to him. "My being positive."

"You told him that?"

"Yeah."

"When?"

"A couple of days ago," said Michael. "Before we went to bed."

Something didn't compute. "Wouldn't he have said something earlier, then?"

"Oh, he was cool about it," said Michael, "and we were safe and all. Unless you count French kissing, which I don't."

"Then why would he all of a sudden . . . ?"

"I think it just ruled out any . . . long-term considerations."

"But that wouldn't make him leave early."

Michael ran his palm along the arm of the sofa. "I dunno. I may have been *looking* long-term." He gave Brian a wistful smile. "You know me."

Now it made sense.

"I don't blame him," said Michael. "Who wants to start something with somebody who . . . you know." He chewed on his lower lip. "He was a nice guy. Some guys won't even *date* outside their own antibody type."

Before Brian could react, Michael added: "You got some sun."

"Did I?"

"Where did you go?"

Brian shrugged. "Down the coast. Point Reyes. Then I went to visit Geordie."

"Who?"

"My . . . friend."

"Oh. How is she?"

"O.K., I guess. Better than I was, actually."

Michael nodded. "I know what you mean."

"How can she do it?" Brian asked.

"What?"

"Act so normal. I'd be throwing things, tearing the house apart."

"She may have done that," said Michael.

"I'd keep doing it," said Brian. "I'd be crazy."

Michael gave him a dim smile. "Sooner or later, it's a question of how you want to spend your time."

"I'm sorry," said Brian. "That's too pat."

Michael regarded him for a moment, then said: "My mother gave me a new address book last Christmas. I haven't written in it yet, because I can't make myself leave out the people who are dead. I can't even cross out their names."

Brian nodded.

"How pat is that? There's one on every page. All of the *H*'s are gone, except you."

It felt a lot like a punch in the gut. "Thanks for telling me," he said.

"Oh, right," said Michael, rolling his eyes impatiently. "Homosexuals, Haitians, hemophiliacs and people whose name begins with *H.*"

"Look, if you're gonna . . ."

"It's O.K. to be afraid, Brian."

"I know that."

"It's also exhausting, and I'm tired of it. So I don't do it anymore. It's probably that way with your friend. There's nothing particularly noble about it. It just happens."

"So that's it, huh? Just don't be afraid. That's your advice."

"You can do what you want to do," said Michael.

He didn't need this. "Great," he said, getting up to leave.

"Sit down," said Michael.

"Just forget it, man."

"Sit down, O.K.? I'm sorry. I'm just being crabby about Thack."

Brian sat down but didn't look at him.

"It just gets old, you know? Talking about it."

Brian nodded.

"If you really want some advice . . . get your shit together with Mary Ann."

"I know," he said.

"You're gonna be all right. I know it. You're feeling guilty right now and that makes it worse."

"Maybe."

"That's most of it, Brian. I can tell."

"What about . . . you know, the night sweats?"

"It only happened once," said Michael.

"Twice."

"O.K., twice. Your mind can cook up all sorts of ugly stuff."

"You think my mind did that?"

"It could have."

"I dunno."

"Your headaches are gone, aren't they? Your sluggishness."

They were, he had to admit.

"You're not gonna die," said Michael. "Somebody's gotta take care of me."

"Hey." Brian looked across at him. "Shut the fuck up."

"O.K., O.K. . . . So nobody's gonna die."

Brian saw the elfin glimmer in his eyes and smiled back at him. "I love you, Michael."

Michael plumped the pillow again. "So marry me."

Brian laughed.

"I mean it," said Michael. "I need a partner."

"A partner?"

"At the nursery, you dildo."

"Since when have you wanted a partner?"

Michael shrugged. "I've thought about it ever since Ned left."

"You talked to Wren," said Brian.

Michael frowned. "What's Wren got to do with it?"

"Everything, I'm sure."

"Oh, don't be such an asshole. I've thought about this for at *least* a year."

"But you still talked to Wren."

"Well, she may have mentioned that you'd expressed an interest. . . . Look, if you hate the idea . . ."

"I don't hate the idea," said Brian.

"I wanna buy that lot next door, expand the greenhouse. I need an investor, and I miss having a partner. You're strong enough, we get along, there'd be no rude surprises." Michael smiled. " 'You hold no mystery for me, Amanda.' "

Brian smiled back. *"Private Lives."*

"See? A breeder who knows Coward. What more could I want?"

Brian hesitated. "It could work, I guess."

"Work? It'll be the best fun we ever had." Michael reminded him of a kid coaxing his buddy into a tree house. "C'mon. Say yes."

"I'll have to talk to Mary Ann," he said.

Walking home to The Summit, he warded off the specter of dread that dogged him across the moon-bright hill. The doorman made a lame joke about the fires still smoldering in the Santa Cruz Mountains. Whole neighborhoods had been incinerated, it seemed, and he hadn't thought about it for days.

On the twenty-third floor, Mary Ann greeted him in Levi's and a pink button-down. There were more candles than usual, and the synthesizer music they used for sex was playing in the background. He wondered if she'd had the tape on all evening, awaiting his return.

"Well," she said softly, once more in his arms.

"I'm sorry," he replied.

"It's O.K."

"I drove out to Abbott's Lagoon. Lost track of the time."

"Have you eaten?" she asked, heading into the living room.

"I'm not hungry," he replied, realizing it wasn't exactly

true; he just hadn't envisioned food in this scenario.

"There's some great fruit salad. Everything fresh."

"No," he said.

She slipped her arm around his waist. "You've lost weight," she said. "It looks good."

He avoided her gaze.

"Cheekbones," she said, touching the side of his face.

He sat on the sofa and kicked his shoes off. She curled up next to him and said: "I taped *Entertainment Tonight.* It looks pretty good."

"So I heard."

"Who told you?"

"Well . . . Mrs. Madrigal, actually. Michael talked to her." He couldn't very well admit to calling the landlady, not when Mary Ann hadn't heard from him.

"I thought *you* did," she said. "Shawna said you did."

"Oh, well . . . yeah, that time. This was another time." Seizing upon his daughter as an evasion tactic, he added: "How's she been?"

"Fine. She sprayed the Sorensons' cat with mousse this morning."

He smiled a little.

"The hair kind," said Mary Ann. "Not the chocolate."

He chuckled.

"She missed you," she said.

"I missed you both."

She looked at him with tenderness, but obliquely, cautiously. "Did it help?" she asked.

"What?"

"Getting away."

What could he say to that? He put his arm around her, pulled her closer. "I wasn't trying to get away from you."

"It's O.K.," she said, her cheek against his chest. "People get sick of each other." She giggled and patted him. "I get sick of you sometimes. You just beat me to it this time."

This stung a little. He had never really been sick of Mary Ann. Even when he'd been with Geordie, it hadn't been because he was sick of Mary Ann.

When he didn't reply, she asked: "What's the matter?"

305

"We have to talk," he said.

It was terse enough—and dire enough—to make her sit up, blinking at him. "O.K.," she said quietly.

"I have this friend who has AIDS," he began, delivering the line as rehearsed.

Her brow furrowed. Her fingertips came to her chin and lighted, gently as a butterfly. "Brian . . . don't tell me Michael is . . . ?"

"No," he said forcefully. "No, he's fine."

"God, you scared me!" Her hand slid to her chest in relief. "Who is he?" she asked.

"It's a woman," he replied.

Man and Boy

I T WAS LATE MORNING WHEN BOOTER FINALLY EMERGED from his bedroom in Hillsborough, enticed by the camplike aroma of sausage frying. He had slept for over fourteen hours, and his system seemed to have recuperated admirably. The aches in his limbs were nothing more than the aches of being seventy-one. He could live with that, as always.

In the kitchen, he found Emma laying out paper towels on the countertop. "That smells wonderful," he said, hovering over the big iron skillet.

"Don't snitch none," she said. "It's for company."

He gave her a teasing glance. "Aren't I company? I'm invited, aren't I?"

"Ask Miss Frannie," said the maid. "You been gone so long, I don't reckon she remembers who you are."

"Oh . . . now." He smiled at her, largely in recognition of her dauntless loyalty. When Frannie pouted, Emma pouted right along with her. It had been that way as long as he could remember. "Where is she?" he asked.

Emma laid some links out to drain. "The patio, I reckon. She's fixin' flowers for the table."

He found Frannie doing just that, up to her elbows in blowsy pink roses. Seeing him, she seemed to brighten a little, so the maid's grumpiness had probably been residual, a lingering ceremonial gesture.

Frannie said: "Aren't these lovely?"

He nodded and smiled at her, his old friend. "There are some nice ferns down behind the tennis court."

She fluttered her eyelids, faintly befuddled. Her face took on a plump-cheeked childishness which always tickled him.

"To go with the roses," he explained.

"Oh, well . . . yes . . . fine."

"Where are the shears?"

She rummaged in her garden things, handed him the shears and said, "Thank you," with a look of mild amazement.

From the border next to the tennis court he clipped five or six large maidenhair fronds, returning to his wife as she adjusted the little linen tepees on the glass-topped table. "Those are perfect." She took the fronds, beaming.

"Who's for breakfast?" he asked.

"Oh . . . just family today. You look much more rested, Booter."

"I am," he assured her. "What family?"

"DeDe and D'orothea."

"And the children?" he asked.

"Mmm," she replied. "Emma's setting up a card table on the lawn. They won't be trouble."

He wasn't so sure about that.

As it turned out, the children were remarkably subdued, keeping to themselves at the other table, showing no interest whatsoever in the grownups. Booter relaxed a little, soothed by the sunshine and the soporific tones of the talking women.

"So," Frannie was saying, "where did you end up going?"

DeDe, he noticed, shot a quick glance at her friend before replying: "Eureka, ultimately. But we drove around a lot. Just . . . taking it easy."

"Did you stay in motels?" Frannie grimaced a little when she said the word.

"No," said D'orothea, with almost as much hauteur. "Bed-and-breakfast places."

"Some of them are very nice," DeDe added defensively. "Carpeting and everything."

D'orothea rolled her eyes.

"I'm sure you're right," Frannie said pleasantly, clearly intent on avoiding trouble. "I'm sure they're very nice."

"What about you, Mother? What have you been up to?" DeDe shifted the spotlight rather deftly, he thought.

"Oh . . . you know me. A little gardening, a few tiresome lunches. Lots of TV. I saw that woman, by the way, the one you like so much. This morning. On Mary Ann's show."

"What woman?"

"You know, that poetess who was on Broadway."

"Poet," said D'orothea. "Sabra Landauer."

"Yes," said Frannie. "That's the one."

DeDe frowned. "She was on Mary Ann's show?"

Frannie nodded. "The whole time. Except for the last fifteen minutes, when they had a dog psychic."

Booter couldn't let that pass. "A dog psychic?"

"She's quite extraordinary." His wife reproved him with a look. "Don't mock what you don't understand."

DeDe kept her eyes down as she spaded her grapefruit. "Did the psychic say what was on Sabra's mind?"

Booter chuckled. DeDe fired off a good one every now and then.

His wife turned to DeDe, looking puzzled. "I thought you admired her. For being a feminist."

"She's all right," said DeDe, as Emma arrived with a parsley-strewn platter of scrambled eggs and sausages. Booter detected another hurried visual exchange between DeDe and D'orothea.

Frannie took the platter from the maid and said: "Well, she was much prettier than I expected."

DeDe grunted. "Did she read her poetry, or what?"

"No," replied Frannie. "She talked, mostly."

"About what?" asked D'orothea.

"Oh . . . her fiancé, for one thing."

"*Her fiancé?*" This came from both young women at once.

"He's an actor," said Frannie.

"He would be," said DeDe.

Frannie added: "He was on *St. Elsewhere* last week. What do you mean, he would be?"

"It's a career move," said DeDe.

"I don't understand."

"She's gay, Mother."

D'orothea began to chuckle.

Frannie was lost. "Then, why would she . . . ?"

"To throw people off the track."

"You mean she would . . . ?"

"She's a star, Mother. Stars aren't supposed to be gay."

"Well, I know, but . . . that poor man!"

"Mother, he's probably gay himself."

"He is?"

"Yes. Now they're both covered."

D'orothea's laughter gathered steam. Pushing away from the table, she threw back her head and gasped for air.

Frannie was plainly offended. "Well, just because I don't know what her—"

"No," DeDe cut in, "she's not laughing at you, Mother."

Frannie stuck out her chest like a pouter pigeon. "I mean . . . *really!*"

"I'm sorry," said D'orothea, rubbing her eyes, recovering control. "When are they getting married?"

Frannie continued brooding.

"Mother," said DeDe, "when?"

"Tomorrow, I think. That's what she came here for."

D'orothea looked at DeDe and shrugged. "I must've been her bachelor party."

After breakfast, Booter withdrew from the women and strolled through the garden, savoring the pleasant predictability of home. Out on the lawn, the children were engaged in a raucous croquet match, which he watched from afar, enjoying their enthusiasm.

When the boy came toward him in search of the ball, Booter seized the moment. "Son," he said quietly. "Could I have a word with you?"

Edgar approached almost guiltily. Good God, thought Booter, am I really that terrifying?

"I wanted to thank you," he said. "For your help the other night."

The boy said nothing, shrugging a little.

"You were very brave, and I appreciate it."

Edgar scratched the side of his neck. "How did you get away?"

Booter decided not to elaborate. "Someone else came along," he said.

Anna yelled to the boy from the lawn. "Edgurr . . . hurry up."

Booter looked at the little girl, then asked: "Did you tell her about it?"

"No," said Edgar.

"Your mother?"

"No."

"Why not?" asked Booter.

"They're girls," said Edgar.

Booter smiled at him and tousled his dark corn-silk hair. "Atta-boy."

"Edgurr," screamed Anna.

"I gotta go," said the boy.

"I thought," said Booter, "maybe we could do something next weekend. Just the two of us. Go to the museum . . . look for dinosaurs?"

The boy hesitated.

"We men gotta stick together, right?"

"I guess so," said Edgar.

"Edgurr, I am leaving right this very minute!"

"Better run," said Booter, smiling.

"She's a pain," said Edgar.

"Well, hang in there. Oh . . . tell me the answer."

"What answer?"

"You know. What's blue and creamy?"

"Tell you later," said Edgar, running back to his sister.

Forgotten Lady

THE WAKE WAS TO HAPPEN IN A HOUSE SOMEWHERE IN the Richmond district. They drove there in Charlie's Fairlane, so Michael kept his eyes peeled for parking places as soon as they crossed Park Presidio. "There's one!" he called when they were still three or four blocks away.

"Fuck that," said Charlie.

"We're not gonna get any better," said Michael.

Charlie tapped the dashboard, indicating a card imprinted with a wheelchair. "Handicap parking," he said.

"Hey," said Michael. "Perks of the eighties."

"Right," said Charlie. "Win a parking place and die."

Most of the other celebrants had come directly from the inurnment at the Neptune Society Columbarium. Michael couldn't help feeling a little fraudulent, like a bum on the sidewalk talking Chekhov with an intermission audience.

"I don't know a soul," he whispered, as they circled the dessert table.

"No one's eating my pie," said Charlie, frowning.

"Here." Michael held out his paper plate. "I'll take a slice."

"No. Not unless you mean it."

Michael laughed. "Give me a goddamn slice."

Charlie gave him one. "That Key lime pie is half gone, and look at the color of it. It's practically Day-Glo."

"Well," said Michael, "it's sort of a postmodern crowd." He took a mouthful of Charlie's gooey-rich pecan pie, enjoying its slow descent. "I never know how to act at these things," he said.

"What do you mean?"

"You know. Whether to laugh or not."

Charlie shrugged. "It's a celebration. That's what they called it."

"I know, but some of these people feel awful right now."

"You'd better laugh at mine," said Charlie.

"Right."

"I've fixed it so you will, actually. I drew up the plans while you were gone. I won't spoil it for you, but it involves several hundred yards of mock leopardskin and an Ann-Margret impersonator."

Michael licked the sweetness off his fingers. "Why not just plain Ann-Margret?"

"Well, she's optional, of course. Use your discretion."

"Who's optional?" It was Teddy Roughton, funereally attired in black jeans, white shirt, and black leather bow tie. He slipped his arm around Michael's waist and surveyed the raspberry tarts.

"It's a long story," said Michael. "Teddy, this is Charlie. Charlie, Teddy."

"We've met," said Teddy, extending his hand. "At the Ringold Alley AIDS do."

"Oh, yes . . . of course." Charlie's tone became ingratiating, Michael noticed, as soon as he remembered that Teddy was three parts *Vanity Fair* to one part *Drummer*. Charlie was impressed by titles.

"Meanwhile," said Teddy, rolling his eyes as he drew out the word, "our laddie here has broken the heart of another unsuspecting tourist."

"What laddie?" asked Charlie, confused.

"This one," said Teddy, giving Michael a shake.

"Me?" said Michael. "What did he say?"

Charlie frowned. "What did *who* say?"

"He was bereft," said Teddy, oblivious of Charlie's question. "Said he was mad for you, but you weren't mad for him."

"Come off it," said Michael, convinced of a hoax.

"Is this Thack?" asked Charlie.

"Teddy drove him to the airport," Michael explained.

"Poor boy," purred Teddy. He was playing it for all it was worth.

"You see?" said Charlie, looking Michael in the eye. "You see?"

"What did he say?" Michael asked Teddy.

"I told you. That he fancied you. And it wasn't mutual."

Michael felt a sudden urge to whoop, right there in the middle of the wake. "Wasn't mutual?"

"Well, those are *my* words, of course. . . ."

"He was the one who was standoffish," said Michael. "He left early, he . . . Is this the truth, Teddy?"

Teddy leaned over the table, examining the tarts at closer range. "Oh, yes," he said vaguely.

"Try the pecan pie," said Charlie, exuding graciousness. "It's extraordinary." Then he turned and scolded Michael. "Didn't I tell you?"

After the wake, Michael was too distracted to work, so he asked Charlie to drive him home. When they reached the Barbary steps, Charlie said: "Don't look now, but your landlady has finally flipped her beanie."

Michael turned, to find Mrs. Madrigal chained to the landing of the steps. Her bonds were of the modest hardware-store variety, faintly ridiculous in this context. She was wearing her semiformal getup, a loose skirt and a tweed jacket over a high-necked white blouse. She was obviously giving it all she had.

"It's a protest," Michael told him.

"Oh, right." Charlie rolled his eyes. "You Russian Hill people are so weird."

Michael smiled and pecked him on the cheek. "I'll call you tonight."

"Not until you've called Thack."

"All right."

"I mean it, Michael. Don't fuck this up."

Michael laughed and bounded across the street. Charlie beeped twice and drove away down Leavenworth. Mrs. Madrigal offered him a cheery wave from the steps, then called down to Michael: "I hope I didn't scare him away."

"No," said Michael. "Not at all." He climbed the steps to the landing, where the landlady sat in dignified splendor, fussing idly with the neck of her blouse, the drape of her chain.

"I'm waiting for Mary Ann," she said, "in case you're wondering."

"She's gonna tape this?" He hardly knew what to say.

She nodded demurely. "I'm afraid she's a bit late."

"What time was she supposed to be here?"

"I'm sure she'll get here soon," said the landlady. The look in her eyes told him not to be so indignant on her behalf. She knew what she was doing, it said.

He asked: "Are there . . . uh . . . demolition people coming?"

"We don't know," she said grimly.

"Doesn't Mary Ann know?"

"No," said the landlady. "She says she doesn't. She needs this for human interest." She threw up her hands and gave him a crooked little smile. "If this is what it takes, then this is what it takes."

He wondered for a moment if Mary Ann's absence was a function of Brian's homecoming. If he had told her, and she had freaked out . . .

"When did you last talk to her?" he asked.

"Oh . . . late yesterday afternoon. She told me I should be . . . uh . . . chained up from noon on. She couldn't be here when I did it, or it would look like we're in cahoots."

"You haven't talked to her this morning?"

"No." Her brow furrowed. "Is something the matter?"

"No," he replied calmly. "I just wondered. Look, I'll call the station for you."

"That would be very kind." She saw his expression. "Don't be cross with her, dear."

He continued up the steps, then stopped. "Oh," he said, "what did you think of Thack?"

"He seems very sweet," she said. "Just right for you."

"He does, doesn't he?"

"Has he gone yet?" she asked.

"Last night."

"Oh, dear."

"It doesn't matter," he said. "I mean, not yet. Right now I'm just enjoying the feeling. You know what I mean?"

"I know what you mean," she said.

He smiled at her.

"Bring me a caramel, dear, when you come back. They're in that crystal dish on my piano."

He climbed the remaining steps in seven-league boots, basking in the glow of her benediction.

When he phoned the station, a peevish associate producer told him Mary Ann had left immediately after the morning taping, and he personally knew nothing about a crew being sent to the Barbary steps.

He tried The Summit. Brian answered with a lackluster hello.

"It's Michael," he said. "Is Mary Ann there, by any chance?"

"Well . . . yeah. She's not really taking any calls right now."

So, thought Michael, he did tell her. "I know it's a bad time," he said. "It's just that Mrs. Madrigal is down here chained to the steps."

"What?"

"Tell Mary Ann. She'll know what it means."

Brian left the phone. Twenty seconds later, Mary Ann came on. "God, Mouse."

He tried to be gentle about it. "It's not too late."

"I'll call the station," she said. "I'll get a crew."

"Good."

"I completely forgot, Mouse! I'm so sorry. Please tell her I didn't mean . . ."

"I'll take care of it," he said. "What time do the wreckers come?"

"Uh . . . three o'clock."

"Good," he said. "If you hurry, you can . . . Are you two all right?"

"Mouse . . ."

"Just yes or no."

"More or less," she replied.

"I love you," he said.

She was silent for a moment, then said, "You guys," with weary resignation, as if she meant every man on earth.

Michael said: "Ask Brian to bring that big butch chain of his."

"What?"

"That chrome job he uses on the Jeep. It'll beat what we've got now, believe me. If I'm gonna be filmed in bondage, I want it to look real."

"Mouse, we don't need two."

"C'mon," he said. "Let's make this fun."

She groaned.

"We'll make those steps look like a fucking charm bracelet."

"All right," she said. "Whatever. We'll see you down there. And listen, Mouse . . ."

"Yeah?"

"If she's smoking grass when the crew shows up . . ."

"Don't worry. I'll tell her. Bye-bye." He hung up, flew to the bedroom, flung off his clothes and showered like a madman. Four minutes later, when he shut off his blow-dryer, he discovered that the phone had been ringing.

He lunged for it. "Yes . . . hello."

"Bad time?" asked Thack.

"Well . . . there's a camera crew coming. We're saving the steps."

"Oh, yeah. I forgot."

"So did we. Almost."

"I miss you," said Thack.

"Do you really?"

"Damn right."

Michael laughed. "That is so great. I miss you too."

"What are we gonna do about it?"

"Well," said Michael, "for starters, I'm gonna write you a long, gooey letter, embarrassing the hell out of myself."

"Mine's finished," said Thack. "In the mail."

"Hey," said Michael, laughing again.

"You're in a hurry. I won't keep you."

Keep me, thought Michael. "I'll call you tonight. O.K.?"

"Great. I'll be here."

Michael hung up and rushed to the closet, where he agonized momentarily over the proper attire for a televised chain-in. He settled finally on a sort of architectonic look: corduroy trousers, plaid shirt, knit tie, Top-siders.

Halfway into the courtyard, he remembered Mrs. Madrigal's caramels and doubled back, scooping up a generous handful from the dish on the piano.

They would need enough for the duration.

Five Days Later

NOW THIS, THOUGHT WREN, IS MORE LIKE IT.

It was almost midnight, and she and Rolando were sprawled across her bed, basking in the blush of her 1939 (all-tango) Empress jukebox.

She had paid for the Empress with Booter's check—Booter's *new* check: ten thousand dollars exactly. That pleased her somehow, knowing her memories of Monte Rio would always be embodied in this tango-lover's wet dream.

He had been so sweet to send the money, and she had accepted it readily, knowing how much it meant to him. He wasn't such a bad old shithead, when you got right down to it. At least, he was a gentleman in bed.

The Chicago night was deliciously balmy. A lake-sent breeze meandered through the loft, tickling the lace on the big industrial windows. She moaned contentedly and nestled into Rolando's warm, bay-rummy flesh.

The phone rang.

"Oh, hell," said Rolando.

"I'll get it," she said.

"Leave it."

"No," she said, sensing something. "I'll be right back." She slid out of bed and made her way naked to the phone in her work cubicle.

"Hello."

"Wren, it's Brian."

"Oh, yeah. How are you, sweetie?" For once, she realized, that question really meant something.

"I'm fine," he said.

"Really?"

"Yeah. It came back negative."

"Thank God," she said, sinking into a chair.

"Really," he replied.

She heard a woman's voice, then the unmistakable sound of Michael's laughter. "Are you having a party to celebrate?"

He laughed. "Well, yeah . . . but not that. We just won a battle with the city."

"Are you at home?" she asked.

"My landlady's house."

This made no sense to her. That high-rise condo had a landlady?

"Is your wife there?"

"Yeah. Not in the room, but . . ."

"Is she O.K.?"

"Yeah," he said. "Pretty much."

"Good."

"Does she know about us?"

"No."

The laughter swelled again. "Is Michael loaded?" she asked.

Brian chuckled. "Just in love, I think."

"Anybody we know?"

"I believe so. They're getting mushy by mail."

"Oh, God."

"I'm gonna be his partner at the nursery. Isn't that great?"

"That is," she said.

He paused before asking: "How's Rolando doing?"

He had remembered; how sweet. "He's fine, actually. As usual."

"He's a lucky man."

"Thanks."

"Well, I just wanted to—Puppy, wait a minute. . . . All right. . . . Daddy's talking."

"Your offspring?" asked Wren.

"Yeah. They want me back at the party. . . . It's kind of hectic. I'm sorry."

"Well, thanks for calling. This Rock Hudson thing had me so worried. . . ."

"Rock Hudson? What about him? Puppy, let Daddy talk."

"Turn on your TV set," she said. The little girl began to yell. "Look, I'll let you go."

"Guess I'd better," he said.

"Have a wonderful life, sweetie."

"Same to you," he said. "And thanks."

"Anytime," she replied.

She hung up and returned to the bed, where Rolando lay sprawled on his stomach, snoring. In the light of the Empress, his magnificent rump looked like two scoops of tangerine sherbet. The effect was too perfect to spoil, so she slipped under the sheets without a word and sat there remembering, waiting for the tango to end.

THE TALES OF THE CITY SERIES

"These novels are as difficult to put down as a dish of pistachios. The reader starts the old childhood game of 'Just one more chapter and I'll turn out the light,' only to look up and discover it's after midnight."

Charles Solomon, *Los Angeles Times Book Review*

Tales of the City
ISBN 978-0-06-135830-2

More Tales of the City
ISBN 978-0-06-092938-1

Further Tales of the City
ISBN 978-0-06-092492-8

Babycakes
ISBN 978-0-06-092483-6

Significant Others
ISBN 978-0-06-096408-5

Sure of You
ISBN 978-0-06-092484-3

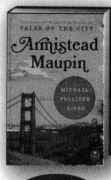

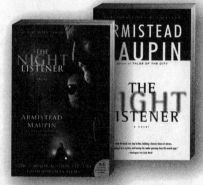